# Honeysuckle Drift

# Honeysuckle Drift

*A Novel*

## Virginia Johnson

Bayside Press

Interior design by Aaron Wedra

Library of Congress control number:
2016913566

Published by Bayside Press
ISBN-13: 978-0692767115
ISBN-10: 0692767118

Email address: contactbaysidepress@yahoo.com

*For Ronald J. Oshima, in loving memory.*

# Honeysuckle Drift

# One

All Ellen's sorrows began when her father struck it rich. He'd come home early from the office one day calling out "Gulfstream!" in such a rousing manner that she thought they were going deep-sea fishing.

Tall, bony, and shapeless as a marsh reed, Ellen Townsend pedaled her bike along Julia Street, wishing she saw more of him. "You're my full moon, my pride and joy, my Mardi Gras parade, you're better than a boy," he said to her sometimes. He was hardly ever home since his latest trial started, and never as much as when they lived in the old house.

Ellen caught a tailwind when she turned onto Government Street. It felt good against her sweaty skin. The street started at Mobile Bay less than a mile away, and the bay breeze swooshed down the lanes like wind across a prairie. It was her favorite street because the decorative wrought iron on the houses looked like pictures of Paris where Ellen wanted to go. Not to see the wrought iron stuff, but to walk in the footsteps of Madame Curie, who was the very reason girls could become scientists, her science teacher said. "Au clair de la lune," she began to sing as she whizzed past the magnolia trees, her rear bumping the seat over the root-raised concrete.

When Ellen reached Weinacker's, she wiped perspiration off her face with her shirttail and hurried inside. She liked hanging out at Weinacker's because of the soda fountain and the import novelties section, where she'd found the shrunken head from Africa, but now she went directly to the pharmacy at the rear. There was a long line at the pharmacy window. Ellen joined it with a grim face. She was proud that her mother had trusted her to pick up a prescription for the first time, and it would look bad if she was gone too long.

"One hell of a line," said a man's gruff voice behind her.

Not wanting to be rude, Ellen turned to him and nodded. He was old, like Grandfather Townsend, and had a wart on his chin the size of a marble. She tried to not stare.

"People ought to let people who have to get back to work go first, don't you think?"

He wanted her to switch places, which would make her later, but how to refuse an adult? "Parlez vous français?" Ellen said.

"Humph. You ought to speak American."

Ellen put on a puzzled expression and faced the front again.

When it was her turn, she handed the pharmacist the bottle in her pocket and asked for a refill in the well-enunciated adult manner she'd begun to use when answering the phone.

"Hey, you tricked me," came the gruff voice, and Ellen winced.

The pharmacist glared at the man for an instant, then read the label on the bottle. "Sorry, but I can't refill it for you, honey."

"I'm thirteen and a half. If that's too young, my mother said you could call her for permission."

"It's not your age," the pharmacist said in a lowered voice. "The problem is that there are no more refills." He pointed to a line on the label. "See, it says zero refills remaining. If there were any left, it would say how many."

"There must be some mistake," Ellen said. It was what her mother sometimes said to salesclerks, and it was all she could think of to say, but she sensed from the pharmacist's manicured fingernails and white starched jacket that any mistake would not be his.

"Not likely, but I'll check." He turned from the window to a file cabinet nearby and began to thumb through a drawer.

"Figures that girl would be trouble," the gruff voice said, and someone behind him muttered something about being in a hurry. Ellen stiffened.

"Here's the prescription." The pharmacist laid a sheet of paper with Dr. Harris' letterhead on the counter. "See, it says five refills. We stamp each time we refill it, and you can see down here it's been stamped five times. Why didn't your father come for them?"

"My mother's the one who runs the errands, but she couldn't because of my sister's birthday party, she turned five, and now my mother's getting dressed in—"

The pharmacist raised his hand. The line was quiet. Listening, Ellen thought. She stuck her head through the window until her lips were a breath away from the pharmacist's smooth, hairless cheek. "Would you call my mother? Please? I can't go home without the pills."

"Look, miss, it's not your parents I need to talk to, it's Dr. Harris. I'll try to find him through his exchange. Come back in five minutes."

Ellen waited in a nearby aisle where she could see the window but couldn't be seen by those in line. The wart man might say something nasty to her on his way out. The clock on the pharmacy wall, round and big as a platter, looked like the clocks at school, and its hands moved just as slowly. Keeping an eye on the pharmacy window, Ellen let her mind drift to the strolls of a new dance she'd seen on American Bandstand. Perfect for tall girls because you wouldn't look silly having to duck under a boy's arm when he twirled you, like in the swing or jitterbug. And perfect for girls who never got asked to dance, like her. Boys in one line, girls in another, and the next boy and girl at the top came together to do the slow six-count step down the middle. She couldn't wait to do it.

When the five minutes became ten, Ellen panicked. The pharmacy window was deserted. She was afraid to ring the bell on the counter, for she didn't want him to think she was impatient.

Finally he appeared with a small brown bag. "Dr. Harris said no more refills until …well, I put a note in for your father."

Ellen thanked him, raced out of the store, and jumped on her bike. From half a block away, she could see her mother standing on the porch in her green dressing gown, red hair ablaze in the shafted sun. Darn. She wanted to give the bag to her father herself and regale him with how she'd managed to get it, but her mother would spoil the moment one way or another.

"I swear you don't know the meaning of hurry, Ellen." Her

mother clattered down the steps in her pointy-toed mules. "If some-one yelled fire, you'd be the last person out of the building." Her bottle-green eyes glinted like cut glass. Green-eyed shrew was Ellen's private nickname for her.

Ellen took a step back. Her mother's arm could spring out like a jack-in-the-box, and her talon fingers would sink into your shoulder before you knew it, but when Ellen explained what had happened, her mother seemed impressed. Then she held her hand out for the bag.

"May I take it to Daddy myself?"

"No. He's still dressing and we're in a hurry."

"Please. It won't take long."

"You know better than to argue. Put your bike in the work-shop and come inside. I need you to keep Wendy out of my hair while I finish dressing."

The workshop, a small building in the corner of the backyard, was used for storage, but that summer Ellen had made it her lab-oratory. Neatly arranged on an old worktable against the back wall were chipped beakers, vials, rusty funnels, and other equip-ment her chemistry teacher let her have on the last day of school. Vinegar was a mainstay in her experiments and its odor hung in the air. Ellen took a chisel from the windowsill and gouged a deep line about an inch long out of the roughhewn table as a tally across the four gouges already there: the first for having to switch to a private school at Christmas break, the second for having to give up Ruthie ("a different social class now," her mother said), and the others for things just as bad. Today's mark was for not letting her take the pills to her father. It seemed like a small thing compared to the others, and the table would be in shreds if she gouged it for her mother's minor cruelties, but this one was especially mean. Her mother would be with her father all evening at that dinner party. She could have given Ellen five minutes with him.

As she left the workshop, Ellen glanced at the cobweb-shrouded cluster of things near the door that came from the old house—fly-ing squirrel cage, fishing tackle, BB guns, bows and arrows, and go-cart. Her father had been home weekends and most evenings then and he had time for those things and for her, but since he'd started working for that big client and bought this house, he'd had no time for them. She bet he missed doing them too.

Ellen heard Wendy bawling the moment she entered the kitchen. Her little sister was sitting under the dining room table, which was heaped with presents and leftover party favors. A limp balloon hung from the crystal chandelier, giving the formal room an air of frivolous disarray. Wendy sat with her legs crossed, and her hiked- up party dress revealed her underpants, which would have mortified her if she'd known. Her throw-myself-off-a-bridge sobs were accompanied by the yelps of a miniature poodle struggling to escape her. Now and then Wendy blubbered mucusy words, "swim," and "Daddy," the latter being the most intelligible.

Smart girl, Ellen thought. This was a resumption of the fit Wendy began that morning when her mother said the swimming after the party was off. Wendy had stopped the fit when her mother threatened to call off the party. Ellen was glad she'd started in again.

"Come out this minute, I tell you!" demanded Ellen's mother, who sat bent over in a dining room chair, scolding Wendy. People said her mother was pretty—the red hair, the prominent cheek-bones, the green eyes—but she didn't look it now, even in the sleeveless white cocktail dress that showed off her tan. Pretty is as pretty does.

Her mother swiped her arm through the air, her silver bangles jingling as she tried to reach Wendy. Ellen grinned at the futility. The cherrywood table was wide and long—"the most expensive firewood in the world," her father teased when it was delivered—and Wendy was positioned dead center. If her mother hadn't been dolled up, she would have crawled under and drug Wendy out by her hair, though it was curled so tight it looked like lamb fur. Ellen's mother's back was to her which was a good thing. If her mother had seen her, she would have made her get Wendy.

"Come on, Wendy," said Dessie, who Ellen thought might as

well live with them for the hours she kept. "I'll make you blueberry pancakes for supper." Dessie, who was lodged in one of the
armed dining room chairs, bent over toward Wendy as far as her
throw-pillow body allowed. "You ought not treat your parents like
this after they done give you a nice birthday party with a fancy
cake and all. Even a clown."

"Dwunk," Wendy said between sobs.

"Hush up, Wendy," her mother said. "You don't know what
that word means."

"Daddy said—"

"Your father was mistaken. The clown was sick, like I told
you kids. Don't you dare go around saying he was drunk."

As a skunk, Ellen thought. She had smelled it when she helped
him unload props from the taxi. Her father caught on during the
juggling act and called a cab to come get him. Later Ellen made
Dessie laugh in the kitchen by imitating his juggling, lemon after
lemon falling to the floor.

"Your parents didn't know he was gonna be sick. You ought to
come out and act nice."

"No."

"Listen, hard head," her mother said. "If you don't stop that
crying and come out by the time I count to three, I'm going to
lock those presents in the closet. One … two…" She paused at the
sound of her husband coming down the stairs.

"Old Dan Tucker was a fine old man. Beat his wife with a can
of Spam," Robert Townsend sang loudly in a deep, rich voice as
he strode toward the dining room. Ellen was struck anew at how
handsome he was. He wore a new sports coat, "Bermuda cream,"
her mother called the color which showed off his olive complexion, dark wavy hair, and big brown eyes. He smiled when he saw
Ellen and winked as he passed her, trailing the scent of Old Spice.

"Where are you going, Old Dan Tucker? Think I'm going to
get my supper." He stopped singing when he reached the dining
room table. "Oh, woe is me," he said in a booming stage voice. "I
made a horrible mistake. It wasn't Spam Old Dan Tucker beat his
wife with. What was it? Where's my newly turned five-year-old,

so bright you have to put her under the wash pot so the sun will come out? I bet she can tell me what Old Dan beat his wife with. I might want to beat mine someday."

"That's not funny, Robert," Ellen's mother said, "especially for someone with high social aspirations. She might repeat it to others."

"What's wrong with that? People admire men who keep their wives under control." He squatted and looked at Wendy. "Please, Birdsong, tell me what Dan Tucker used."

Wendy shook her head back and forth as though trying to dislodge something, a dramatic gesture she used to show resolve. Ellen watched hopefully, for sometimes the shaking made Wendy vomit. Her father would not go off to the dinner party then, and they would go swimming.

"Let me know if you change your mind, Birdsong, and we'll play a quick round of Grab Money before I go." He stood, resumed Dan Tucker, and circled the table, his slight frame moving gracefully.

"Time to go, Robert."

"Hold your horses." He knelt and stuck his torso under the table. "I bet you don't know why the chicken crossed the road."

Wendy sniffled. "You promised we'd go swimming."

"I know, and I'm sorry. That was before I knew about this important dinner which I must attend to make us more money. I know how much you like money. We can go swimming next Saturday as early as you want."

"Noooo. You said after my party."

"Oh, please, Birdsong. Don't be mean." He made the sad clown face—lips turned down, droopy-lid eyes—he often used to tease them out of sulks. "Do you want to see a grown man cry?"

"Yes!"

Ellen smiled. Wendy knew his tricks.

"This is ridiculous." Her mother bent over to look at Wendy. "He's not breaking his promise if he takes you next Saturday. Next Saturday is also *after* your party, isn't it? Just a little more *after*, that's all. So straighten up and—"

"That's not fair," Ellen stepped forward. "It's not what Daddy meant," she said turning to her father. "It's too tricky, isn't it, Daddy?"

"Ah," he said, "the 'too tricky, unfair objection. I think you're on to something, Counselor. Objection sustained."

Ellen felt like grinning, but her mother's glare said "Don't you dare."

"Stop this, Robert. We're going to be late. She'll be fine the moment we leave."

"You don't know that, Elizabeth. Birthdays are important. I didn't realize last night when you mentioned the dinner party that she would take it so hard. Let's cancel. Call the Whitmans and tell them one of the girls is sick."

Yippee, Ellen thought. She'd been waiting all summer to show her father her new strokes.

Bang. Her mother's fist came down on the dining room table. "No. We're dressed up, Dessie's here to babysit, and it's a dinner party, for God's sake, with the seating and everything else planned out. The Whitmans would never forgive us."

Ellen felt like banging something herself. If her father wanted to change his mind, it wasn't her mother's business.

"Damn, Elizabeth. Why didn't you tell me about this dinner much earlier?"

"What? You told me about the dinner in May and asked me to wrangle an invitation. I volunteered at the Junior League for two damn weeks with Barbara Whitman to get it. Besides, when do I get a chance to tell you anything?"

"You find chances to nag me about Sondra Miller."

"Because you encourage her flirting, and it embarrasses me."

The two of them were off and running then, faces reddening, other problems mentioned. Her mother's shrill voice reminded Ellen of a screaming meanie, a firecracker that slithered around in the grass with a high-pitched sound loud enough to burst an eardrum. No longer feeling smug about her sustained objection, Ellen scratched at a mosquito bite on her thigh and watched Dessie quietly rise from her chair and pick up wrapping paper from the floor. When she bent over, her varicose veins on her thighs wiggled, which made them look like fat worms crawling under her dark support hose. Ellen knew she ought to help her, but her parents' arguing froze her to the spot, as it always did.

After a minute or so, all was suddenly silent, just like with the screaming meanie.

"How long since we've had a chance for a nice evening out together, Robert?" Her mother's voice was surprisingly soft. Like the wolf who eats chalk in Little Red Riding Hood. Her father's eyes darted around the room like those of a cornered animal, then met Ellen's. She scurried to the table, and looked under it. "I'll play with you, Wendy. Pick out the gifts you want to play with most. You like bugs. How about the ant farm ?"

"That's an excellent idea," said her mother, and smiled at Ellen. There was lipstick on a front tooth, but Ellen wasn't going to tell her.

"Ants aren't bugs. I want to play with the beads."

"The jewelry kit! Perfect," her father boomed, and began to shuffle through the pile to find it. "Right up Ellen's alley. You can make a necklace for Dessie."

Ellen's jaw dropped. Kiddie kits! It had been a hundred years since she'd played with kiddie kits. Didn't he know her anymore?

"A necklace!" Dessie said. "It would be like my birthday too."

"Here it is." Her father pulled a long, shallow box from the pile. He handed it to Ellen, and smiled at her—the broad smile that usually made her smile back no matter how she felt, but she didn't smile now.

The lamb fur poked out from under the table. "I want to see."

Ellen pointed through the cellophane to the many shapes and colors of the beads. When she looked up, her mother was out the front door and her father stood in the threshold. He blew her a kiss. "Thanks, Muskogee, and by the way, congratulations. Heard you grabbed that pharmacist by the collar."

# *Two*

Ellen stood at the screen door watching Wendy, who was crossing the monkey bars in the back yard hand by laborious hand, with the rest of her hanging dead weight. "Swing your legs, Wendy, like I showed you. You have to swing them," Wendy yelled back a resounding no. The jewelry making had ended in an argument that set Ellen free to read or play records or watch television. But feeling adrift in the darkening twilight, she hung around Dessie in what they called the laundry room, a buffer area between the kitchen and the back door. It was a pleasant place to be at this time of day—the harsh sun replaced by a dreamy lavender sky and the scent of honeysuckle blown in by the evening breeze.

"She'll never make it without momentum," Ellen said.

"Show her again." Dessie sat nearby at the Townsends' newly purchased mangle, a wrinkled, dampened linen napkin spread on the waist-high padded board before her. She licked a forefinger, tapped it on the large metal plate suspended above the board, and muttered, "Not hot yet."

"Why should I? She dumped those beads on the carpet and left me to pick them up."

It would be perfect at the pool now, Ellen thought. Most of the kids would have gone home, and the water would be a shimmery blue in the underwater lights. She could be showing her father the breast and butterfly strokes she'd learned in swimming class. The only stroke he knew, the one he'd taught her, was closest to what her instructor called the "freestyle," and she'd been surprised to learn in class that he did it wrong. The idea of her father being wrong was always a slippery thought. Ellen circled her arms around as though swimming and remembered the forward thrust she'd felt when she pushed the water back with her hands cupped like the instructor said, instead of slapping at it like her father.

"What in the world are you doing?" Dessie said.

"Swimming. What I would be doing this minute if Mama hadn't dragged Daddy off."

"Sounds to me that dinner party was his idea."

"But can't a person change his mind without getting browbeat to death?"

Dessie tested the heat of the metal plate with her finger again, then pulled a lever on the side of the machine and lowered the plate to the board. Clean, sweet-smelling steam hissed out around the edges. After a few seconds, she pushed the lever back, and the plate rose to present the napkin perfectly pressed. "This contraption is really something. I can do tablecloths and napkins and lots of other things lickety-split." She wiped the beaded moisture from her caramel-colored face with her apron and lifted the napkin to fold it.

Ellen sighed. Dessie had ignored her question because she would never say anything bad about her mother. But this time her mother had been so obviously unfair that Dessie would have to agree. "Even if you don't think Daddy had the right to change his mind, you have to admit Mama was mean to Wendy, trying to confuse her with all that 'after the party' business."

"Listen, Ellen," Dessie said, turning toward her, "Your mama's a hard-feeling woman, and she'd put a lot of effort into them having a night out together. You'll understand her better when you're—"

"Mature, you're going to say. I am mature, and I'm tired of people treating me like a kid."

"I ain't talking 'bout that. I was gonna say when you get married. I seen how mature you're getting. Like this afternoon when you offered to play with Wendy so your parents could leave."

Ellen felt a tingle all over. Dessie didn't pay compliments often, and when she did you could believe her.

"Thank you. I try to be helpful." Ellen nodded at the stack of ironed clothing on the folding board. "I can put those away."

"That would be nice. I know you're lonesome without Ruthie. Changing schools in the middle of the year can make it hard to find friends. But there's plenty nice girls at that Julius T. Wright's

School for Girls. You'll make friends when school starts again."

"No I won't. And I'm not just saying that. I know it for certain."

"What are you talking about?"

"Sorry, but I can't tell you."

"I thought you told me everything," Dessie said in a let-down tone.

"I do, except for this." It was ninety percent true.

As she climbed the stairs with the ironing, Ellen felt again the sting of what happened in French that day in April. It was the first really hot day of spring, and the classroom, which was in the remodeled attic of a restored antebellum mansion, was a scene of adolescent female torpor—girls sprawled at their desks with the bodices of their gray cotton uniforms opened to the second button. The mandatory bar ties for keeping the collars closed, without which one got demerits, were nowhere in sight, and the skirts were hiked to mid-thigh by knees splayed to catch the air.

The petite Mrs. Delacoix, who'd lost an arm in France during the war, announced that they couldn't use the overhead fan. She was an epileptic, she said, and overhead noises often reminded her of the bombers and brought on seizures. When she turned to write the day's translation paragraph on the board, Dottie, one of the most popular girls in seventh grade, tiptoed to the wall and flipped the switch. The blades began to turn, and as they picked up speed, the low droning of the fan became louder and louder.

The girls, including Ellen, who'd never seen a seizure, waited with fearful excitement. In less than a minute, Mrs. Delacroix turned from the board with her body jerking head to foot like a dashboard hula doll, and fell to the floor where she continued to jerk around. When Dean Goodwell and the school nurse rushed in a few minutes later (someone must have gone for them), Mrs. Delacroix's dress and slip were up around her hips, exposing her garter belt, bare flesh, and a bit of pink underpants.

Ellen had burst into tears. Girls from all over the room turned from staring at Mrs. Delacroix to stare at her. Ellen didn't know why she was crying—she liked French but wasn't friends with Mrs. Delacroix—and she desperately tried to stop, but she couldn't. After Mrs. Delacroix had been helped from the room, the nurse took Ellen to the first-aid room and calmed her down.

Ever since that day it seemed like all the girls, even the ones she'd been getting in with on the basketball team, drew in like a tight ring of sticker bushes when she approached. Ellen had been desperate for advice on what to do about it, but she had no one to ask. Her mother, who wanted her to be popular, would be angry because she'd embarrassed herself, her father's time was so limited that she wanted to save him for fun stuff, and she figured Dessie wouldn't know how things were at a snobbish girls' school. After school let out in May, she decided that she didn't care and hell would freeze over (one of her father's expressions) before she would speak to the girls who'd snubbed her. The loneliness of this summer showed her that she did care, but she still didn't know how to change things.

Room by room, Ellen put the ironing where it belonged, taking the last of it to her parents' bedroom. Her mother's new bathing suit lay on the dresser, its whalebone bosom rising voluptuously. Made of a stretchy fabric covered with gold sequins, it was so expensive that her father said he'd have to melt it to pay for it. A waste at any price, for her mother was afraid to go into water above her knees. Ellen dumped the ironing on the bed, grabbed the suit, and held it up to herself in front of the dresser mirror. It looked like the suits Esther Williams wore in movie posters. Ellen widened her eyes in horror and flung out an arm as though summoning help the way Esther had in *Million Dollar Mermaid* when the glass of her swimming tank cracked.

Ellen laughed, turning this way and that to admire the glamorous transformation of her flat chest. Just imagine if she walked into the Teen Room at the club wearing this suit. The very idea gave her chills. She felt self-conscious there because she usually didn't have anyone to hang around with, but still, she went in as often as possible. The flirting, which she hoped to be part of someday, was more appealing than the wet-towel fanny-snapping that went on around the pool. Best of all was watching the dancing on the twenty-by-twenty-foot square of linoleum that served as a dance floor. She hoped a boy would ask her to dance, but so far none had.

"You look too young is why," said Amanda, an older girl whom Ellen sometimes sat with in the Teen Room. Amanda suggested that Ellen wear a padded bathing suit and start smoking. Ellen had thought both ideas too bold for her age, but now that she'd stood her ground in the pharmacy and Dessie had said she was getting mature, she decided to learn to smoke. That very night was perfect, for her parents were gone and Dessie would watch TV after Wendy went to bed.

When she'd put the bathing suit back as she found it, she checked the pockets of her father's suit jackets for open cigarette packs he'd forgotten. Nothing but a few broken cigarettes. Last was his hunting jacket. Nothing but bird feathers smeared with dried blood in the outside pockets. No cigarettes in the deep inside pockets either, but she found a piece of thick paper rolled into a scroll. Qu'est-ce que c'est? she said to herself.

"Ellen." Dessie called up the stairs, not wanting to climb them, Ellen knew, because of her varicose veins. "Will you play with Wendy so I can finish these linens for your mother's party Monday?"

Ellen wanted to shout no. She was sick of Wendy. And worse was the fact that she if she had friends, she wouldn't be such a sitting duck for babysitting. "Okay."

She unrolled the paper carefully, then gasped. A photo of a naked woman bending over the back of a chair, and a naked man behind her with his thing poking her bottom. A spasm of giggles came from Ellen's mouth. This was the most disgusting thing she'd ever seen. She hurried to the window, and held the photograph to the light.

The people weren't completely naked. The woman wore boots with heels so high Ellen wondered how she could walk in them. The man had on dark socks and a wristwatch on the arm that was reaching forward as though to grab the woman's breasts.

His thing, which was huge—the words 'fat carrot' popped into her head—was partly sticking into the woman's behind. The half of the man's face showing in profile was scrunched into a grimace, and his neck muscles bulged like twisted rope. Ellen knew a little about sex from girls talking about it, and then last year in Health class, she learned all about it. This photo certainly didn't look like the "cozy event," as the teacher called the sexual act, which she said felt marvelous for both partners. The man looked like he was in pain, and the woman, although her face was mostly hidden by her long hair, probably was too. It would hurt to have a fat carrot stuck in your butt. Suddenly, Ellen felt afraid. Maybe this was how sex really was.

"What are you doing?" Dessie stood in the doorway, arms akimbo. Ellen slapped the picture to her chest. "Nothing."

Dessie glanced around the room, noticing, Ellen was sure, the open door of her father's closet. "What have you got there?" she said as she walked toward Ellen.

Ellen was tempted to hand the picture over and ask if this was the way sex really was. Dessie would tell her the truth and wouldn't tattle on her. But she didn't want Dessie to think badly of her father.

"Nothing, Why did you sneak up on me?"

"Sneak! I been calling and calling up them stairs, and when you didn't answer I come to see was something wrong."

"Well, nothing is wrong, so you can go back down. I don't want to be checked up on like a child. You said yourself that I was mature."

"I said 'getting mature,' and that ain't the same as being mature. There's grown-up things you got no business fooling with. Now let me see." Dessie extended her hand for the picture.

Ellen whipped it behind her back, her heart thumping like a tom-tom. She couldn't let Dessie think her father was dirty-minded.

"I said give it here."

"I don't have to. You're just the nigger maid."

Dessie dropped her arms, her whole body seeming to drop with them. In a second, she thrust her open hand toward Ellen again. "Now that's the gospel, but I'm the nigger maid in charge of you."

"Dessie, please, pretty please don't make me."

Dessie shook her head, stomped out the door and down the stairs, the sound of each heavy footstep feeling like a condemnation. Ellen ran to the balcony and called down that she was sorry. Dessie kept going.

"I'm really sorry Dessie. I don't know what got into me." Ellen was breathless as she entered the laundry room after putting the picture back and running down the stairs.

Dessie had just resumed her seat at the mangle. She looked toward the screen door. "Wonder where Wendy went. She was sitting on the stoop when I left."

Ellen fell to her knees next to Dessie. "Really, I didn't mean to say that word. I hate it. Please forgive me."

"What was you looking at?"

"A dirty picture." She had to offer something, and telling wasn't as bad as showing.

"Humph, that's what I thought. Men's foolishness. You oughtn't be snooping."

"I know. Will you forgive me for what I said?" Surely, any second Dessie would reach out and pull her into her soft, warm bosom.

Dessie spread another dampened napkin on the padded board. "Will you see about Wendy? She's too quiet."

"Okay." Ellen reluctantly rose to her feet; she sorely missed the hug. "I'll play with her as long as you want. I love you, Dessie. One time I even dreamed I was your daughter." It had been a good dream, but Ellen remembered how relieved she felt when she woke and found that she was white.

"What happened in the dream?"

"I forget the details, but it was nice."

"Humph."

Wendy was hiding, Ellen thought as she looked around the big yard. She had to be there somewhere because the gate latch was closed and too high for Wendy to reach anyway. The workshop,

Ellen thought with a gasp. Her mother had the handyman put a hook high up on the outside of the screen door, thinking the things in Ellen's laboratory might be dangerous to Wendy, and she had forgotten to hook it back after putting her bike away. She heard Wendy's voice as she reached the screen door.

"I'm thirsty, Fifi. Let's us drink Sissy's Kool-Aid,"

"No," Ellen yelled and burst in. Wendy dropped the plastic glass of vinegar mixed with mercurochrome on the table.

"Sissy, you made me—"

Ellen grabbed Wendy's shoulders. "Did you drink any of that?"

"No. You made me drop it."

"Blow in my face." A sugary smell. Leftover birthday cake, maybe, but she had to be sure.

She grabbed Wendy's jaw. "Open your mouth."

"No. Let go." Wendy twisted and kicked. "You're hurting me,"

"If you let me see in your mouth, you can sleep with my Madame Alexander doll tonight." Her mother would kill her; Madam Alexander dolls were sold only by Gayfer's Department Store and were collector's items.

Wendy stopped struggling and rubbed her cheek. "You promise?"

"Yes. Now open wide."

Ellen looked at every inch of the sweet-smelling cavern, depressing Wendy's tongue with the handle of her measuring spoon to see her throat, stretching the skin around the mouth to see the cheek walls, turning her lips inside out as one would do to a horse to check the gums. All clear.

"That hurt. Why did you look in my mouth?"

"To see how many words you have left in your lifetime. No wonder Daddy calls you Birdsong, the way you chirp, chirp, chirp without stopping." Boy, was I lucky, Ellen thought. For the first time in her life, she felt the meaning of that word in her bones.

"You're just jealous. My Indian name is better than yours."

"No, it's not. Muskogee is Daddy's favorite Indian chief. He was smart and brave."

# *Three*

Groggy on his drive to work Monday, Robert detoured along Water Street to give his wake-up pills more time to kick in. He relied on Sundays to catch up on sleep, but with Wendy's party and the Whitman dinner Saturday, he'd spent yesterday doing office work neglected last week because he'd been in trial.

As the Cadillac crawled forward, Robert craned his neck to see between warehouses the grand central station that was the port of Mobile—river traffic flowing into the tea colored bay from the mouth of the Mobile River and worldwide commerce coming from the Gulf of Mexico. Cargo ships, freighters, ocean tugs, river tows, oyster boats, shrimp trawlers, and so on changed position every second like tinted shapes in a kaleidoscope. The sight enlivened Robert as it usually did, and he once again congratulated himself for leaving the humdrum of the DA's office in Montgomery to go into practice here. A port city always had a lot of crime, and who better to defend it than a lawyer with ten years' experience as a prosecutor.

The pungent aroma of shoe polish met him as he entered the marble lobby of the Van Antwerp, a distinguished neoclassical building in the heart of town. Robert proudly said "the Van Antwerp," when someone asked where his office was. He had moved there from a piss-colored one-story building with a Bail Bond sign on top within a week of Gulfstream putting him on retainer.

"Good morning, Hi-Jinx. You winning or losing?"

"Winning, just like you Mr. T," said the colored man who was arranging polish and brushes on the two-seat shoeshine stand. He wore his trademark dress of dark blue pants, a blue shirt and a gold brocade vest, which Robert found appropriately spiffy for the Van Antwerp.

"How 'bout a shine?"

"Sorry. Got court in twenty minutes."

"Case about old Willie in the Quarters getting killed by that loan man?"

"That's the one. He died, but there's no proof he was killed." Still sluggish when he reached his office, Robert took a bennie from a bottle in his pocket and swallowed it. Evidently two wasn't enough for a kick-start anymore, and he wasn't going to chance being seriously fatigued in court again as he had been in December. During his closing statement in the last of two trials he'd done back to back, his mind went blank for a few terrifying seconds. He'd high-tailed it to the family doctor when court adjourned. "Some claim Benzedrine's the Holy Grail," said Dr. Harris, "that it cures everything from impotence to blindness, but I can only vouch for fatigue. The military gave it to pilots, paratroopers, night patrols and the like in the war." Robert had remembered then that men in his barracks dumped Benzedrine from the infirmary-issue inhalers into their coffee and drank it as they sat around singing little jingles, like "Who put the Benzedrine in Mrs. Murphy's Ovaltine."

At quarter to eight, Robert packed his briefcase and left for the ten minute walk to the courthouse. These walks were usually a mental recess, but the Fry case was unsettling. If he let his client, a collections gorilla for Gulfstream, get convicted of manslaughter, he'd be moving his practice back to the Bail Bond building. He'd had an even chance of winning until that insurance agent testified that he'd seen Fry's car in the Quarters the night the old man died from a fall. Added to the other circumstantial evidence, the agent's testimony could undo him.

Still lethargic, Robert trudged for the first couple of blocks, but by the halfway point he was striding right along. The third bennie kicking in, thank goodness. He sang in his mind snatches of the song they'd raucously sung at the Whitmans' Saturday night, the volume increasing to a rousing crescendo for the last line: "It's a honeysuckle heaven and they call it Mobile." A grand evening—the twenty of them sitting around the living room trying not to spill their liquor on the expensive carpet while some of the wives attempted to out can-can each other Rockette style. He remembered with a smile how Sondra Miller had positioned herself close to him. "Deliberately so you could get a good look," Elizabeth had whispered. Her jealousy of Sondra amused him. Sondra didn't look bad girdled in a cocktail dress, but in a bathing suit and slathered with suntan oil, she looked like a pig on a spit.

When the county courthouse, a grim four-story fortress, came into view, Robert quickened his pace. There was no reason for him to worry about that agent. Thanks to a law school buddy who was legal counsel for Ford Motors, he had an ace in the hole that would destroy the agent's credibility provided Judge Simmons let it into evidence. And if not, he had other, albeit less effective, ways of discrediting the idiot.

As usual, Robert entered the courtroom and greeted the bailiff, the judge's clerk, and the court reporter like they were his party guests. Then he bent over the shoulder of the pudgy, balding man reading the newspaper at the prosecution table. "Hope you've got a couple of handkerchiefs for wiping the sweat off your brow, Carl. This case might go to the jury today."

"Deed I do," Carl said, and grinned at Robert. "I'll lend them to you when the verdict comes in."

Robert felt a rush of affection as he laughed. They were best friends, a case of opposites attracting, everyone said.

Maintaining his jovial air, Robert approached the defense table and shook hands with Jack Fry. The deputy had already removed his handcuffs as required by court rulings to avoid jury prejudice. Under the same rulings, Fry had been allowed to wear trousers and a sports coat instead of the jail uniform, but at 6'4" with a head and chest that looked like a small boulder on top of a large one, a scar across his cheek, and a perpetual scowl, he would have looked violent in a Santa Claus suit. And he was violent by nature, Robert knew. At their first meeting, he'd advised Fry to admit he'd been collecting in the Quarters the night of Willie's death and Willie, being scared of him, fell trying to back away. "Eighty-year-olds have fatal falls all the time, Jack. The DA would let you plead guilty to a lesser charge and you'd be out in three years." He recoiled when Fry leaned toward him and roared, "Are you crazy. I got me a young wife to keep an eye on. Your job is to get me off."

At precisely eight o'clock, Judge Simmons, a short man with silver hair and a long sharp nose (Robert called him "the Rooster" behind his back) opened his chamber door and paused at the threshold while the clerk called for all to rise. His feet concealed by the floor-length robe, he seemed to float as he moved forward and up the two platform steps to the bench. There he is, Robert thought, his Rooster face desecrating once again the bronze Alabama seal on the wall behind him. Simmons liked to demean lawyers in front of juries, Robert more often than others. But today Robert would act like the judge's biggest fan until that Ford report got into evidence.

When the jury filed in, Robert draped his arm across the back of Fry's chair and talked to him as though Fry was a solid citizen and not the gorilla they thought he was. It was obvious from the disgusted expressions he'd gotten from the jurors in this case that they, like most juries, were prejudiced against loan sharks and would be eager to convict Gulfstream's collections agent.

Around mid-morning, Carl finished his examination of Rupert Tanner, the insurance agent, and it was Robert's turn to cross-examine. He rose and approached the stand with the eagerness of a hawk spotting prey.

"Mr. Tanner, you testified Friday that you were sure you saw Mr. Fry's car in the victim's neighborhood the night of the incident, is that correct?"

"Something like that, can't remember exactly."

"Your honor, May the court reporter read that part of Mr. Tanner's testimony on Friday?"

"Go ahead, Miss Thompson," Simmons said.

"I'm in the Quarters collecting insurance premiums every week the same night the defendant's there for loan payments, and I saw his car there the night of the incident."

"So that's your testimony, Mr. Tanner," Robert continued, "that you were sure you saw the defendant's car in the Quarters the night of the incident. How were you *sure* the car was Mr. Fry's. Did you recognize the license plate number?" He knew the man hadn't, or Carl would have brought it out on direct exam, as well as any other observations which would support Tanner's identification of the car as being Fry's. That was Carl's Achilles' heel–no proof that Tanner's identification was accurate. But this jury, prejudiced and eager to get at a loan shark company, might not care.

"Didn't need to look at no license plate. Guy lives three houses from me and I seen him coming and going a thousand times in that '47 Ford."

"Is it fair then, Mr. Tanner, to say that you assumed the car you saw in the Quarters belonged to the defendant because it was the same year, make and model?"

"Yeah. What's wrong with that? Things usually is what they look like."

"Don't you have any qualms, Mr. Tanner, about convicting a man based on an unproven assumption?" He emphasized the word "unproven."

"Objection. He's harassing the witness."

"Sustained. Out of order, counsel."

"I apologize, your honor. I got carried away."

"Mr. Tanner, I'm not asking if the car you saw that night was the same year, make and model as Mr. Fry's. My question is why you are so sure it actually was Mr. Fry's car. Do you think that Mr. Fry is the only person in Mobile who drives a 1947 Ford sedan."

"Course not."

Tanner's face, meaty like the rest of him, had taken on an angry reddish hue. Short, fat men were often hostile witnesses. It probably had to do with frustrated sex lives.

"Then I'll ask the question again. Why are you sure that the '47 Ford you saw that night belonged to Mr. Fry instead of someone else? The similarity to Mr. Fry's car could easily have been a coincidence, couldn't it?"

"Nope. Ain't enough of 'em in town for coincidence."

Robert smiled to himself. Perfect. "How many '47 Ford sedans would have to be in town, as you say, for you to think the similarity could be coincidence—two hundred, three hundred?"

"I don't know. Three maybe."

"Objection. Counsel is asking the witness to speculate."

"Sustained. The answer is to be struck from the record."

"Sorry your honor."

Robert returned to the defense table and took a vellum binder from his briefcase with a flourish. "Your honor, I'd like to submit into evidence a certified record of the Ford Motor Company, Automotive Statistics Division for the limited purpose of disproving the witness's assumption that the car he saw was the defendant's because, and I quote, 'Ain't enough of 'em in town for coincidence.' "

He handed a duplicate binder to the clerk to hand to Simmons, who took it with a frown, and he gave another one to Carl.

"The record shows the distribution of new 1947 Ford sedans throughout the US, broken down by state."

"Counsel, you need somebody from the corporation to testify that this is authentic," Judge Simmons said in a chiding tone.

"I talked to a Mr. Thomas Howell, Ford's legal counsel, about that, your honor. He said they send certified records all over the country to be used in litigation when the records reflect company activity in the ordinary course of business and are certified by their respective custodians. As you'll see, the certification is on the last page."

Carl scanned the few pages in a snap, but Simmons, forehead wrinkled with concern seemed to review them one by one, and then stared at the certification a few seconds like it was a frog he was about to dissect.

"Humph." Simmons said.

"Seems to me, it's a good practice, your honor. Saves time and money for the company, the litigants and the courts."

"Mr. Taylor, any objection?"

"No, your honor," Carl said.

"Well, alright." Simmons handed the binder to the clerk to be marked as the next exhibit. "Proceed, Mr. Townsend."

Robert handed his copy of the binder to Tanner and instructed him to turn to the tabbed page. "As you can see, Mr. Tanner by the heading on the chart, the page shows the number of new 1947 Ford sedans distributed to each state. I've circled in red the number sent to Alabama. Would you read that number for the record please?"

Tanner looked at the judge as though asking if he had to comply, and Simmons told him to go ahead.

"Twenty-five thousand."

"So, Mr. Tanner, if Mobile received a third of those twenty-five thousand—more is likely since we're the second largest city in the state—then over eight thousand new '47 Ford sedans would have been on the market here thirteen years ago. Even assuming half of those are no longer on the streets of Mobile, four thousand still would be. Don't you think four thousand is a large enough number to refute your assertion that, and I quote, 'Ain't enough of 'em in town for coincidence?'" Glee ran through Robert's veins as he heard the shifting in the jury box. Even prejudiced, the jury couldn't ignore the damage the figures did to Tanner's certainty that the car was Fry's, and thereby to the man's credibility. This moment was his reward for the embarrassment of having to discredit such asinine testimony.

"Objection. Counsel's drawing a legal conclusion."

"Sustained."

Fine with Robert. The jury got the point.

"So don't you agree, Mr. Tanner, that the similarity of the cars could be a coincidence?"

"Objection. Again. Calls for speculation."

"Maybe if it weren't for the hubcaps," Tanner blurted out without waiting for the judge's ruling about the objection. "I just remembered. That's the main reason I knowed it weren't no coincidence. Fry's car don't got no hubcaps, and neither did the car I seen. I don't suppose you got papers on missing hubcaps, counselor."

The jury burst into laughter, happy, Robert knew, to be back on track to stick it to the loan shark's gorilla.

You son of a bitch, Robert thought. A bald-faced lie.

"I don't need papers for that, Mr. Tanner," Robert said when the jury laughter subsided. "It's common knowledge that twelve-year-old cars often lack hubcaps. If you thought the missing hub-caps to be significant, as you seem to now, why didn't you mention it in your preliminary interview with Mr. Taylor?"

"I forgot. I was nervous in his office."

"Objection, your honor. The witness's state of mind during that interview is not related to his testimony on direct exam."

"Your honor, I disagree. It's relevant to—"

"Objection sustained, and the answer is to be struck from the record. You're out of bounds, Mr. Townsend. Do you have any further questions for this witness? Preferably, unobjectionable ones."

"Yes, your honor," He didn't, but he had to come up with some. He glanced at his watch. "Since it's five till twelve, your honor, I request that we break for lunch before I commence a new line of questioning."

Judge Simmons glanced at the clock on the wall near his desk as though to confirm the time, then announced they would adjourn for lunch and reconvene at one o'clock.

# *Four*

When Robert returned to the defense table, Fry said "Put me on the stand, counselor. I'll tell them I had hubcaps in February. That'll show them he's a liar."

Robert shook his head. "The jury wouldn't believe you, and it could cause other problems." Like Fry roaring at Carl during the cross-exam thus proving his violent nature firsthand.

"I guess you're doing all right without it. You had ole Rupert going there."

"Ole Rupert? When I showed you the witness list you said you didn't know him except for a quick introduction at a Christmas party."

"I don't really know him. We had some words is all and—"

"Excuse me, Mr. Townsend, jury's gone and I've got to put the cuffs on."

"That's fine, Ralph. Take him to the meeting room; I'll be there in a minute."

As the deputy led Fry away, Robert felt the heavy hand of Red Doakes, the vice-president of Gulfstream, on his shoulder.

"Good job with those statistics, counsel, even though courier service from Michigan was damn expensive. The missing hubcaps thing is a monkey wrench, though."

"And a lie. Without a license plate identification, Carl would have grilled him about the particulars of that car like a chef deboning a catfish. It's not the first time a witness lied to get back at me for making him look foolish. "

"I'm not worried," Doakes said. "I've got full confidence in you, Robert, and it's finally our turn at bat."

Our turn at bat, Robert scoffed as he made his way to the basement meeting room. Doakes knew they had no defense.

"Goddamn it, Jack," Robert said as he entered the small, hot room which was rank with sweat. "Tell me everything that happened between you and Tanner at that party."

"Weren't no big deal, a few words is all. Me and Candy was talking with some people. Tanner come up and we was introduced. A little later, after I'd been joking around with my buddies, I came back and he was handing Candy a drink. I told him to get lost, he gave me some guff, and I said we should step outside. The coward turned tail and I ain't seen him since 'till this trial."

Robert pictured the scene—buxom, blue-eyed Candy in a short skirt, blond hair to her fanny, flirting with the pot-bellied Tanner, his face flushed with excitement when Fry returned. She was sexy, nothing like Helene, of course, but provocative in a one-night-stand sort of way.

"Has Candy seen him since?"

"He wouldn't be around to talk about it if she had."

"Damn it to hell, Jack. You should've told me this at first so my investigator could've checked him out. I might have found something that showed he has a reason to lie."

"Just get me off, counselor. Like I keep telling you, nobody seen me in the Quarters that night."

"And like I said when I advised you to plea-bargain, that doesn't mean the jury can't find you guilty."

Robert bought a Coke from the snack bar in the courthouse and drank it slowly, relishing the relief for his dry mouth and throat. The dryness, a side effect of the bennies, had gotten worse since he supplemented Harris' prescription with one from another doctor. He would cut back on the pills as soon as his workload eased. When he finished the Coke, he slung his jacket over his shoulder and headed to the harbor. He wasn't hungry, and the walk might untangle the knot in his stomach.

Robert crossed Water Street, the swath of grass beyond it, and two sets of railroad tracks to reach a concrete walkway that ran parallel to the water, which swelled and churned from the heavy port traffic. Still a three-ring circus of vessels like he'd seen that morning, but it didn't interest him now. Tanner's lie about the hubcaps made the Michigan figures less definitive. He could imagine the jury's deliberations: "Even four thousand is a large number of them. I think it could have been coincidence." "But what about the missing hubcaps? Coincidence on top of coincidence. That ain't likely." Granted, Carl still had the problem of proving Tanner's identification was accurate, but it was the nature of prejudiced people to mistake belief for proof.

He followed the walkway toward a cargo ship that was being unloaded fifty or so yards away. The Ionian Wind flew a Greek flag, but its cargo could be from anywhere—Belgian lace, French perfumes, English china. Suddenly he wished the girls were with him. Before Gulfstream when his work days were riddled with money-less holes, he often brought them down to watch ships unload. He didn't see enough of the girls now, but that would change as soon as he'd replaced Gulfstream with less demanding wealthy clients, and he was working on it.

He watched a squadron of ducks follow a towboat entering the forested banks of the Mobile River. Towboat captain. Now that would be the ticket—up and down a lazy river for a living. Robert chuckled at the thought. His family couldn't live for a week on the salary a towboat captain earned in a month. Plus, he'd be so bored he'd be farming alligators on the side.

So how to discredit Tanner, Robert thought as he headed back. Tanner being motivated by anger would do it, but that little tiff at the Christmas party wouldn't support such a claim. There was the appearance of a classic triangle which would impeach Tanner, hands down, if he could prove there was one. But he knew there wasn't. Candy wouldn't be caught dead with the likes of Tanner. Still, he could paint such a strong possibility that the jury would need to consider it in their deliberations. He'd have to be cautious, though; if they thought he was overreaching, they'd be only too happy to keep their sympathies with the prosecution.

"Mr. Tanner, let's return to the hubcaps," Robert said when his cross-examination resumed. The droopy-eyed, after-lunch jury sat up straight. Curious, Robert knew, about why he would revisit testimony unfavorable to him. "You stated that the car you saw on the victim's street the night he died was missing hubcaps and that the defendant's car was also missing hubcaps, is that correct?"

"That's right."

"And you testified that the defendant was not a friend or even a casual acquaintance of yours, only a neighbor you'd briefly met at a neighborhood Christmas party, is that correct?"

"Yeah. What of it?"

"Don't you think it's peculiar, then, that you would take such an interest in the defendant's car as to notice his hubcaps were missing?" He emphasized the word "peculiar" as to connote something untoward.

"No. He lives down the street from me. I seen him coming and going every day."

"Objection. Not related to the witness's testimony on direct."

"Sustained"

"I see my neighbors coming and going, Mr. Tanner, but I don't notice—"

"Objection. Irrelevant."

"Sustained. Way out of order, counsel."

"Sorry, your honor. When you met Mr. Fry at that party, was his wife with him?"

"Yeah. I met both of them."

"You and Mr. Fry got into a dispute at that party, did you not, having to do with Mr. Fry's wife?" Ah-Ha, shifting in the jury box. "You brought a cocktail to Mrs. Fry when Mr. Fry left her to talk to someone else, isn't that correct?"

"Yeah."

"Why would you take a drink to another man's wife?" Ah-Ha, more shifting.

"I had a drink and she didn't. It was just good manners."

"Good manners. So that means you were taking drinks to every empty-handed woman at the party?" Robert paused to hear chuckles, but the jury box was silent.

"Of course not. Me and her was talking, that's why."

"Do you mean it was just the two of you alone, off in some cozy corner having—"

"Objection, your honor. Leading question."

"Sustained."

"Isn't it true that you and Mr. Fry got into an argument when he returned and he asked you to step outside to discuss why you brought his wife that drink?"

"Discuss it, ha. He don't know the meaning of discuss."

"Why didn't you reveal this dispute with the defendant about his wife on direct exam?"

"I didn't think about it. It weren't no big deal."

Robert scanned the jury. Completely absent was the liveliness of eyes, the tilting of heads, the forward-leaning posture of people thinking they were on to something. They weren't buying a triangle. Fry was going down, and Robert was going with him because the idiot refused to plea bargain. *Three years, are you crazy. I got me a young wife to keep an eye on.*

Stalling for time, Robert walked slowly to the defense table as though to review his notes. Fry was leaning over the table toward the witness stand, fists clenched, face red. Fry *was* buying a triangle. An idea flashed across Robert's mind like a shooting star. Continuing to stand next to Fry, he turned to the witness.

"Mr. Tanner, would you say Mrs. Fry's attractive?"

"Objection, your honor. Irrelevant."

"On the contrary, your honor, Mr. Tanner's thoughts about Mrs. Fry could be extremely relevant, given his testimony about the dispute between him and the defendant involving Mrs. Fry."

"Overruled. Answer the question, Mr. Tanner."

"Yeah, she's attractive. Got a nice figure, if you get my drift."

"I'm sure every man in this room gets your drift, Mr. Tanner."

"Objection."

"Sustained. If you're out of bounds one more time, counselor, I'll hold you in contempt."

"Yes, your honor." He glanced at Fry whose heavy breathing—a rough gravelly sound—had become audible. "Mrs. Fry has long hair, doesn't she, Mr. Tanner?" After she'd visited Fry in jail wearing a too-short skirt, Robert had overheard a guard say that her hair was the only thing keeping the dust off her fanny.

"Yeah, it's long."

"To her shoulders?"

"Oh, longer than that. It's past her... Well, you know."

"Past her what?"

"Objection. Irrelevant," said Carl, but Tanner, eager to show off his manly observation spoke before Judge Simmons' ruling.

"Her ass."

Clenched fists, fiery face, savage intake of breath. Fry was teetering over the vortex of insinuations his lawyer had made to save them both. Robert bent over and whispered in Fry's ear, "Diddling your wife is my guess."

Bellowing like a lunatic, Fry began to scramble across the table, one knee on the top before the deputy wrestled him back to his chair. The bailiff had reached them by then, and together they got the cuffs on.

Judge Simmons rose to his feet. "You'll stay in handcuffs for the rest of the trial, Mr. Fry. You've clearly demonstrated your capacity for violence, and I won't have it in my courtroom."

Robert covered his mouth with his hand to keep from laughing out loud.

"Are you finished with this witness, Mr. Townsend?"

"Yes, your honor," he said in a tone as appalled and apologetic as he could muster.

"Any redirect, Mr. Taylor?"

"No, your honor."

"Mr. Tanner, you're dismissed," Judge Simmons said.

Jurors weren't allowed to talk in the jury box, and their faces were usually somber when an important witness left the stand, but this jury was like a crate of zombies suddenly come alive, all of them bubbling with chatter.

Judge Simmons pounded them into silence with his gavel and reminded them that talking was forbidden in the jury box. When they quieted, he said, "Let's proceed," and asked if Carl was through with his case. Before Carl could answer, Robert asked for permission to approach the bench, and Carl joined him.

"Your honor," Robert said in the hushed voice out of jury

earshot used for such conferences. "I object to my client being put in handcuffs in front of the jury."

"What's wrong with you, counsel? He was about to attack the witness."

"With all due respect, your honor, I disagree. Mr. Fry was trying to sit back in his chair when they put the cuffs on. I move for a mistrial on the grounds of jury prejudice."

"Motion denied, and as I said, he stays in handcuffs for the rest of the trial."

"I intend to appeal that ruling, your honor. I have a second motion. I object to the court's characterizing my client as violent in front of the jury. I quote: 'You've clearly demonstrated your capacity for violence, Mr. Fry.' I move for a mistrial on the grounds of judicial misconduct."

Judge Simmons leaned over the bench until his flushed face came within a foot of Robert's. "Something's rotten in Denmark, counsel. What did you say to the defendant before he jumped up?"

"Sorry, your honor, but it's confidential. Attorney-client privilege, you know."

"There are exceptions to that privilege, counsel, investigation of unethical attorney conduct being one."

"No breach of ethics by me, your honor. I'm just defending my client."

Judge Simmons glared at him for a few seconds, then sat back in his chair. "The court adjourns until tomorrow morning to consider motions made by defense counsel."

Robert stood on the courthouse steps raised by adrenaline to the balls of his feet. He was a winner—a mistrial plus Simmons over a barrel in one fell swoop. Simmons would have to grant the mistrial. Judicial misconduct was a shoo-in. With luck, he'd have enough other clients before the new trial date to kiss Gulfstream goodbye.

It was only two o'clock and he had nothing scheduled that afternoon because he thought he'd be in court. There was plenty to do at the office, but the euphoria of victory demanded an exciting reward. A feeling akin to the primal urge of conquerors to rape and plunder, no doubt. He decided to go to Helene's. He'd seen her Thursday, so he'd be violating his once-a-week rule, but what difference would a single violation make? He intended to break it off with her soon anyway; an affair longer than a couple of months was prone to messy complications. For the moment, though, carpe diem.

# *Five*

Dessie put too much curry in the shrimp salad, and by five o'clock Monday afternoon the seven women in Elizabeth Townsend's card club, eight including Elizabeth, had consumed four pitchers of Famous Ramos Gin Fizz. Elizabeth had bribed the bartender at the Roosevelt Hotel in New Orleans for the recipe—gin, cream, orange water, and powdered sugar. Like a delicious milkshake, everyone said. Poker and gin instead of bridge and tea had been a huge gamble. "You're too new to Mobile society to break with tradition, Elizabeth," her friend Glo warned. But it was a risk Elizabeth needed to take. So far it was paying off, she thought as she stood on the portico waving at the three women leaving to beat their husbands home from work. And paying off for the reason she'd figured: give highbrow women lowbrow fun and you'll be popular. None of those three had made any overtures of friendship in the eight months she'd been in the bridge club, but that afternoon each of them in turn privately pulled her aside and suggested dinner sometime soon with husbands in tow.

She was overjoyed. The husbands were what she was after. Surely the president of an aluminum company, the head of an international paper company, and the owner of a construction company could use a brilliant, personable attorney, and thanks to her, Robert would soon be meeting them. He was desperate to get out from under Gulfstream, although he wouldn't admit it, and since he had no time for rain making she had done it for him. And would continue to do so although Robert thought a wife shouldn't interfere with her husband's business. No longer would she helplessly have to watch him ruin his health with those pills.

Through the screen door behind her came the soft, melodious voices of the four remaining women—the sound of Southern women of leisure, with one woman's sentence ending high in the air, and another catching it there and bringing it down. A complete musical phrase. Of course, Elizabeth thought as she turned to join them, she wasn't home free. Emily, Sondra, and Glo, who were part of the Townsends' little clique within their country club, were no concern. But there was Marjorie Simmons, who'd come as a last-minute substitute, expecting like the others had, to play bridge. She was matriarch of the club, and if she found poker and gin too risqué for Mobile's socialites, word would get out and the three who'd left would never call. Elizabeth was worried because Marjorie was much older than her other guests and reputed to be very proper.

The conversation, Elizabeth realized as she resumed her seat at the poker table, was the familiar one of how Mobile's being a major wartime port had changed the city. Not having known Mobile then, she only half listened as she gathered the cards and shuffled.

"I'm telling you that it hurt us in the long run," said Sondra Miller. Her long red fingernails sliced the air as she spoke, for she talked with her hands (which did not explain, as Robert claimed, why she touched him incessantly when they conversed). "How could it be otherwise, country hicks converging on the city like locusts, cluttering our parks with the tents and shipping crates they lived in. Remember how our sewers were constantly clogged, garbage cans overflowing, and God help any one of us who needed a hospital room."

"Yes," said Glo, "but look at how our economy flourished with new industries and the ones we had expanded because we had the manpower. Our shipyards and the State Docks, for example. The expansion was a good thing."

"I'll drink to expansion," said Emily, "and I don't want any cracks about my figure." She took a hefty swig of her gin fizz and continued. "Especially as it pertained to Brookley Field. More good-looking soldiers per square foot in this town than you could bat your eyes at, and don't look at me like that, Sondra, you know what I'm talking about."

Afraid Marjorie, who'd been quiet, was probably as bored with the topic as she was, Elizabeth pounded the deck on the table as though it were a gavel. "Last hand, ladies. What'll it be? Five card stud or draw?" Those were the only games the club social director, whom Elizabeth had paid to come for the first half hour, had taught them. Elizabeth shoved the deck toward Sondra. "Want to cut?"

"Hold your horses, Elizabeth," Sondra said. "I have one more point to make. It's true that our businesses thrived because we had such a large workforce, but over half of that riffraff stayed when the war was over. So we still have trashy trailer camps, ridiculous-looking 'homettes,' and ramshackle houses on the outskirts of town, plus their lice-ridden children crowding our schools. It's a damn shame. Mobile will never be the pretty little French city it used to be."

Marjorie leaned forward, back rigid and chin high. "And France, Sondra," she announced, "will never be the pretty little country it used to be—mortar holes in buildings dating back to the Renaissance, farmlands cratered, and grave sites head to toe across the southern provinces—but it will still be France thanks in a large part to our city's contribution. One hundred ninety-two ships, one hundred sixty-seven tankers, seven destroyers, and hundreds of other vessels were built here, and countless weapons, munitions, and other war material packed, loaded, and shipped off around the clock by that 'riffraff' as you called them." Her lips pursed, she sat back in her chair and nodded with satisfaction.

A pall fell over the group. Elizabeth remembered that the Simmons's son was killed at Normandy. Damn. As hostess, she should have changed the topic early on.

"Thank you, Marjorie," said Glo. "You've put things in perspective."

That's my Glo, Elizabeth thought, her intelligent, unassuming, *Gone with the Wind* Melanie-like friend. The only real friend she had in the club, and luckily, Carl and Robert were best friends.

Sondra agreed with Glo's comment. Emily said her husband, who was French, was grateful to the Americans for what they did over there. "But Louis doesn't like losing money to them, so I need a chance to recoup my dollar fifty. What were those choices again, Elizabeth?"

"The only games we know, Emily. Five-card stud or draw."

"I'll take the stud," Emily said, "and the sooner the better. That's what I told Louis last week when we were hanging a mirror in the guest room. He said we needed to find a stud, and I said one of us did anyway."

Elizabeth, who'd begun to deal, laughed with the rest of the women until she saw Marjorie's frown.

"Don't be vulgar, Emily," Marjorie said. "We've had a long afternoon and a lot of gin fizz. It's time for us to go home."

"Go if you want, Marjorie, but I'm not leaving, and neither is anyone else. We're not playing the usual 'Simmons Says' this afternoon." She glanced at the others as though acknowledging their complicity.

Oh, God, no, Elizabeth thought. Emily is drunk. Elizabeth looked at Glo, expecting to see an "I told you so," for Glo had warned about Emily drinking for such an extended time, but Glo just looked concerned.

"I don't know what you're talking about, Emily," Marjorie said.

"Of course you do."

Elizabeth wanted to tell Emily to shut up, but losing her temper would destroy a year of nerve-wracking efforts to blend in with these well-bred women, which Robert wanted her to do. In the periphery, she saw Sondra's smirk. Sondra had no doubt been waiting for something to spoil the party and would make a hundred phone calls before supper, the first three to the women who'd left.

"I said I didn't know, Emily, and if you're not going to tell me, I might as well leave." As Marjorie scooped her winnings from the well in the table into her purse, the women's voices begging her to stay swelled like the sudden sound of cicadas at dusk. The voices stopped when Emily, her hands pressed together as though in prayer, turned to Marjorie. "Please forgive me. I didn't mean it. You've known me longer than God. You know what a kidder I am."

The tautness in Marjorie's face disappeared. "Stop looking

so pathetic, Emily. Maybe not longer than God, but too long to let your bad manners spoil my fun." She dug the change from her purse, dropped it back into the well and resumed her seat. "Frankly, I don't know when I've enjoyed myself this much, Elizabeth. Deal me in."

Goose bumps rose on the back of Elizabeth's neck. Bingo. Praise about the party from Marjorie—something like Elizabeth Townsend's being a fun and imaginative hostess—could easily lead to potential clients, for who wouldn't want a fun, imaginative hostess and her husband in their social circle. As a matter of fact, she realized, the Society section of *The Press Register* often printed a blurb about Marjorie's social doings. Maybe today's party would be mentioned there.

As though to corroborate her proud moment, the light of the lowering sun, perhaps just freed from a cloud, suddenly flooded through the small leaded and beveled diamond-shaped panes of the living room window. Fractured by the bevels, the light fell in golden beads across the room, suffusing the oriental carpet, the velvet upholstery, and the rosewood tables with a magical glow. All the women oohed and aahed, including Elizabeth, who always felt a rush of pleasure when it happened. She'd chosen this house for the joy of looking out of those fairytale windows, instead of peeping in as she'd done to the grand houses near her high school while waiting for the school bus.

Elizabeth expected Marjorie to lead the women's departure when the hand was over, but instead Marjorie pushed her chair back to better admire the antique poker table.

"So graceful, almost feminine, and smaller than I would picture a poker table," she said. "A perfect antique side table in a room this size."

"Thank you. That's what I thought. I'd been looking for such a thing for ages and came across it at an antique shop in New Orleans. The owner said poker tables on the gambling boats were scaled down so more could fit in the cabin. He said this one had been on the *Delta Queen*."

"*Delta Queen*, my foot," Sondra said. "Those antique dealers in New Orleans will tell you anything."

Heat rose to Elizabeth's face. What else to expect from a woman who would show her ass in the pretense of being a chorus line dancer? "Not this time, Sondra. He gave me a certificate of authenticity." The sound of her voice dismayed her—back was the harsh, clipped speech of rural Mississippi that she'd spent her adult life trying to get rid of. Luckily, no one seemed to notice, except maybe Glo, who quickly interrupted to say she would ask Dessie to make coffee.

"A certificate with the ink still wet, no doubt," Sondra retorted.

"Well, it could have been on the *Delta Queen*, Sondra," Marjorie said, "so it doesn't matter. The point is that it's lovely. Everything is, Elizabeth." She swept her hand through the air to include the whole room. "This is the first time I've been here, and I'm impressed. Tell me more about yourself, my dear."

"She's married to a man who looks like Tyrone Power. What else is there to know?"

"I know Robert is attractive, Sondra, but she wasn't born married to him. I mean your family, dear. Where are you from?"

"Jackson."

"Oh, really. Markham and I know some old families in Jackson. What's your maiden name?"

"Thomas." Elizabeth strained to keep irritation from her voice. Answering questions about her family background had been the hardest part of their joining the club.

"Well, of course," Marjorie said. "I know the Thomases of Jackson. They're descendants of Jackson's first wartime mayor. The Great War, I mean. As I remember, he had four successful sons and three married daughters. All of them had children, who've probably had children by now, spreading Thomases across Jackson like kudzu."

"It's not that family. My parents died when I was young and I was raised by my aunt and her husband." A half-truth. Her mother died, but her father hadn't wanted her.

"Oh, I'm sorry," Marjorie said. "What did your uncle do?"

"He was a farmer." Another half-truth, but how better to characterize the slovenly planting and harvesting of vegetables he did when he was sober.

"Oh, so you're our little farm girl," Sondra said. "I thought so."

And you're our loud-mouthed tart, Elizabeth thought. "Not in the way you're thinking, Sondra. My uncle was a dairy farmer—hundreds of lucrative cows. And of course we didn't live on the dairy farm; we had a mansion in town."

"My cousin has a dairy farm," Sondra said, "so I know a little about the business. What kind of cows did—"

"Oh, here's the coffee," Elizabeth said with relief as Dessie came toward her with the silver service. After the clinks of spoons on china stirring sugar and cream, Emily called for gossip. "And nobody leaves until we do a thorough job. We have a tradition to uphold."

After a minute, Glo broke the thoughtful silence. "This is not gossip exactly, but I saw something surprising when I met Carl downtown for dinner last week. Mr. Bearden was hobbling into the Esquire Club, his colored man holding the door open for him."

"Where have you been, Glo?" said Sondra. "Mr. Bearden's been going to the Esquire Club for years, even before his wife died."

"I don't understand why a man in his seventies, or any intelligent man, would watch those...what do you call them?" Marjorie said.

"Striptease dancers," said Sondra.

"Who knows why men do anything," said Emily. "You can't predict them and you can't control them. The most you can do is spend their money. That's what a friend in Birmingham says. Her husband's hobby is young women. She doesn't fuss because he's usually discreet, but last month, he bought his newest chickee boom-boom a new convertible and they whizzed around town with the top down. My friend spit fire when somebody told her they'd seen it, and one day when she saw the convertible parked with the top down, she had her gardener rush over and dump in a truckload of manure—front seat and back seat. Then she called her husband at work and said, 'Honey, you know that new convertible you bought? I just turned it into a flowerpot.' "

Elizabeth joined in the laughter to avoid suspicion. These respected ladies had not been cheated on as she had, or they would realize that the woman's antic was an attempt to not feel pathetic.

"I don't understand," Elizabeth said when the laughter stopped. "Why doesn't she divorce him? It looks like she'd get plenty of money."

"She's almost fifty," Emily said. "Who wants to be divorced at fifty?"

"Or any age over thirty," said Sondra. "There's no future in it."

Marjorie was the last to leave. "Thank you so much, Elizabeth. I've never played poker before, and it was fun to do something new. I'm really sorry about your mother, dear. If you ever need some mothering, let me know. We all do sometimes. And now I have a question. The Order of Myths, my Mardi Gras Krewe, is having its young court luncheon in August. That's where we look over the members' children and grandchildren to pick maids and pages for the next King's court. Since I have no descendants in that age range, they let me nominate a proxy, and I was thinking of your Ellen. I saw her helping your younger one at the club's Easter egg hunt, and she seems like a lovely girl. The luncheon doesn't mean she'll be chosen, but if she'd like to be considered, we'll send her an invitation."

"Dessie, guess what," Elizabeth called as she hurried to the kitchen with the silver tray of dirty cups. Unbelievable—their knock-kneed, cat-got-your tongue Ellen as trailblazer to the Order of Myths, the oldest and most prestigious krewe in Mobile. Remembering that Dessie would have gone to the club to pick up the girls, she called Robert's office to give him the good news, but there was no answer. He would be proud of her impressing Marjorie and thrilled that they might have an in with the Order of Myths, the best organization in Mobile for ensuring lucrative clients.

After she'd taken a bath and put on fresh makeup, Elizabeth padded across the carpet to her walk-in closet, which was larger than her room in the ramshackle farmhouse of her childhood. Thirty or so expensive, fashionable garments grouped by seasons and formality hung on two ten- foot rods running front to back in the rectangular area. Shoe racks filled the space underneath them, and the shelves above were laden with hat boxes and bags. If her uncle were alive, she would show him this, then laugh in his face. How many times had she gone to school in a dress with the hem above her knees and a bodice so tight the fabric gapped between the buttons. Clothes at Kresses were dirt cheap—it wouldn't have taken much of his liquor money to spare her such embarrassment.

She and Robert would celebrate her good news when he got home, so she decided to wear her new lounging gown, the tag read: At Home with Him. It was a soft silk in lime green, a color Deborah Kerr often wore because it was said to look good on red-heads. The plunging V neckline with wide lapels called attention to her cleavage, and the A-line ankle-length skirt was cut on the bias, which the saleslady said minimized middle-age spread, thus, no girdle was needed.

Elizabeth slipped into the gown and admired herself in the mirror. Only a tall, broad-shouldered woman like herself could carry off the gown's Hollywood-like flair. Marjorie could if she was twenty years younger. It wasn't so surprising that Marjorie had taken to her. They were a lot alike—notorious at the club for walking too fast on the golf links, and neither were gossips. The phone rang, and she hurried to the nightstand to answer.

# *Six*

When she finished dressing, Elizabeth came downstairs and stood on the porch to watch the girls jump rope on the sidewalk in the darkening twilight. The streetlight directly over them came on, and they appeared to be on stage, the dark blue sky as a backdrop and the silvery Spanish moss hanging from the oak as a half drawn curtain. And she was their audience watching from the back row. She often felt distant from her daughters, not truly feeling their joys or sorrows like other mothers did with their children. But she was vigilant about keeping them well and safe. The only bad accident was the four year old Ellen's' broken arm from falling off a swing when Robert pushed too high.

Elizabeth swayed so that the silk of the dressing gown caressed her calves. Robert would like the soft feel of the gown and its sophisticated yet sexy look. He would tease that she looked like Tallulah Bankhead when he saw her. Too bad Red had insisted on taking him to dinner. She could tell over the phone how excited he was about getting a mistrial and wished he could have come straight home. Well, when he came they would have a grand time celebrating each other's good news.

"I see London, I see France, I see Wendy's underpants," sang Ellen and Marie, a neighborhood friend of Wendy's. As they turned the rope, Wendy's foot caught for an instant, but she recovered and kept jumping, her light cotton skirt lifting and falling like butterfly wings. "I'm jumping longer than you, Marie, and you're older than me."

Elizabeth smiled. Wendy was smart, lively and cocky like Robert, and favored him too—olive skin, doe eyes, thick luscious hair. If Wendy hadn't inherited her quick temper, she would be the perfect daughter. Who would ever think that Wendy and slow, quiet, mousy-haired Ellen were sisters.

Suddenly, heat lightning danced in the near distance.

"Come in, girls. Marie, you run on home."

"I didn't hear thunder," said Ellen.

"I've told you that doesn't mean you can't get struck."

When Robert wasn't home for supper, Elizabeth and the girls ate at the built-in breakfast nook in the kitchen, a cozy place with red leather seats, a ceramic tabletop the same color, and a window that ran from the table height to the ceiling. The nook was the only feature of the house that Ellen, who'd balked at the move, had liked. The window made her feel like she was eating in the dining car of a train, which she had done when she'd taken the Hummingbird to visit her grandparents in Montgomery.

The spicy tomato aroma of Dessie's shrimp creole filled the air as they slid into the booth already set with steaming bowls of it.

"Daddy's getting a mistrial, which means we'll be seeing more of him for a while."

"Yippee. When will he be home? He said we'd play ping-pong if he got home in time since he worked yesterday."

"I don't know, but the ping-pong has to wait. He'll be tired. Let him sit down and relax with me."

"You just want Daddy for yourself," said Wendy, looking at Elizabeth defiantly. "Like on my birthday when he…"

"Come on, Wendy Beanie. That's over with. Let's have a nice supper to celebrate the good news." This would probably be their last supper without him for some time, Elizabeth thought, and felt the urge to make it pleasant instead of lackluster as their suppers often were when he wasn't there. "Let's play that train game you made up, Ellen."

"I thought you said we couldn't because Wendy got too distracted to eat."

"We'll try again if Wendy will promise—"

"I promise. I won't get 'stracted. Can I go first?"

She couldn't, Ellen said, because it was Dessie's turn from the last time. Dessie said she had to study the black bottom pie she was cooking for Miz Elizabeth's bake sale, so she would listen and make guesses. Ellen said it was her turn then because Wendy took extra turns the last time.

"No I didn't."

"Since we don't know for sure, I think Ellen should begin," Elizabeth said, and winked at Ellen. "That way you can get a head start eating, Wendy."

"All aboard that's coming aboard," Ellen called out. She made the hissing sound of a steam engine, and then the clikety-clack sounds of train wheels rolling on the track. "Here we go." She looked out the window, and as though dusk had transformed the honeysuckle bush, crepe myrtle tree and jungle gym into a field of turnip greens, she began. "See those men, women, and children wearing straw hats bending over picking greens and tossing them in a bushel basket? Must be fifteen to twenty pickers. Oh look, that mule-drawn wagon poking along that trail close to them has stopped. Watch the pickers hurrying over to dump their basket loads into the wagon while the farmer writes who picked how many baskets in a little notebook."

She put her ear to the glass as though listening. "Now they're teasing each other and telling jokes to have a little fun before they start picking again."

"I want to have fun. I'm going to pick greens too when I'm growed up."

"No, you're not. I grew up on a farm, Wendy, so I know those people are not having fun. Their backs ache because they bend over all day, the skin on their fingers is raw, and the chigger bites on their ankles itch all the time. Plus, they're worried because they know the farmer's record book will fall short of the number of baskets they picked. There's nothing fun about farm work."

"Now, that's the gospel," said Dessie. "I'll take the kitchen any day."

"Oh, I didn't know," Ellen said. After a pause, she turned back to the window. "Look at them standing around resting before they go back to picking. See the farmer juggling the reins to tell the mule to go, but he doesn't move an inch. Now the farmer's whipping the reins and calling out for the mule to go on, but the mule still doesn't move. The workers smile at each other. The farmer

stands and lashes the mule on the back with his whip. Then…
then—"

"Ellen, for Pete's sake go on," Elizabeth said.

"The mule bolts. The farmer falls back in his seat, and the
wagon goes lickety-split down the trail. Just look, the workers
are laughing, every man, woman, and child, holding their sides,
wiping tears from their faces. And they're laughing still as they go
back to the field to fill their baskets."

"Cute story, Ellen, even though it's not realistic," Elizabeth
said when she'd stopped laughing. She looked at Ellen as she
would a piece of jigsaw puzzle that didn't seem to fit anywhere.
The girl went around in a fog, frustratingly inattentive to deadlines or the task at hand. But once in a while she surprised you by
doing something admirable.

"I like that story," said Dessie, who'd also been laughing, "but
a field of greens could be anywhere, except maybe Chicago or
New York. You got to give us real clues."

"And they're 'sposed to be clues I can understand," Wendy said.

Next, Ellen saw a huge, round three-story building with a roof
shaped like an upside down bowl and three flags flying, and then
she saw a train station where an old man in a suit and hat was
sitting on a bench with two young girls who were licking all-day
suckers.

"I know, I know. It's Montgomery. Me and Ellen is watching
trains and that's Grandpa with us, isn't it Mama," Wendy said.

"It certainly is." The old coot. Living with Robert's parents
while he was in the Pacific had been almost as bad as living in
Jackson. Suddenly a scene she wanted to describe came to mind.
"Let's get out of Montgomery. Chukka, chukka, we're moving
again."

"Noooo. I guessed right so it's my turn, isn't it, Dessie?"

"Yes, but why not be nice and let your mother go?"

"That's right. Especially since it's Mama's first time ever."

"No." The lamb-fur head shook violently.

"Sometimes you let your father go when it's not his turn,"
Elizabeth said. "I've heard you."

"Uh-uh."

"Yes, you do, but never mind. What if I go now and you get two turns in a row?"

The lamb-fur head stopped shaking. "Okay."

"Thank you. Chukka. Chukka. We're moving fast through a pitch-black night. But oh, look. Big city lights ahead—buildings ten stories tall with so many windows lit it looks like stars are sitting in them. Now we're pulling into a station that's ten times bigger than Montgomery's. We're in Atlanta, Georgia, and—"

"No, Mama," Wendy said, head shaking again. "You're not 'sposed to tell us where. That's what we're 'sposed to guess."

"My turn is different. Hiss-hiss, the train's coming to a stop—see the steam coming up from the wheels. And look at the dozens of beautiful girls on the platform in fancy dresses with skirts that twirl out when they dance. Hear the loud clicks. That's the sound of the doors in every train car opening automatically. See the soldiers rush out, all spiffy in dress uniforms, spit-shines on their shoes and hat brims, every one of them smiling. Watch now, that handsome soldier, wavy dark hair and big brown eyes, walking over to a long-legged young woman in a lavender dress with long hair the color of a new penny." Elizabeth pressed her ear to the window.

"Listen. The soldier says, 'Hello, good-looking. Have you been waiting for me as long as I've been waiting for you?' The young woman says, 'Hardly. I'm waiting for my husband, who's a champion boxer, and he's standing right behind you.' The soldier whips his head around to look, then laughs." Elizabeth paused, remembering how witty she'd felt at that moment, and how thrilled by Robert's laughter. "The soldier takes her arm and escorts her to an auditorium across the street with a sign in front saying USO Dance Tonight." Elizabeth remembered the glitter ball shining on Robert's luscious hair as they danced, and her fear that he would think she was a country hick.

"Did the husband go too?"

"There was no husband, Wendy," Dessie said. "The young woman was kidding him."

"Here's the question for y'all to answer: Who is the couple?"

"You and Daddy," Ellen said. "I know you met in the war and went dancing."

"Un-uh. Mama said the lady had long hair. Mama's hair is short."

Elizabeth's hand flew to her pageboy, a tight spinsterish roll only a few inches below her chin. When she learned at the club that it wasn't appropriate for women over thirty to have long hair, she'd had hers cut to just a little above her shoulders, but the hair-dresser that morning had cut too much.

"It certainly is your parents, Wendy," said Dessie, who was taking the pie crust from the oven. "This is a story about before you were born. Tell us more, Miz Elizabeth. I'm enjoying this."

"Me too," Ellen said.

"Not me," Wendy said. "We were supposed to guess where. It's my turn now."

"The game is over because you haven't touched your food. Pick up that spoon and—"

"But it's my turn and you said I get two—"

"Not another word. Eat." Elizabeth turned to Ellen. "Did you meet a Mrs. Simmons at the Easter Egg Hunt, a tall gray-haired woman with glasses?"

"I don't know. Maybe it was the woman who asked me to give the little kids clues, you know, 'hot' or 'cold.'"

So that's how it happened, Elizabeth thought: Marjorie was too busy running the hunt to really look at the gangly body with the narrow face. "Today Mrs. Simmons said you were a lovely young lady and…well, never mind." Elizabeth decided to wait until they got the luncheon invitation before telling Ellen. Maybe then she wouldn't balk so much about going.

"Are you making friends in the swimming lessons yet?"

"No. We mainly swim."

"What about in the Teen Room?" Surely in that concrete brick room next to the hot dog grill the adults called Chaos Cavern, Ellen would rub elbows in a social way.

"Not really."

After a half dozen more questions—getting information from Ellen was like trying to shake coins from a piggy bank—an unwanted picture emerged: Ellen in her shapeless swimsuit ensconced on a stool in a corner, usually alone, unless this snotty sixteen-year-old named Amanda deigned to sit with her, while ping-pong, cards, dancing, and so forth went on around her. And she would be that way at the King's Court luncheon—too shapeless and too shy to be noticed.

"Look, Ellen, you'll never make friends by just watching. You have to mix with people. Play cards, play ping-pong, tell jokes. You can't be a bump on a log."

"Sissy is a bump on a log, a bump on a log, a bump—"

"Shut up, Wendy."

"I am not."

"You are if you don't talk to people. Just walk up to someone and say. Hi, I'm Ellen. I like your bathing suit or whatever. Can't you do that?"

"Not alone. The kids are usually with somebody. If I had a friend with me, like Ruthie then…Please, can Ruthie go—"

"No, damn it. Must I explain again? We're in a higher social class now than the Kellys, and it will look bad if you pal around with Ruthie—that wild hair, that gap between her teeth. Martha was my best friend, remember, and I had to give her up because of her appearance. I wish you understood, but I can see by your face that you think I'm being mean, don't you?"

Ellen shrugged.

"Of course you do, because you've had an easy life, Ellen. You don't know what mean is. Tell you what, look out the window."

"But it's my turn," Wendy said.

"Hush up and eat." Elizabeth pointed outside. "That tool shed in the back yard of that ramshackle farmhouse. See that girl about your age on her knees next to a large tabby lying on the ground. The girl's counting the newborn kittens at the mama's teats. Now a scruffy-looking man in overalls comes in and drops kitten after kitten into a croaker sack. When he's got all the kittens, he heads off with the sack across the field toward a creek. The girl's running after him yelling, 'Please don't.' When they get to the bluff at the edge of the creek, he pushes the sack toward the girl and she takes it thinking to run with it, but he grabs her and makes her drop the sack in, and then—" She stopped. Hadn't meant to go that far, yet she felt hollow inside because there was so much more to be told.

The kitchen was silent except for the ticking of the wall clock, a black plastic cat whose eyes looked from one side to another with a comic furtiveness as its tail swung like a pendulum ticking off the seconds. The three of them looked at Elizabeth expectantly as though she would continue.

"That's all. I just want you to see the difference between "mean" and my wanting you to be careful about what people think of you." Elizabeth sighed. There was nothing in Ellen's face that said she saw the difference.

"Did the girl drop the kittens in the creek?" Wendy said.

Jesus Christ. Elizabeth hadn't considered Wendy. "It's a made-up story. Forget about it."

"The girl drownded the kittens," Wendy said, her voice quivering.

"Nobody drowned anything, hard head. I said it's just pretend. There was no girl, no kittens."

"I got to beat some egg whites now," Dessie said. "Who wants to help?"

"I do." Wendy said, and rose to her knees.

"Not until you finish eating. You can leave a little rice, but you have to eat the shrimp."

"I did. See?" Wendy gestured to her bowl, where only a mixture of rice, bell peppers, and stewed tomatoes could be seen.

Elizabeth dragged her fork over the rice to uncover a pile of shrimp. "You liar."

Eyes ablaze with defiance, Wendy popped one shrimp after another into her mouth with her fingers.

"No. One at a time and use your spoon. Chew with your mouth closed."

Cheeks bulging, Wendy moved her jaw back and forth like a cow chewing cud. In a few seconds came a muffled noise which sounded like she was coughing with her mouth closed.

"Stop that. You'll choke." Elizabeth said.

Wendy nodded but rasped again and began to gag. Her chest heaved and her arms flailed.

"Dessie!" Elizabeth yelled.

"Cough it in your bowl, honey," said Dessie, who'd hurried to the table.

Wendy opened her mouth and coughed. Creole shot across the table like water from a firehose.

Elizabeth looked down at the sauce-splattered bodice of her gown, then jumped to her feet. "You little devil. You did that on purpose." She grabbed Wendy's bowl and turned it upside down on the girl's head. The sticky rice sat in a mound like a macabre pillbox hat, red sauce dribbling down. After a shock-frozen instant, Wendy let out a soul-wrenching wail.

"Mama!" Ellen said.

"Mama nothing. Look at me." Elizabeth dropped the bowl on the table and shook Wendy by her shoulders. "You did it to spite me, didn't you?"

Continuing to wail, Wendy shook her head, and clumps of rice brushed her cheeks as they fell. She swatted at them as though deflecting bees.

"Calm down, baby. You all right." Dessie stood close to Wendy, a dishcloth in her hand.

"Stop that yelling this minute, damn it! You're not hurt."

The wail turned to heaving sobs. Tears mingled with tomato sauce ran down Wendy's pudgy cheeks. Elizabeth snatched the dishcloth from Dessie and wiped Wendy's face.

"I'm through eating," Ellen said. "I'll take her upstairs and clean her off."

"All right. Get in the tub and wash her hair."

"In the tub? You agreed I was too old to—"

"You heard me."

"You hear that, baby?" Dessie said. "Ellen's gonna take a bath with you. You like that."

"Let's go," Ellen said, touching Wendy's shoulder. Wendy's

sobs diminished to whimpers as she scrambled from the booth. Ellen followed, and Fifi trotted after them.

Feeling as though her bones had turned to water, Elizabeth eased herself down onto the bench, and looking toward the window, saw the reflection of the girls as they left the kitchen holding hands, one skinny and tall with stringy hair, the other short and plump with curls—her Olive Oyl and Betty Boop. She shouldn't have done it. Where did dumping food on your child's head fall on the continuum from light switchings and spankings, which she'd administered, to beltings, which she'd been careful to refrain from?

Suddenly she heard a voice. "Lady, I'd say you're a mother by the skin of your teeth." Words once hurled at her by a tattooed carnie barker. Irritated by five-year-old Ellen's dawdling, Elizabeth had threatened to leave her at the carnival. When Ellen continued to lag, she hid behind a tent to teach her a lesson, but in the few seconds it took to dig a cigarette out of her purse, Ellen disappeared. After the worst ten minutes of her life, Elizabeth heard an announcement over the loudspeaker, and when she reached the office, the carnie was waiting with Ellen. The anger she'd felt toward the barker came back to her. He didn't know a goddamn thing about being a mother. But Dessie did. She was washing dishes, and Elizabeth could tell from the rigid way her back bent over the sink that she disapproved.

"I wouldn't have done it if the creole had been hot, Dessie. It will wash out of her hair easily enough, you know."

"Yes ma'am," Dessie said, without turning around.

"Come on, Dessie. You know Wendy did it deliberately. Otherwise, she would have coughed into her bowl. That temper has got to be stopped. 'Fight fire with fire,' my uncle used to say as he took off his belt."

"Yes ma'am." Her back still rigid.

On her way to change out of the ruined gown, Elizabeth put her ear to the door of the bathroom at the top of the stairs.

"You're finished, Wendy. Get out so I can stretch my legs."

"Okay. Do you think that girl with the kittens was Mama?"

"No. She told you it was just a story."

"Do you think Mama would drown Fifi like those kittens?"

"Yes, if you don't keep her off my bedspread."

"Ellen Townsend!" Elizabeth said as she opened the door. "Shame on you. Of course I wouldn't drown Fifi, Wendy, and I didn't drown any kittens. It was all pretend."

Wendy, looking so innocent and vulnerable naked, slunk back from her. Elizabeth felt a pang. "I shouldn't have lost my temper, Wendy, but I hope you learned a lesson."

"Yes ma'am."

"Go put on your nightie, and I'll come read you a story when I've changed clothes."

"I want to watch TV."

"No. A story is better." Better for putting her to sleep before Robert gets home, Elizabeth thought. Otherwise, Wendy would tell him about the creole the minute he came in the door, and any amorous inclinations he might have would vanish. "Go on, now. I'll be there in a minute."

Elizabeth glanced at Ellen, who was rinsing off. Still flat as a pancake. No change from April, when she'd told her pleading daughter she didn't need a bra. Why weren't her breasts growing? If Ellen had something up there like the girls in their carpool, she would have more confidence. Elizabeth would ask Dr. Harris to check her out. Meanwhile, maybe it was time for padded bras and a padded bathing suit.

"Challenge someone in the Teen Room at ping-pong, Ellen," she said abruptly. "You can almost beat your father, can't you?"

"I have. Twice."

"So there. Even if you don't beat the person you challenge, you'll have given them a good game. And you'll have made a friend. People want friends who are good at something."

"I guess. Can I ask you a question?"

"Don't ask me if you can ask me, just ask me. What?"

"Was that you and Uncle Boyd with the kittens, and did he make you drop them in the creek?"

"Yes. I shouldn't have told about it. I just wanted you to know that having to give up Ruthie may seem like a horrible thing, but it's nothing compared to how cruel life can be."

# Seven

Putting the high-strung Wendy to bed was never easy, but that night, with her hair smelling faintly of tomato sauce, it was torture. Wendy insisted that her usual routine of water, story, and toilet be repeated three times, along with the added steps of checking her closet and under her bed for monsters. She had either sensed her mother's remorse and was taking advantage of it, Elizabeth thought, or was still in a frenzy about the incident.

When Wendy finally fell asleep, Elizabeth crept downstairs and sank into the velvet cushions of the living room sofa. She lit a cigarette and tried to succumb to the mesmerizing effect of the revolving gold balls of the mantel clock, but couldn't get Dessie's disapproval off her mind. Dessie probably thought Wendy was too young to have coughed the creole at her on purpose, but she knew better. When she was five, she'd deliberately turned the garden hose on the tobacco pouch her uncle left on the porch. At any rate, the incident was over, and she wasn't going to let it ruin her evening, *their* evening really, for she and Robert had a lot to toast.

The living room looked especially nice. The floral arrangement she'd bought for the party enlivened the room with color. And the poker table, the top of which she'd covered with a fringed silk shawl, bestowed the grace of an antique.

Even if the table hadn't been on the *Delta Queen*—she supposed Sondra could be right—she wouldn't part with it for the world. The table *had* made her party. The women, who'd come expecting bridge, had burst into enthusiasm about poker the minute they saw it: "Such cute little cubbyholes." "That felt's as soft as a baby's butt." "Elizabeth, where's the cigars." She'd not known a poker table would have such an effect, but instinct told her to get one, so she'd desperately combed the antique-cum-junk shops in New Orleans until she found it. Then she paid a fortune to get it refinished in time for the party.

Elizabeth smiled to herself as she remembered the motherly way Marjorie had mediated the dispute between her and Sondra about the table. Then she played and replayed in her mind other good moments of the afternoon. After a while, the pride and self-confidence she'd felt before the creole incident returned.

Around nine thirty she fixed the drinks tray for their toasting—a filled ice bucket, Bourbon, brandy, and glasses—then returned to the sofa and flipped through her latest *Ladies Home Journal*. Most of it was as boring as the Methodist hymnal. She'd give anything for a *True Detective*, but her subscription had gone the way of smoking in public, answering the door barefoot, and other things Robert told her cultured people didn't do.

The only part of the *Journal* she faithfully read was an \advice column entitled "Making Marriage Work." Mostly common sense, like "Greet him with a smile, not a frown, when he comes home late from work," but she read the column anyway so as not to miss something useful. In this issue, a letter from a wife who'd written in for advice grabbed her attention: "I hate sex. I've been married four years and have two children. I have never had an orgasm, I get no pleasure at all from sex, yet my husband wants it at least four times a week. I fear for my marriage. What should I do?"

There must be something wrong with the husband, Elizabeth thought. Stupid, ugly, or boring. Or no…no finesse. He should be the one seeking advice, she thought, then laughed at the idea of a man writing a letter like that. She felt sorry for the woman. She had liked sex as a teenager and absolutely loved it since she met Robert. She almost always had an orgasm, sometimes more than one. It was truly wonderful. *Had* been wonderful, that is, for Robert had had trouble performing the last few months. Exhaustion, stress, or possibly a side effect of the pills, he thought. If it was exhaustion or stress, she might get lucky tonight, for the stress of the trial was gone temporarily, and his voice on the phone had been full of energy.

At ten thirty, Elizabeth refreshed the ice bucket; at eleven, she began to pace. The good restaurants closed by ten on weekdays, except Constantine's, which was reputed to never close on a customer. That's probably where they'd gone. It was Robert's favorite restaurant because the hostess wore a dress that fit her rear end like a glove. The last time they'd eaten there, they argued all the way home about whether it was proper etiquette to tip a hostess, which Robert had done. Or maybe—the thought hit her hard—he'd had an accident. Red was a big drinker, and on special occasions Robert was too. As she rose to call the police to check on accidents, she heard his key in the door.

She looked lovely, Robert said, and kissed her. That lounging gown was his favorite. He was too tired for toasting tonight. A hot shower and bed was all, except he was eager to hear her good news. Elizabeth bubbled forth, skipping the parts that could wait and ending with Marjorie's invitation to Ellen. "Can you believe it? The Order of Myths. What's that expression you lawyers sometimes use—the camel has his nose in the tent."

Robert looked at her for a second as though stunned, then burst into laughter. She pointed upstairs and shushed him. Seeming to get control of himself, he sang in a lowered voice, "Old Judge Simmons is a fine old man, beat his wife with a frying pan," and then he laughed again.

"I don't get it."

"I've got Rooster in an embarrassing bind about this mistrial, and he's spitting fire. I'd like to be a fly on the wall when Marjorie tells him about that invitation."

"Oh, Robert, no. She'll take the invitation back." She'd never regarded Roberts' gripes about Simmons as anything more than the complaining of a too cocky attorney about a by-the-book judge, but this sounded bad.

"I was teasing. Don't worry, Elizabeth. His honor will never know about the invitation. He's on too much of a high horse to care about stuff like that."

Robert was still in the shower when Elizabeth, who'd cleared up downstairs, came into the bedroom. Showers refreshed him, she thought with a smile. As usual, he'd tossed his clothes on the bed.

She hung his suit on the valet and picked up his dress shirt to put in the hamper. As she checked to make sure he'd not left a pen in the pocket—he'd ruined a lot of shirts—she smelled something sweet. She brought the shirt to her nose and sniffed it with vigor. He kept Old Spice at the office for last- minute dinners with clients, but this wasn't the astringent, refreshing smell of Old Spice. It was cloyingly sweet. Her heart raced. It couldn't be. Out of the blue with no problems between them, no suspicious occurrences. But then his affair in Huntsville had come out of the blue—the matter-of-fact voice of the desk clerk when she called Robert's hotel telling her that Mr. Townsend and the missus were at dinner. Elizabeth sniffed the shirt again. Perfume. She was still holding it to her nose when the bathroom door opened.

"What are you doing?" He stood on the threshold, a towel around his waist.

"What are *you* doing is the question? Who the hell is she, damn you?"

Robert hurried to close the bedroom door and returned with an expression of puzzled innocence. Elizabeth knew better. Artful posturing was one of the reasons he made a good trial lawyer.

"Objection, your honor," he said. "The question assumes facts not in evidence."

"Oh, but they are. Smell this." She wadded up the shirt and threw it at him.

His nose wrinkled in exaggerated fashion as he sniffed. Then he laughed. "Looks like you caught us."

"What!"

"Me and Red. Don't let on that you know, but Red has a penchant for the bump and grind. He drug me to some strip tease joint in Chickasaw with a broken air conditioner, so I took my jacket off and a herd of horseflesh cozied up to us to buy them drinks. Their perfumed perspiration must have rubbed off on me. Take another whiff and see if that's not midnight in Chickasaw." He tossed the shirt back to her.

It was possible, Elizabeth thought with relief—Red the bawdy bachelor whose dirty jokes Robert enjoyed telling her. She smelled the shirt again—the same sickly sweetness, a far cry from the sub-tlety of her Chanel No. 5, but that proved nothing. Even if it was some strip teaser's perfume, it didn't mean Robert had spent the evening with Red.

She tossed the shirt aside. "This doesn't prove anything."

"I look forward to coming home all evening and what I get is suspicion. Why don't you trust me?" Now an expression of extreme disappointment, which she didn't trust either.

"You know why."

Robert shook his head. "I have no idea. I...Huntsville! For God's sake, Elizabeth. That was six years ago. Ancient history."

"Five."

"Five, then. Still a long enough statute of limitations in a marriage worth keeping, don't you think, Pocahontas?"

"Maybe." His plaintive tone and use of her pet name, which she'd not heard for some time, softened her. He turned away from her to get pajama bottoms from his highboy, and she watched him put them on. She thought, as she had many times, that Robert was not especially attractive undressed: slight frame, narrow, bony shoulders, and the thin, almost hairless boylike chest. But by the time she'd first seen him naked, his physique hadn't mattered. His handsome face, exuberance, and wit had been irresistible. That court reporter in Huntsville, especially after seeing what would have been his excellent courtroom performance, would have felt the same way.

"Call Red and ask him," Robert said when he turned to face her. "He should be home by now. Of course, he won't like it that I told you. His number's in the den. Do you want me to get it?"

Yes and no. She heard Emily's voice: *His hobby is young women.* But this wasn't comparable to that. For all his flirting, Huntsville was the only time Robert had been unfaithful, and then only to relieve the loneliness of a month-long murder trial too far away for weekends home.

"Well, do you want the number?"

"No." She would take a chance rather than damage the bond between them.

Robert opened his arms to her. They embraced with fervor, as though consoling each other for a rift they'd almost had. His body was warm and moist and she wanted to melt into it. The rest of the day had been meaningless hullabaloo compared to this moment.

The bedroom was dark when Elizabeth came from the bathroom. She'd washed and powdered down there, but hadn't taken the time to douche for fear he'd fall asleep. Robert lay on his side facing the wall. She eased in and curved her bare body along the lines of his, but not so close as to seem aggressive; even uncultured women had pride. Besides, she didn't want to embarrass him. If he was up to it, he would turn to her. She felt the heat of his body and her nipples hardened.

In a few seconds, Robert reached his hand around and patted her thigh. "Sorry. That trial has suctioned every ounce, plus I've had to increase the pills to keep up with the work, and you know how they affect me. How about going to the island after I take the girls swimming Saturday? An overnight at the cottage would do wonders."

"You mean that sandbox with a mortgage," she said, hoping their running joke about the cottage would mask her disappointment. "Next Sunday is July Fourth at the club, a command appearance, you know."

"The weekend after, then. This mistrial thing will be handled by that time, and most of my backlog at the office."

"Sounds good. Why not stay a couple of days and you could start getting off the pills? You need to, Robert, and not just for bedroom purposes. You're losing too much weight and too much sleep."

"Maybe I will, all things considered." A hopeful answer, Elizabeth thought.

A half hour later under cover of Robert's snores, Elizabeth tiptoed to the bathroom, locked the door, and took his boxers from the hamper. After he'd fallen asleep, she remembered that he hadn't seemed tired when he arrived—his laughter about Judge Simmons and the peppy way he'd climbed the stairs. Holding the boxers to the overhead light, she saw a spot the size of a half dollar near the fly. It was colorless, clear as water, but if it was water, wouldn't it have dried by now? She sniffed it. To her relief, the scent was not the mulched-grass odor of semen but the thick, sweet aroma of Robert's perspiring genitals. She'd been an idiot to suspect him. She lay back on the bathroom rug and held the boxers to her face.

# *Eight*

Ellen reached for the lighter below the dashboard as soon as it popped out and then pressed the glowing coil to the tip of Elizabeth's unlit cigarette. She hadn't extended this courtesy to her mother in a long time, but today she deserved it. They were going to Gayfer's for Ellen's first brassiere. She'd wanted one for months, but her mother kept putting it off, then suggested it herself this morning.

"Thank you," Elizabeth said when she'd blown the smoke out, its shape reminding Ellen of a mare's tail cloud. Ellen decided that was how she would blow it out when she learned to smoke.

"You're welcome."

Halfway to town, they stopped at Dr. Harris' office. Elizabeth said she had to ask him a question and that Ellen should come too.

"Why? I'm not sick."

"I know, but you're entering puberty and it's routine to check things out. It won't take long."

Ellen cracked her knuckles, a nervous habit, as she waited on the examination table in a gown. For the first time, she'd had to remove her underpants along with everything else. The sensation of air on her tussy and the caress of the gown on her bare fanny felt shameful here, though at home she thought nothing about it.

Ellen was also scared. She'd overheard a tenth grader say that her doctor put her feet in metal braces attached to his examination table, pushed her legs so far apart she felt like she was doing the splits, and stuck a metal stick, or something like that in her tussy. She said it hurt like hell but the doctor was casual about it as though he was toasting a marshmallow. Ellen figured that's what she was facing. Why else remove the underpants? Her mother should have warned her. And for that matter, shouldn't have brought her here. They were supposed to be getting a bra.

When the loud clicking of the sprinkler outside the window stopped, Ellen heard her mother and Dr. Harris talking in the adjoining room—something about her father's pills and his sex drive, whatever that was. She heard her name then, and hurried over to put her ear to the door.

"The problem is that she's thirteen and flat as a board while most other girls her age have at least some bosom. When I was her age, I wore a size B cup. I'm afraid she might be retarded."

Retarded! So her breasts not developing like other girls meant her brain wasn't either!

"I doubt it, Elizabeth. But as long as you brought her, I'll take a look."

Ellen hopped back on the table just as the door opened.

Ellen liked Dr. Harris, or Dr. Owl, as she and Wendy privately called him because of his hooked nose and heavy black-rimmed glasses. He told knock-knock jokes as he examined them. He was silent now as his fingertips pressed around on her breast area as though crimping a pie shell.

"Ooh," she said.

"Tender?"

"A little." Her face flushed at the thought that maybe he could tell she'd been pulling on herself. She'd overheard some older girls at school say it helped things along.

"Tender's normal at your age."

The gown, which opened in front, had two ties. Dr. Harris tied the top one, which he'd untied to examine Ellen's breasts, then undid the one at her waist and folded the gown back. He squeezed and poked at the flesh around her waistline, hips, and stomach, then started downward over her belly.

"I never have cramps like some girls," Ellen blurted. The metal-stick girl had said she'd gone to the doctor because of bad cramps.

"Of course not," said her mother, who sat in a chair a few feet away. "You're not menstruating yet, and breasts come first, don't they, Dr. Harris?"

"Usually."

"Wait." Ellen gripped the sides of the table. "Mom, I need to talk to you."

"Ssh. Let him finish."

"I have," Dr. Harris said. "You can sit up." He said she was par for the course, her growth spurt since last year was normal, and there was new tissue in her breasts, which was why they were tender. He turned to Ellen, who'd sprung upright. "Young lady, I think you'll start to fill out any day."

"That's good to know, isn't it Ellen?"

"I guess." She was actually thrilled, but in no mood to convey that to her mother.

"Well, I'm excited for you," Elizabeth said as they pulled from the parking lot. "I better step on the gas to get those bras if you're going to fill out right away."

"He didn't say right away. He said any day."

"Watch your tone. What's wrong with you?"

"It wasn't routine like you said. You thought I might be retarded."

"Retarded…How did you…oh, eavesdropping. I didn't mean the word the way you're thinking. I meant I was worried that something was interfering with your development and maybe he could give you something to speed things up. A little shape like the other girls would give you more confidence. I want you to be happy, you know."

Maybe, Ellen thought, but those gouges in her worktable showed otherwise. "You shouldn't have shushed me when I said I wanted to talk to you. I was scared to death."

"Scared of what?"

"This girl in school said her doctor stuck a long metal stick in her tussy and it hurt like the dickens and he acted all casual about it like he was toasting marshmallows. I thought Dr.—"

Her mother was laughing, not a scoffing laugh as though at Ellen's naiveté, but howls of hilarity. "Toast…toasting marshmallows…oh dear, my eye makeup." She took a hand from the wheel to blot the tears starting down her cheeks. A smile played on Ellen's lips. She had made her mother laugh.

The Lingerie Department of Gayfer's, which Ellen hadn't known existed, was on the third floor. The colorful ladies' undergarments, sheer nightgowns, fancy robes and other frivolous apparel displayed in the vast carpeted area created the ambiance of a party, a private one for ladies and older girls like her, Ellen thought. She might enjoy coming back here.

"They call these training bras," the saleslady said as she brought boxes of brassieres into their dressing room.

"Training?" Ellen looked at her mother.

"It takes a while to get used to a bra."

"Indeed it does, Take your camisole off, dear, and we'll get started."

Ellen, who'd expected she and her mother would be left alone, stood in grim-faced embarrassment as the saleslady hooked and unhooked, tightened and loosened, and wiggled her fingers inside the cups. ("Sorry dear, these darn fingernails.") Finally she declared one of the bras to be the perfect compromise between no padding, which Ellen wanted, and a lot of it, which her mother wanted. "This padding is whisper-thin," the woman said, "just enough to give a nice shape."

"How does it feel, Ellen?"

"Fine." It was uncomfortable like all the others, but she could tell her mother's patience was wearing out.

Elizabeth said to keep it on and they would take three more like it. The saleslady beamed as she rang them up. "I knew we'd find a fit if we persevered. It's like I always say: there's a girl for every bra and a bra for every girl."

Ellen's eyes met her mother's, and they barely managed to keep from laughing until the woman was out of earshot. They stopped at the second floor to look at bathing suits because Ellen needed one, her mother said. It didn't take long to find one Ellen liked—a stretchy fabric that would cling to her body when she was swimming instead of filling with water and blousing out like her cotton gingham one. Her swimming would be more streamlined. Ellen hadn't wanted padding in the bosom, but all the ones with the stretchy fabric had it, so she asked for the matching cover-up to wear when she wasn't in the water.

Ellen was eager to go home to look at herself in the suit in the privacy of her bedroom, but her mother said she needed a really nice dress. Her heart sank. "A really nice dress" meant war. Ellen reminded her mother that she had two nice dresses as she followed her across the aisle to the Teen Department. "Please, let's go home. It's almost lunchtime and I don't need another dress."

"Yes, you do," her mother said, then continued in a hushed voice. "I wasn't going to tell you until the invitation arrived, but you've been invited to a luncheon of the Order of Myths where they're going to choose pages and maids for the King's court next Mardi Gras. If you're picked, you'll be part of all kinds of events and get to ride in the biggest parades."

"No. Being stuck on a float would ruin my Mardi Gras."

"Listen Ellen, any girl would give her eye-teeth to…" She stopped, noticing two well-dressed women a few feet away, and ushered Ellen into the nearest dressing room. "You *must* attend that luncheon," she continued when the door clicked shut. "This town is a tight society of rich people who've lived here since Moses and look down on anyone who hasn't. Your father and I are trying our hardest to get in with them, and now you can help. Whether you're picked for the King's court or not at that luncheon, the right people will notice that you were invited, and if you are picked, your picture as part of the court will be on the front page of the paper."

"Grandma Townsend said a lady should be in a newspaper only three times—when she's born, when she gets married, and when she dies."

"Are you trying to irritate me?"

"I don't want my picture in the paper."

"You're being selfish, Ellen. We need your help. You're going to that luncheon if I have to drag you there myself."

"But you can't make me smile, or talk to anyone. I'll…I'll be a bump on a log." Ellen was elated for an instant at having hurled her mother's hurtful words back at her, but then her knees felt weak.

The jack-in-the-box arm sprang out and the talon fingers seized her shoulder.

Someone knocked on the door. "Hello in there," said a cheery female voice. "Do you ladies need any help? Different sizes of something, perhaps?"

"No. Nothing,"

"All righty. My name is Susan. Let me know if you change your mind."

As the tapping of the woman's heels on the linoleum faded away, her mother continued to give Ellen what her father called "the evil eye"—a long unflinching hostile eye to eye stare. Breaking the evil eye a few seconds later, her mother said. "Consider this, a secret you're never to tell anyone, especially not your father. He's desperate for rich clients who won't work him to death like Gulfstream. If you were on the King's court, he and I would be invited to the Myths ball and he would meet those kinds of clients, and there'd be a photo of the three of us that could hang in his reception area, Mr. Miller's bank, the club, and other places. You've seen Mardi Gras ball pictures like that around town. People are impressed by them. Do you understand now why you have to go to that luncheon?"

Ellen shrugged. Her father *was* working too much, and she had noticed pictures like the ones her mother described, but it was hard to believe that her father, who was good at everything, needed her help to get business. This was probably another trick of her mother's like the "routine" doctor exam had been.

"Tell you what, I'll make you a deal," her mother said.

An hour later, the large dressing room was strewn with ruffled, scalloped, and lace-trimmed dresses chosen by Elizabeth and simple shirtwaists selected by Ellen, all rejected by one or the other of them. The air was tense with the question of fault: Ellen's skinny body or her mother's flamboyant taste. Her mother had the stature for fancy dresses, Ellen had heard someone say once, but on her they looked like they were walking around by themselves.

"We'll have to go to Maison Blanche," Elizabeth said as she helped Ellen out of the last dress to be tried, a bright green that gave Ellen's complexion a jaundiced hue. "It's probably too late to get anything made."

"I'll take the red one, then." Anything to avoid the drive to

New Orleans and another bout of trying things on.

"No. The waistline was up to your ribcage, remember?"

Leaving the department, they saw a young man putting a dress on a mannequin—a blue-and-white pinstriped shirtwaist with a red sailor collar and a wide red patent-leather belt. On a stand nearby stood a copy of *Seventeen* with the dress on the cover. The model, tall and slim with long blond hair, stood at the bow of a ship with three young men in Navy whites standing in a row on each side of her. Ellen nodded to her mother, who summoned a saleslady, who told them the shipment hadn't arrived and the dress on the mannequin couldn't be sold because it was the buyer's sample.

Elizabeth insisted on talking to the store manager, and when he came, a dapper-looking man in a three-piece suit, Ellen moved away from them so as not to be embarrassed by her mother's badgering, but she watched with admiration and silently rooted for her. She would eagerly go to that luncheon if she was wearing that dress. And it meant she would be eating her cake and having it too, for if she agreed to go to the luncheon and be her most charming, Ruthie could spend the night within the next few weeks.

A few minutes later, Ellen followed her mother to a fresh dressing room to wait for the dress. Her mother's threat to buy one at Maison Blanche and tell everyone at her country club where she got it, had cut the mustard with the manager. Ellen mentally crossed her fingers for it to fit when the saleslady slipped the dress over her head.

"There," the saleslady said when she'd fastened the belt. "Why, it's absolutely lovely on you."

Not daring to look in the mirror, Ellen turned to her mother.

"I'll be dammed." Elizabeth's voice was studied and gentle. "Look for yourself."

Unlike the stiff shirt Ellen had worn, the dress, made of soft, lightweight cotton, draped gracefully over the modest mounds made by the bra, and the gathers of the full skirt, which the belt pulled tightly to Ellen's waist, gave her hips. For the first time, Ellen saw herself with the hourglass shape of a woman. The songs that played in the Teen Room—"Come Softly to Me," "Little Darlin,'" "Teen Angel,"—could be about her too.

"Turn, all the way," her mother said in the same gentle voice. Ellen inched around as though the dress might fall off.

"You certainly favor your mother, dear."

Did she? Not having put her hair in a ponytail that morning, she noticed in the mirror the auburn sheen of it as it fell to her shoulders. And there too were her mother's high cheekbones and slight overbite, but she'd soon be getting braces for that.

Ellen looked down at her white flats, bought the summer before. They were scuffed even though recently polished, and the straps across the top of her feet looked juvenile.

"These shoes are awful. May I get new ones?"

Her mother laughed. "More shopping and less deep-sea fishing for you from now on. We'll get red patent leather to match the belt. But not today. Put on your clothes so she can cover the dress for us to take home."

Ellen glanced at the mirror again. She couldn't bear to take the dress off without more being made of it. "Let me keep it on and run show Daddy while you're paying. I'll only take a minute. Pretty please."

"All right. I need to get some makeup, then I'll come over. Maybe he can take us to the Admiral Semmes for lunch."

Instead of turning toward her father's office at the corner, Ellen walked across Bienville Square to savor the anticipation of showing herself off to him.

The square, a one-block oasis of grass and trees in the middle of town, was crowded at the noon hour—clerks with bag lunches, shoppers resting, people feeding peanuts to the pigeons. Feeling like all eyes were on her, Ellen walked with her shoulders back as her mother had told her to do a thousand times. She kept a distance from the three-tiered fountain, which she would normally rush to on hot days like this to catch the spray. Now and then she glanced at the amazing rise in her bodice. "Whisper-thin padding," the saleslady had called it. It was fine with her, and soon she wouldn't need padding, for Dr. Harris said she would fill out "any day."

Not wanting to wait a minute longer to see her father, she hurried toward the Van Antwerp.

The lobby of the Van Antwerp smelled like shoe polish, an aroma Ellen loved, for in their old house she polished her father's shoes on Sunday nights while he read the newspaper. Hi-Jinx looked up from buffing a customer's shoes when she entered. "Well, Miss Ellen. I wondered why your daddy's shoes is been such a mess and now I know. You is growed up and out of the shoeshine business."

"That's right, Hi-Jinx. I'm leaving it to you." She felt a thrill when Hi-Jinx nodded as though it was perfectly natural for such a ladylike phrase to come from her lips.

As the elevator rose, Ellen looked at herself in the mirrored panels. She could probably pass for sixteen. Now her father would know that she was way past the stage for kiddie kits. Or—and this would be disappointing—would he raise his right eyebrow as he did when he smelled a bluff as if to say "we both know you're putting on"? Or—and this thought dismayed her—would he think she'd no longer be a good fishing buddy or even want to be? She'd be quick to reassure him about that.

As Ellen stepped out of the elevator, a familiar-looking woman came out of the bathroom and crossed the hall to her father's office, closing the door behind her. Miss Pascagoula! She'd been riding on a Mardi Gras float called Sleeping Beauties of the Coast. She looked attractive with her rhinestone crown sparkling in the torchlight. But at the bonfire party afterwards where she, her father, and Wendy were introduced to her, she looked like what her mother would call a hussy. Her bosom was half bare in her bathing suit, and her makeup was too heavy. She'd acted like a hussy too, asking for a ride home when she didn't really know them and "home" was all the way to Pascagoula. When they dropped her off, her father jokingly called her Sleeping Beauty because it was the name of her float. Ellen had cringed. The darn hussy didn't deserve a nickname from her father. Whatever the woman's reason for needing a lawyer, Ellen hoped her father would be finished with her soon.

The door to his office was locked. Ellen saw through the glass panel to the reception area that Mrs. Mims wasn't there. Her father and the woman must be in her father's private office, the door to which was closed. He would hear if she banged, but that would be childish.

The top half of the inner door was made of rippled amber glass. Ellen pressed in close to the outer glass hoping to see into his private office through the two panes. She saw two silhouettes cast by sunlight from his window. The silhouettes suddenly moved toward each other and became one. A trick of the light, Ellen thought. One of them must have moved in front of or behind the other such that their shadows overlapped. She pressed in even closer, tilted her head for a different angle, and saw the figures themselves. They were kissing.

Ellen jumped at the rumbling sound of the elevator door down the hall. Her mother!

The scuffed white flats flew toward the elevator. It was empty except for the janitor, who was rolling his cart out. He held the door open for her.

"You're out of breath," her mother said when Ellen intercepted her at the street corner. She was carrying a Gayfer's bag, which now included Ellen's skirt and blouse as well as the other things they'd bought. "I told you not to run in that dress."

"I forgot," Ellen said.

"Don't forget again. Why didn't you wait up there for me?"

"He's busy with a client."

"Let's go up. Maybe he'll be through soon."

"No, he won't. I could tell. Let's go home. I feel sick to my stomach, like I might throw up."

"Don't you dare. Not on that dress."

# Nine

Blue was Ellen's favorite color. Her bedroom was done in shades of blue—walls, carpet, curtains, bedspread. Swimming pool blue she'd thought when her mother let her pick from the decorator's chart. Her bedroom was her favorite place to be when she was home and it was too cold or hot in the workshop. She could play records and practice dance steps from *American Bandstand* in privacy. Now, however, Ellen sat on the bed staring at her sad-sack face in the dresser mirror. Not even in the blue-hued domain of her daydreams could she deny what she'd seen at her father's office.

"Did you hang that dress carefully?" Her mother, who often forgot to knock, stood in the doorway wearing an old stretched-out bathing suit.

"Yes, ma'am." A lie. She'd thrown it in the back of her closet. It was a hateful reminder of her eagerness to model it for her father.

Her mother approached the bed with a fruit jar in her hand. "I see you're admiring your new bra."

"No, I'm not. I'm just deciding what to wear."

"Well, do my back first." Her mother handed her the jar, which contained iodine mixed with baby oil, a suntan lotion recipe from a woman's magazine.

This was Ellen's most hated chore—the sickly sweet medicinal smell, the greasy, viscous red mixture—but feeling sorry for her mother because of that hussy, she resolved to do a good job. Which wasn't easy. Her fingers had to navigate layers of peeling skin from previous sunburns to dab the lotion on gently.

"For God's sake, Ellen, you act like you're petting a snake. Hurry up. I'm losing the best sun."

"I can't. The skin—"

"Never mind." Her mother grabbed the jar. "I'll do it when I get outside."

Fine. Do it yourself, Ellen thought. The green-eyed shrew was back in the snap of a finger even though they'd had some fun together that morning. Watching her mother screw the lid on the jar, Ellen felt a thrill at having a secret over her. Her bosom sagged in the old suit, her stomach pouched out like she'd swallowed half a basketball, and when she walked toward the door, little half-moons of fat jiggled on her thighs. Who could blame her father for kissing that beauty queen?

"Come down when you're dressed. Dessie made consommé to settle your stomach before she left."

"She's gone?" Just minutes before, Dessie had been in the kitchen raving about the new dress. Ellen had planned on talking to her about her father. "She didn't tell me she was leaving."

"Lester's band just got back in town, so I let her off until Friday. You clean up after yourself in the kitchen. And by the way, the bra looks fine on you. Wear one every day and you'll grow into them faster."

Grow into them, Ellen scoffed when her mother had gone, as though breasts were plants and a bra was the sun. A silly idea, and the bra looked silly—a forlorn bivouac of two miniature tents, the blue embroidered flower between them a mockery of her boyish chest. She pushed in on the peak of one of the tents and watched it cave, then little by little rise again. Ridiculous. She didn't want her breasts to grow now. What if they bulged from her bathing suit like overgrown balloons the way Sleeping Beauty's did on that float? They'd almost fallen out altogether when she leaned over to put beads around Wendy's neck. If only they had. Her father would have laughed, and that would have been the end of Miss Pascagoula. That hussy had set her sights on her father that night. Bad luck that her mother had been sick and couldn't go.

She put on a baggy shirt so no one would notice the bra, and went downstairs. The kitchen felt gloomy without Dessie, and still as a grave except for the cat clock whose bulging eyes looked right to left and back again as though desperately seeking something.

Ellen looked out the window as she sipped the consommé. Wendy was digging for what she childishly called roly-polys even though Ellen had told her the proper name was pill bugs. Her mother lay on a chaise lounge on the patio facing the white-hot sun. Best tan in the club, people said. When Ellen told Dessie she thought it was a dumb thing for her mother to do, Dessie said, "Dumb like a fox. White men like tanned-up white women and your mother don't want your father's head to turn." Ellen knew that. The slightest hint of it set her mother off even when there was nothing to it, like the argument Saturday about fat Mrs. Miller and arguments on the way home from restaurants when her mother claimed he'd flirted with the waitress although he'd only been friendly. She couldn't imagine what her mother would have done if she'd caught him with that hussy today.

As she washed her mug, Ellen vaguely remembered something in the long-ago past about her mother being angry with her father because of some woman. She concentrated hard, and slowly bits of it rose from the compost of her memory. She was woken in bed at her great-aunt Mabel's house by her mother screaming on the hall phone at her father, and days or weeks later he came and they all went home. She didn't remember Wendy being there. Maybe she hadn't been born. It suddenly struck her that her mother might still catch him with that hussy—could spot hair or lipstick on his clothes, or hear about the woman from some friend who'd seen them together like on the soap operas Dessie watched. She had to do something to prevent her mother from finding out, but what? Dessie would know.

Ellen snuck her bike out of the workshop. She figured twenty minutes round trip in the car to what was called the Quarters, where most of the coloreds lived, meant at least an hour and fifteen minutes by bike. If she didn't talk to Dessie for more than fifteen minutes, the note she'd left on the kitchen table—"Weinecker's back by 2:30"—should cover her. Regardless, she had to go. If she phoned, Dessie, who didn't like advising Ellen about her parents, would say it was none of her business. But if Dessie saw how desperate she was, she would help.

For the first two miles, shade from the big oaks on St. Catherine Street gave intermittent relief from the sun, but then came St. Stephens Road, a treeless commercial thoroughfare that ran past the Quarters. Waiting for the light to change at St. Stephens, Ellen reached beneath her shirt to wipe away the itchy sweat under the brassiere. A pickup truck pulled up to the light, and one of the boys in the bed yelled, "Hey, lemme help you with that."

Her face flushing, Ellen turned away until she heard the truck move on. Dang brassiere. When the light changed, she crossed the street and rode on the shoulder, which was so narrow she had to concentrate to keep from veering into traffic. Exhaust fumes burned her eyes, and vehicles speeding past were so close that if her elbow swung out from her side even a little, it would get knocked off, leaving a stump that would swing grotesquely for the rest of her life, like Mrs. Delacroix's. Ellen was relieved when she turned into the Quarters.

Mobile's neighborhoods were mostly checkerboards of house styles, but the houses in the Quarters were uniform one-story clapboards. Drainage ditches ran along the frontage of the yards where sidewalks would otherwise be, and because there were no driveways, cars had to park on the narrow streets or in the weedy lots along with old discarded appliances and furniture.

When Dessie's old Rambler was broken and Ellen's mother had to pick her up and take her home, Ellen liked to ride along. She would press her face to the window to see everything she could through the yellow-brown dust raised by the Cadillac: little kids chasing chickens or playing in the ditches, older kids standing around in clusters smoking as though it was nobody's business, adults lounging on the old furniture as though in the privacy of their living rooms, even mothers nursing babies with their blouses raised to the world, plus a hundred other things she couldn't have imagined, like the last time—a boy about Wendy's age wringing a chicken's neck, and dead pigeons hanging from a porch roof as though they were Christmas lights. The pigeons, Dessie had said, had something to do with voodoo. Like a tourist who visits the same foreign country over and over because it's strange, Ellen loved the Quarters.

Now, with dust settling on her bare legs, Ellen felt uneasy.

There were lots of people in the yards, most of whom paused to look when she passed. Even two butt-naked toddlers stopped fighting over a water hose to stare. The fancy bike made things worse with its lavish chrome and its handlebar streamers, which she scrunched up at the end of the first block and held beneath her sweaty palms. She wished she had a sign on her back: Here to visit Dessie Moore. The ride was rough because of deep ruts in the road, and rabid-looking mongrels barked at her heels. Once, she caught a whiff of barbecue sauce that smelled like her father's.

Ellen came to a run-down baseball field with a torn chicken-wire backstop. Kids of all ages had joined hands in the field as though getting ready for Snap the Whip. She stopped to wipe sweat from her eyes, and when she looked again, the kids had formed a circle. A boy lugged a small white goat to the middle of the circle, released it, and ran to join his friends amid cheers. Bleating loudly, the goat darted around trying to butt through the hands, but the kids held fast, laughing and mocking his bleating. Ellen laughed too, her worries forgotten for the moment. She would ask her father to borrow a goat for Wendy's next birthday party. Then it struck her that they wouldn't still be with her father then if her mother found out about that woman, and that maybe her mother had remembered some suspicious little thing and was rising from the chaise that very minute to inspect her father's clothes. Ellen rode on toward Dessie's house as fast as she could.

Dessie's Rambler wasn't there. Ellen felt like crying. She was about to sit on the shady porch and think of what to do when she heard a saxophone playing. Lester! Maybe Dessie was on a quick run to the store. Ellen knocked loudly on the screen door, and Lester soon appeared, a heavyset, good-natured man who drove Dessie crazy, or so she said.

"Why, hello, Miss Ellen. Your mama come for Dessie to work after all?" Lester opened the door and peered out at the street as though looking for the car.

"No, just me. I need to talk to Dessie."

"Mother Moore's down in the back, and Dessie went to cook for her. You can walk on over there. It's just across the creek."

"The creek where y'all fish?"

"Yeah, Three Mile Creek, just the other side of that field next to them willows," he said, pointing to where the street dead-ended. "There's four little cabins in a row just up the bank, and Mother Moore has the first one you come to. I'll show you. I'll play my sax, and you follow me, like some story Dessie read to little Charles about a bunch of kids following this man who was blowing on something."

"That's the Pied Piper. You don't have to show me, Lester. I'm not a kid anymore, you know. I'm going into eighth grade."

"Well, I'll be. What's your favorite study?"

"Science and French, but I can't talk about it now. I'm in a hurry."

With any luck, Ellen thought as she crossed the field, Mother Moore would be taking a nap. She was the only mean colored person Ellen had ever met. She complained if Ellen rode along when Dessie drove her to the doctor or the farmer's market or such, and she once said in her witchy voice that it was a sin for the races to mix. Dessie replied that she wasn't mixing with the girls, only raising them, and winked at Ellen in the rear-view mirror.

At the end of the field was a slight descent down a dirt bank covered with rotting tree trunks, thickets of brambles, and trash-strewn weeds. The creek was forty or so yards across, wider than Ellen expected, but they'd had a lot of rain from April on. She remembered Dessie complaining about the creek overflowing and leaving water snakes in the field.

Ellen squatted at the creek's edge and splashed water on her face to cool off as leaves, branches, cigarette butts, and other debris rushed by. She could see the smooth pebble bottom for five or six feet out, but beyond that the water darkened quickly. From what Lester said, there must be a place to cross. She walked her bike upstream, looking for a sandbar or a spot where the water was shallow all the way across.

She paused when she saw three colored boys sitting on logs in the shade of a willow about fifty feet ahead. Probably on a lunch break, she guessed from the open paper bags and sodas on the ground nearby. One of the boys noticed her and said something to the others, and they looked at her too. She stiffened. She wished she'd let Lester come. She pivoted quickly to walk the bike downstream. She heard the boys' voices calling, but the sound of the rushing water muffled the words. She glanced back. They were standing and waving at her, yelling something she couldn't hear. Were they summoning her? Were they drunk? Despite the water snakes and no matter that her bike would get wet, she had to get across.

"Hey, miss, wait," called one of the boys, who'd almost reached her as she turned the bike to go into the creek. "If you wantin' to cross, there's a footbridge. That's why we was calling to you." He must have run like the dickens, because he was out of breath.

"Footbridge? Well, where is it?"

He pointed downstream. "See where the creek starts to go around that land sticking out, and the big willow at the edge of the water? The bridge is attached to that willow."

Squinting into the sun, Ellen saw a crude bridge of planks and rope extending from the willow's leafy branches to those of a willow on the other side. The brownish contraption almost blended in with the water.

"I didn't see it." Her face flushed with embarrassment for having been afraid of the boys and for not having seen the bridge. He probably thought she was stupid.

He grinned. "City ain't seen it neither. We picked a good place to put it so they wouldn't. They'd say it was dangerous, you know, kids wanting to jump off or somebody fall off, stuff like that, and make us take it down. It's mostly just the people who live around here who knows about it and needs it when the creek is up. You won't tell anybody, will you?"

"No, I won't." She started to say "cross my heart and hope to die," then realized how juvenile it would sound. "I promise I won't. And thank you for keeping me from getting wet."

A path on the other side of the footbridge led to a clearing in the pines where four shotgun houses stood in a row. Ellen crept up the steps of the first one and peered through the screen door. It was like looking into a tunnel–the darkness of a long, narrow hall with light at the end coming from the back screen door. The sound of a radio and the earthy, peppery aroma of Dessie's collards wafted through the screen.

"Dessie," Ellen called at a volume she thought Dessie would hear but not Mother Moore.

Thump-thump came the sound of the old woman's cane, then Ellen saw her prune face behind the screen.

"Dessie's busy girl, What you want?"

"I want to—"

"Who are…You is Ellen, ain't you?"

"Yes, ma'am. I need to talk to Dessie." She'd raised her voice in the hope Dessie would hear.

"'Bout what?"

"It's private."

"Dessie be to work Friday. You get on home." The witch started to close the door.

Ellen took a deep breath and called out, "Dessie?" She heard footsteps in the darkness behind Mother Moore and Dessie appeared at the screen. She wore a pretty blue dress, and Ellen, who'd never seen her out of uniform, suddenly felt shy. What if Dessie didn't want to be bothered now in her own time and place?

"Why, Ellen, I was in the back and didn't hear you. Your mother wanting me after all?"

"No. Mama doesn't know I'm here. I'm on my bike. I need to ask you something in private. I need your advice. It's very important." Ellen felt its importance as she spoke, and her voice quivered at the end.

"Advice." Mother Moore spit out the word. "It ain't your place to be giving advice to no white girl behind her mama's back, Dessie."

"I'm not. I'm just trying to find out what's wrong—"

"That's as bad as advice, with her mama not knowing she's here." Mother Moore thumped her cane and stepped in front of the door to block Dessie. "And you listen here, Dessie Mae. If her mama you say has got a bad temper finds out you talked to her, she'll fire you, and tell them rich women why. Who gonna hire you then?"

Baloney. Ellen and Dessie both knew that if her mother found out she'd gone to the Quarters alone for any reason, she would be the one in trouble, not Dessie. She noticed that Dessie's lips were pressed together as Mother Moore spoke, no doubt holding back a grin. But Dessie's face was serious when she turned to her.

"You better go on, Ellen. I'll be there Friday."

"But Friday might be too late because—"

"Like I said," Dessie interrupted, "I'll be back to work Friday."

"Okay then," Ellen said after a pause. It was hard to believe her ears. As she mounted her bike, Dessie called out to her to be careful, that she wasn't used to busy streets. Ellen didn't even look toward her; she wanted Dessie to know she was hurt.

Ellen was glad to see the boys were gone when she reached the other side of the footbridge. If she opened her mouth to say anything to anyone, she would burst into tears. She would have bet her life that Dessie wouldn't send her away like that. Before Mother Moore started in, Dessie had that "uh-oh, tell me what's wrong, Ellen honey" look on her face. But then she sided with Mother Moore. It had felt like an arrow in her heart. Dessie wasn't the person she'd thought her to be. And neither was her father. She would have bet her life that he would never kiss a woman other than her mother even if some hussy was throwing herself at him.

# Ten

July 4th was the Skyline Country Club's biggest celebration, and the Townsends were on their way to join the fun. Lying on the northern ridgeline of the sea-level city, the club was a fine place to be on a sweltering day—five degrees cooler and fifty percent fewer mosquitoes than for the folks below.

As the car climbed the hill, Ellen's father began to sing. "You're a grand old flag, you're a high-flying flag, and forever in peace may you wave." Her mother joined in, and Wendy echoed a word now and then. Ellen pretended to read a comic; she was too nervous to feel like singing. When Dessie got to work Friday and Ellen explained her problem, Dessie had advised her to tell her father right away. "Even if it will embarrass you like you say. If he knows you seen him with that woman, he'll realize how close he come to your mama catching him, and he'll drop that chickee boom-boom like a hot potato."

Intending to tell him that evening when he got home from work, Ellen had waited in the front yard so they could talk in private, but from the moment of his usual greeting—"Hey, Muskogee. You winning or losing?"—she was taken aback. He looked and sounded like he always did, but she felt distant from him, as though he were an imposter, and that made her feel like an imposter too. She'd avoided him the rest of the evening.

Last night she'd come close to warning him, for he'd seemed more like his real self. As soon as her mother went to bed, she'd hurried to the den, where he was watching a western on TV. They liked watching westerns together, so she joined him, laughing throughout at his usual quips, like "Watch now, he's about to bite her on the nose." When the movie was over and he turned the television off, she thought to commence, but the words she'd rehearsed were leaden on her tongue. "I saw you" would sound like "I caught you," which would be like pointing her forefinger at him and scraping the length of it with her other forefinger the way grade-school kids shamed each other. Now it was day three. She *had* to tell him today. She would pick a time at the club when there were a lot of distractions so the conversation would seem casual, or at least more casual than serious.

"You're the emblem of the land I love…" Her father's bellowing continued, and the car began to weave from one side of the lane to the other.

"That's dangerous, Robert. A car could come around one of these curves and you'd sideswipe it."

"It's out of my hands. It's the God of family sing-alongs doing it. He won't be satisfied until everyone in the car is singing."

Ellen looked at the rear-view mirror and saw him grinning at her.

The car continued to swerve. "The home of the free and the brave. Every—"

"Stop it, I said. You're going to get us killed. I know you're teasing, but you don't know when to stop."

"Every heart beats true 'neath the red, white and blue," Ellen sang out, "where there's never a boast or a brag," and the car steadied again. Their arguing was making her more tense.

Ellen trailed behind her family through the crowded parking lot at the club, past the festooned brick clubhouse, and into the patchwork of families on the lawn near the pool, where they found the Taylors, Millers, and Boudreauxs in a semicircle of lawn chairs.

"I rise for two things," Mr. Taylor said as he stood and gestured for Ellen's mother to take his chair. "Dixie and Hollywood stars."

Robert plopped into the chair. "Much obliged. I've been told I'm the spitting image of Tyrone Power."

Mr. Taylor nodded at the other men, and the three of them spilled her father to the ground. Laughter rippled outward from the semicircle to others who'd noticed, which was everyone in the club, Ellen thought with embarrassment.

"If that's the way y'all feel, I'm going swimming with my

daughters. Come on, girls."

"Not so fast," said Mr. Taylor, and scooped Wendy into his arms. "First a hug from the queen of the curly-haired snaggle-tooths." When he'd put the squealing Wendy down, he took Ellen's hand, stepped back and looked at her top to bottom. "Where's the thirteen-year-old I saw at Easter? This young lady's ready for the Miss America contest."

"Oh, Mr. Taylor," Ellen said, glad she'd closed the snaps on the cover-up. Her mother had made her wear the new suit, and these people would notice that the bosom was padded.

"You should have seen her Thursday, Carl. We bought the most perfect dress at Gayfer's. She looked sixteen if a day, didn't she Robert?"

Ellen looked at the ground, her heart pounding.

"I didn't see her."

"Yes, you did. When she came up to see if you could take us to lunch."

"What?" He turned to Ellen, his expression cautious.

"I...I saw you were busy and didn't want to interrupt," Ellen muttered.

"Oh." He laughed. "Looks like I got off cheap. You two would have wanted soft-shell crabs at the Admiral Semmes."

"I suggested we wait in your office, but she suddenly got nauseous."

"May I take Wendy in the pool?" Ellen said.

"If I can come too. Last one in's a rotten egg." her father said.

"Noooo. I can't keep up," Wendy wailed.

"You wait, Miss Priss. I have to put lotion on you."

Ellen impressed her father with the breast and butterfly strokes she had learned. "Fine as a horsehair split three ways," he said. Then she challenged him to race the width of the pool round trip. "I won!" Ellen said when she reached the edge half a stroke ahead of him.

"By a nose," he managed to gasp. "That's the last time I'll give you a lead."

"You didn't give me a lead. Remember I said I didn't want a lead and you said I'd be sorry."

"Objection, your honor. Counsel is lying through her teeth."

"Hardy-har-har." She splashed him. His dark hair was plastered to his forehead as though painted on, water rolled down the hump of his nose, and his white teeth sparkled. She loved him best when he looked this way.

"You were out of practice. Let's do it again," she said.

"No." Wendy stood on the side of the pool with her arms folded imperiously. "It's my turn with Daddy now, and I want submarine."

Ellen helped Wendy get on her father's back and watched as they slipped away, her father submerged just enough for the water to tease Wendy's face. Her squeals soon became indistinguishable from those of other kids titillated by their fathers' half-scary teasing in the water, a cacophonous choir of fear and delight. A father's teasing in the pool is one of the best things in the world, Ellen thought.

"Hey, Ellen," called Amanda. She came toward Ellen in more of a glide than a walk, as though carrying a book on her head. "Thinks she's better than us because she goes to boarding school," Ellen heard a girl say once. Jealous, Ellen knew. Amanda was eye-catching pretty and sophisticated. She was the only girl who crossed her legs when she sat on a stool in the Teen Room instead of propping both feet on the rungs, and she smoked pastel cigarettes.

"Wow. You have a new bathing suit. Looks like you took my suggestion about the extra help up top. Wanna go in the Teen Room? It's wild in there today."

"After a while. I'm swimming with my dad."

At that moment, her father and Wendy appeared, both sputtering and laughing. "That's him." Ellen pointed proudly.

"He's handsome. I wish my dad liked to swim. Well, come soon as you can. I'll save you a seat."

It was Ellen's turn for submarine, her father said, but she didn't want to. It had felt awkward the summer before—her body too heavy for it and her legs too long, like when she'd outgrown her old bike. She told her father she was too big for submarine, but he said nonsense.

"Okay, but I want you to promise to come up if I signal. No teasing."

"People in hell wanting ice water too. All aboard."

Ellen wrapped her arms around his neck and her legs around his waist with her ankles crossed in front to anchor her. It was her usual submarine position throughout the years, but felt awkward last year, and now made her feel self-conscious. The soft fabric of his bathing suit brushed her calves, and her crossed ankles touched his groin unless she consciously held her feet outward. Worse were the foam pads in her suit pressing into his back. He must feel them. Did he think those were her breasts?

"Umph!" he groaned. "You've grown since last summer."

"Twelve pounds and three inches, Dr. Harris said. I'm getting off."

Before she could untangle herself, he clutched her ankles with his hand. "Down periscope."

Soon they were tacking through an underwater forest of legs and shafts of light with the shadows of surface swimmers passing over like scudding clouds. Ellen grew increasingly uneasy at the feel of her father's muscles moving under her, the tickle of his waistband on her inner thighs, and mostly the feel of the foam pads in her suit pressing into him. It was creepy. She tapped on his shoulder, which meant he won because she needed to come up before he did, but for once she didn't care.

Instead of upward, however, her father followed the downward slope of the pool toward the diving area. Ellen tapped harder. He continued downward. When the underwater swirls of divers off the boards were less than twenty feet ahead, she pounded his shoulders with her fist. When he didn't respond, she kicked and twisted, but he gripped her ankles tighter. In a panic, she inhaled and water rushed in. She dug her fingernails into his Adam's apple as hard as she could until he released her ankles.

Ellen arrived at the surface gasping for air. Her father

followed. Plank-shaped shadows bounced up and down on the surface nearby. They were in no-man's land where only divers swimming to the ladders were allowed.

Her father touched a spot of blood on his neck and looked at his finger. "What's the idea?" he said, and chuckled uncertainly.

"You tried to drown me."

"I what?" They were treading, and he motioned for her to follow him to the side of the pool.

"You almost drowned me. Why didn't you come up when I signaled?"

"We'd been under less than a minute, and I wasn't going to let some uppity teenager boss me around. Why did you want to come up so soon?"

"I got water up my nose."

"I'm sorry. I didn't know. I was only teasing you."

"But you don't know when to stop."

He frowned. "Now, who does that sound like?"

Ellen felt a pang. "I didn't mean it. But still, I'm mad."

"About my not coming up, or maybe something else? You didn't come in the yard this morning when Wendy and I were playing with Fifi, and you didn't want to sing with me in the car." He'd been squinting into the sun, but now, using his hand as a visor, his eyes pierced hers with that knowing expression she'd never dared lie to.

"Tell me what's on your mind, Muskogee."

This was a good opportunity—the noise of springing boards, of divers splashing, of the lifeguard's whistle, good enough distractions for her to talk.

"Well, it's that I —"

She stopped. A white piece of foam rubber with curved edges surfaced between them. They stared at it for a second as it bobbed on the water, concave side up like an upside-down magnolia petal.

Her father laughed. "A falsie. Somebody's lost—"

He stopped at the sound of her gasp and closed his hand over the foam. "Don't worry. Nobody saw. I didn't know you—"

"It's Mama's fault. She made me get this suit."

He held the foam toward her underwater. "Here. No need to be embarrassed. Get her to put it back in," he said, then added with a wink, "else you might keel over like a sailboat overloaded on one—"

She snatched the pad from him. "That's mean." She swam to the ladder, ignoring his calls, and climbed out.

Ellen whisked her cover-up from the towel she'd spread on the grass near her parents and strode toward the pool bathroom. Her face was flushed from her breasts having come to her father's attention, especially in that way. He would think she was like Sleeping Beauty and wanted people to notice her bosom. Which wasn't true. She'd wanted the bathing suit even though it was padded because it swam better. And she got the matching cover-up so that she could hide her chest when she wasn't in the water. She was nothing like Sleeping Beauty. She worked hard in school and would become an important person one day—a scientist or lawyer or famous swimmer like Esther Williams. She went into the bathroom, a concrete echo chamber reeking of chlorine, took safety pins from the basket labeled "Necessaries," and pinned the pad back in.

When she came out, her father was back with her mother and their friends, evidently telling them a funny story, for they were looking at him and laughing. He wasn't worried about her feelings a bit. "Keel over like a sailboat," he'd said. Downright cruel since he could see she was embarrassed. She wasn't going to waste any more of her July Fourth worried about her mother catching him with that hussy.

Any summer weekend would find fifteen or so kids in the Teen Room, but now there were at least thirty—some the holiday guests of members, others the older teens who considered the club scene square but were forced to join the family holiday. It was wild, like Amanda had said. Loud talking, laughter, and the belted-out strains of "Bony Maroney" bouncing off the concrete walls made a deafening racket. The dance floor was a spasm of bobbing heads and bodies, and much of the room was in a haze of cigarette smoke thick as cotton candy. There was a no-smoking rule, but on special occasions the room monitor ignored it. Darn, Ellen thought. She would be able to smoke without worry now if she knew how. She vowed to learn the first chance she got.

"I thought you'd never come," Amanda said when Ellen sat on the stool next to her. She tugged at Ellen's cover-up. "Take that off and you'll get asked to dance, I bet."

"Maybe in a little while." She didn't intend to take it off or do anything that would draw attention to her bosom.

"Up to you. Did you have fun with your dad?"

"Yeah."

"You're lucky. Mine is boring. Is your sister fun?"

"Fun to tease, but mostly she's a brat." Ellen had a qualm of disloyalty, but saying it had made her feel more mature.

"Sisters and brothers are like that, I'm told. I'm glad I don't have any. See that tall boy at the jukebox, the blond? Do you think he's cute?"

"I guess so," Ellen said to be polite. She didn't really know how to judge, but she knew she preferred boys with dark hair like the boy who delivered their evening paper.

"I've danced with him twice."

*Peggy Sue* started playing and the blond boy asked Amanda to dance again. The muscles from Ellen's brain to her toes managed a perfect invisible triple step to the lightning-fast beat of the music. The triple was tricky, and most kids did a single. Amanda, she noticed, was doing triple. Her partner was—what was he doing? His feet were barely moving, yet Amanda was smiling at him as though to say, "Aren't we having fun?" Well, she would smile for no reason too if it meant she could get on the dance floor.

She turned to glare at two boys who were cursing and slamming their paddles on the ping-pong table nearby. The room monitor should throw them out. Maybe they'd been drinking. Maybe they weren't even teenagers. They looked older than the other boys and a little like hoodlums because they were unshaven and wearing T-shirts, although the rules required boys to wear shirts with collars unless they were in bathing suits. One of them grinned at her, and she turned back toward the dance floor.

"He can't dance worth a flip," Amanda said when she took her seat again, "but he's nineteen and has a car. If I had a boyfriend with a car, I wouldn't be so bored in this town, except I'd have to sneak around to ride in it. My stepmother wouldn't care, but my father would—"

"Your stepmother?" Ellen had never met anyone who had a stepmother. "Where's your mother?"

"In Dallas. I spend June and July with my father, and August with her. We don't get along, but she works for Neiman Marcus and buys me lots of clothes for school. I love my school. It's in Memphis and I can't wait until September so I can go back."

"Why?" Ellen had assumed Amanda's parents made her go away to school.

"It's fun, like a slumber party every night in the dorm. We have a pool as big as this one, and we ride horses three times a week. I love horses. Do you like to ride?"

"Who doesn't?" Ellen said. She'd never ridden a horse, but she thought her answer sounded sophisticated.

"The school is expensive, but I'm sure you'd like it. Maybe you could...Oh, my favorite, the Mashed Potato."

"It's the greatest. It's the greatest. Mashed Potato. Yeah, yeah yeah ..." Someone turned up the jukebox as kids scrambled for partners, and in seconds the dancers overflowed the linoleum onto the concrete. Anyone could do the Mashed Potato—aiming your feet at each other pigeon-toed like, then away from each other repeatedly so it looks like you're mashing something into the floor. Doing it well, however, Ellen knew, meant flipping out your heels with each mashing motion and coordinating your arms with elbows bent and pounding the air with the beat. Coordination was the trick, and she was perfect at it in her bedroom mirror.

The blond boy appeared. "Hey, Miss Pixie Doll, let's do it," he said, and extended his hand toward Amanda.

Ellen watched as they joined the throng. She felt sorry for Amanda. That school in Tennessee sounded a little like fun, but she'd bet Amanda would rather have a place she could think of as home and a sister or brother. Uh-oh. The ping-pong player who'd grinned was strutting toward her.

"Come on, baby, let's mash some potatoes."

A resounding no rose in Ellen's throat. She didn't want to dance with anyone who didn't have respect for a ping-pong table. But the beat of the song throbbed through her body so strongly she could barely keep her feet still. Plus, she would be dancing for real, not just in her mirror.

"Okay." After all, this wasn't a dance where partners touched.

Having longed to get on this dance floor for months, she threw herself into it— feet flying, head bobbing, elbows bent and arms moving in sync with the beat.

"Boy, looks like you being paid to mash taters," her partner said.

"Thanks," Ellen said. She was thrilled. This was the beginning of something new about herself and it was exciting. Her eyes caught Amanda's across the floor, and they smiled. Maybe the regular boys noticed her now and would ask her to dance in the future. Some of them were pretty good dancers. This boy was horrible. His wiggle looked like he had to go to the bathroom.

"I bet you're older than you look. Take this off," he said, tugging at the sleeve of her cover up.

"No." She jerked her arm free.

"Aw, come on." He grabbed a panel of the cover-up so hard the snap came undone. "You must be hot in—"

Wrenching away from him, her arm half out of the sleeve, Ellen saw her father peering through the plate-glass window.

She nodded toward it. "There's my dad." Her partner turned to look and she ran out.

"Whoa. Guess you're not still mad at me," her father said when Ellen threw her arms around him. "It's so dark in there I couldn't tell if it was you dancing or not. Come on. Your mama and Wendy are saving our place in the line."

Ellen walked arm in arm with her father toward the terrace, where colored men in white jackets and chef's hats hovered over smoking half-barrels, waitresses bustled around putting food on the buffet tables, and club members with drinks in hand spilled down the wide steps to the lawn like some giant draping plant. Ellen spotted her mother halfway up the steps, the gold sequins of her bathing suit sparkling in the low-angled sun like the scales of a large Koi she'd seen in a magazine. Hip height to her was the lamb-fur head.

"Beating me in a race and dancing with boys," her father said. "A lot for a father to learn about his daughter in one day. Carl's right. You are growing up fast. Next thing I know you'll be marrying one of the lifeguards. Maybe I ought to call out and warn your mother." He cupped his mouth with his hands as though to make a megaphone.

"Oh, Daddy. Stop it," Ellen said with a laugh. In a few more steps, her heart beating hard, she pulled him aside from the path.

"I saw you with that Sleeping Beauty woman when I came to your office Thursday. Are you going to leave us for her?" Leave us, she thought. Where did that come from? All along, she'd only intended to warn him.

"I thought you'd probably seen us from what your mother said, and I'm sorry. I'd never, never leave y'all, Muskogee. What you saw was…well, sometimes when men my age, middle-aged they call it, see old age not that far off—hair falling out, teeth falling out, and so on—an attractive young woman is hard to resist although you know you should. Like when you gobble ice cream on a hot day knowing it'll give you a headache but you can't stop. Like with ice cream, the attraction, doesn't last very long and we middle-agers don't intend it too. It doesn't harm anyone. Don't worry about that woman another minute. I'm going to drop her now like a hot potato. All right?"

Ellen nodded. The relief she felt was too big for words.

# Eleven

Early in Robert's liaison with Helene, he told her he would never risk losing his daughters, so if she was looking for a husband she had better look somewhere else. It wasn't an easy thing to say, but necessary. Women were quick to make romantic assumptions.

"I am looking. What do you think I do when you're not around?"

Robert, kneeling at the safe in his office closet, remembered how they'd laughed at her response. It hadn't surprised him. Why would she be dating a married man twenty years older with children except to use him as a place holder? Helene might shed a tear or two when he broke it off, but she wouldn't be hysterical.

As he turned the dial, he saw in his mind's eye four-year-old Ellen bundled in a blue wool coat, wispy hair brushing her frost-reddened cheeks as he pushed her swing in the park. At her urging, he'd pushed her higher and higher, and when she yelled, "Too high," he said, "One more," and pushed especially hard. Then he'd watched in horror as her swing went as high as the crossbar and the blue bundle fell to the ground. He'd felt like a razor blade had slit him up the middle, and he felt the same way on July 4th when Ellen asked if he was going to leave them for that woman. He'd suspected she'd caught them when Elizabeth mentioned her going to his office at lunchtime, but he never thought she'd be afraid he would abandon them. He shouldn't have broken his rule against meeting Helene in Mobile. "Please, Robbie. Just once. I've never seen a lawyer's office."

Robert took two hundred-dollar bills from the stack—enough, he hoped, to keep Helene from missing the cash he sometimes pressed on her. He would say the money was part of her birthday gift, along with the ruby pendant he'd bought that morning, for she was sensitive about his giving her money. "Is that what you think this is?" she'd said the first time he offered it, her gypsy eyes widening with dismay. He'd said of course not, then spent a while reassuring her. And he meant it. No paying arrangement would feed a man's ego like she had his. Robert hesitated a moment, then took another hundred from the stack. Guilt money. Her birthday was bad timing for his exit, especially since he'd be spending the night, which was also against his rules, but he'd promised weeks ago. "Please. Just for my birthday."

It had been convenient that Helene lived in Pascagoula. It was thirty-five miles southwest of Mobile where the scenic coastal highway across Mississippi began and they could dine in the swank restaurants on the strip without being seen by people he knew. Plus, his hunting club was halfway between Mobile and Pascagoula, so he could pop in for pit stop coming and going on his way to her place. As he drove past the weathered sign— Theodore Dove and Quail—he glanced fondly at the fields and the ramshackle house the members called the lodge. It served as shelter from sudden downpours and as a venue for all-night poker games and private indiscretions of the members.

The hunters here were more fun than the ones in his hunting club in Montgomery. Some of them were outright racy, like Buster, who gave Christmas presents of pornographic photos taken by his cousin in New Orleans. All the men claimed responsibility when the sofa smelled of perfume or a lipstick was found in the bathroom and laughingly called each other liars. The Montgomery lodge had no sofa. Stories here about unfaithful husbands were considered funny, but in Montgomery they brought dismay. Come to think of it, he'd never heard a sad story here about a marital infidelity. His would have been the first if Elizabeth had caught him instead of Ellen. She would have taken the girls and left him in the snap of a finger as she'd done with Ellen when she found out about that court reporter in Huntsville. He shuddered to think of how close he'd come.

It was dusk when Robert arrived at Helene's, the tall sign in the parking lot already blinking its neon orange: Best Deal Motel—Daily, Monthly, Weekly. Kitchenettes. The motel looked as mundane as its name—a flat-roofed concrete block building with a gravel parking lot for landscaping.

Robert parked in front of Unit Eight, combed his hair in the rear-view mirror, and then, because he'd be spending the night, took two pills from the bottle in his pocket instead of his usual evening one. "Head to scrotum, some of my male patients on Benzedrine tell me," Dr. Harris said once.

And they're right, Robert thought. He'd not had instantaneous erections since he was in his twenties, and he'd never been able to sustain them for as long as ten minutes, after which the orgasms were so intensely pleasurable he could hardly bear it. But he also thought that Helene had a lot to do with it. He drove home from their trysts in a sexual stupor.

Helene, who must have been watching for him, opened her door when he stepped from the car. She was wearing a tight red dress with a slit up the side. As head to scrotum as it gets, he thought as he headed toward her. She laughed when she opened the envelope with the three bills and she rhapsodized about the ruby pendant.

"It matches my new dress perfectly. It must be fate," she said.

"More like finances. A ruby was the only stone in the jewelry store I could afford."

"It's a real ruby?"

"Does a goat stink?" His fingers trembled from the heat of her skin as he fastened the gold chain around her neck.

Their evening began the same way as their dates—a drive along the coast highway (Helene loved his "cushy Caddy") with golden beaches on one side and the mansion-like summer houses of the rich on the other. As usual, his right arm lay along her shoulders, and the fingers of his draped hand teased at the low-cut neckline of her dress, while her left hand rested on his thigh, now and then squeezing the inner area. This evening brought more finger teasing and squeezing than usual, and such rowdy banter and laughter that they could have been kids on the last day of school before summer vacation. "Can you believe it, the whole night together," Helene said several times. They toasted their whole night together,

her birthday, and the sunset view numerous times with champagne in the dining room of the Beau Rivage, the coast's most elegant restaurant.

"Goddamn," Robert muttered the next morning when his funny bone hit the wall in Helene's broom closet of a shower. He was hung over and had a hollow feeling in his stomach that he recognized as dread. He hoped the three pills he'd taken when he woke would kick in right away. His goodbye talk with Helene was going to be especially difficult after what happened last night.

Robert dropped his head toward his chest so the hot water could ease the tension in his neck. Son of a bitch. Three months of careful calibration gone to hell: mixed bouquets instead of roses; candlelit dinners with anecdotes instead of meaningful looks; appreciative comments in bed, but no sweet talk, no speaking of "we" or "us" or future plans. And it had worked—her passion never flagged, and she never pressed him for more intimacy, unless he counted the time she asked to call him Robbie. He'd tried to finesse the intimate connotation a yes would have had by saying, "Call me anything except Wanted, Dead or Alive," but she laughed and called him Robbie.

Robert sighed and turned so the water could hit the front of his neck. When he closed his eyes against the splash, he saw them dancing as the silver-haired xylophone player in the dimly lit lounge of the Beau Rivage would have seen them: another older man and younger woman falling further into some rendition of nightclub love with each stroke of his mallets. "It must have been moon glow that brought me to you," Robert had sung in a whisper through the silky strands of Helene's cascading waves. He was a good dancer, and they moved like two upright candles melting into each other. "Sing it again," Helene had asked at four in the morning, and when he said he was "champagned out," she said it was their song now and he was to sing it for all her birthdays. Son of a bitch. If he could, he would leapfrog the next half-hour to land behind the wheel of his car and be on his way to his ten o'clock plea bargain session.

When Robert came from the bathroom, Helene, in a flowing

rose negligee, was filling the jar of flowers he'd brought with fresh water. Sunlight through the window, softly diffused in the still-dewy air, swept across her face and upper chest, where the ruby pendant marked the beginning of her cleavage. Robert paused at the sight. Something about it—her attractive features, the lighting, or the pose—reminded him of a famous painting of a beautiful woman he'd once seen. He wished he'd bought it.

"You woke up," he said.

"Oh, hi. I missed you. I don't have a coffee pot, but how about a Coke and some toast?"

"No toast, but a Coke's the ticket. On the rocks, please."

He was charmed and unnerved by the domestic sounds of Helene rustling around the kitchenette as he dressed—a freshly laundered shirt from his small overnight bag and the suit and tie he'd worn the day before. As he sat on the bed putting on his shoes, he glanced around the room and realized he would miss its intimate slovenliness—the dresser top jumbled with cosmetics, costume jewelry, and scarves, the worn carpet strewn with stockings, garter belt, bra, and slip, the red dress flung over the armchair by the door. Inexplicably, because he was normally a neat person, the disorder relaxed him. And in addition to the sex, he would miss Helene for her easy nature—no nagging, no third degree.

"Sorry it took me so long. I couldn't find the bottle opener." Helene brought the Coke to him. "You wouldn't think things could get lost in such a small place."

Her breasts, beneath the sheer veil of negligee, were eye level, their hard, coppery nipples begging to be fondled, or teasingly scraped up the length of his chest, or taken into his mouth.

"Not much of a breakfast, Robbie."

"Breakfast enough for Tarzan."

He felt slight stirrings of energy from the pills he'd taken when he woke, but given his lack of sleep, he needed much more energy for the day ahead, so he took two more pills. Then he patted the bed beside him for Helene to sit, and glanced at his face in her dresser mirror—a tentative expression that wouldn't convince anyone of anything. He'd planned on telling her that since she was 22 and almost an old maid, she needed to look for a husband in earnest, so he was letting her go. But after last night, the words sounded callous. Only a cad would romance a woman all night knowing he would break things off the next day.

Helene looked at him with a happy, expectant expression he would rather not have seen. He stood and faced her with his shoulders back, as though facing a jury. "Helene, your birthday has brought me to my senses," he began. He gave his "old maid" reasoning, added that her heart wouldn't be in the search if he was still in the picture, and ended with, "I'm thinking only of you. It's important for me to know that you've found a wealthy, educated husband to take care of you before you get much older."

"I know that, Robbie," she said, smiling. "And I have. You."

My God. "Helene, you know that can't be."

"Yes, it can. And it wouldn't be hard. You know all about how to get a divorce. I know in my heart that you want to. I've thought so lots of times, but I wasn't sure until last night."

Robert shook his head as he damned himself to hell. "I'm sorry, but last night was off course. Champagne, music, dancing does things to people. It was a lovely evening, but I'm not going to leave my family."

Helene's face went blank for a second. Then she rose and walked toward the kitchenette slowly, as though lost in thought. With each step, the nylon negligee clinging to her rear shifted from one small rounded buttocks to the other. She stopped at the tiny table on which sat the champagne bottle they'd brought home with them, now empty.

"Helene," Robert said softly. Her shoulders were hunched. Was she was going to cry? Was she already crying but not wanting to make a spectacle of it? Damn. Maybe he had been too hasty, should have given her notice, weaned her off.

"Look, I didn't mean this had to be our last time. We could meet once, maybe twice a month while you're looking. Finding someone appropriate is going to take you a while."

"Five minutes at the most." She turned to face him, dry-eyed, head defiantly cocked.

"Come on, Helene, let's talk about it."

"All I have to do is make a phone call. He's younger than you and looks damn good in a Stetson. I've never lived on a cattle ranch, never seen one, but I might like it. Get out, Robert."

Stunned, Robert paused a moment in the breezeway. Then, squinting painfully in the glaring sunlight, he strode to his car with his head held high, as though not in the least humiliated. Although it was only nine o'clock, the Cadillac felt like a steam bath. Robert started the engine, turned the air conditioner on full blast, and pulled from the parking lot onto the busy road with his tires spitting gravel. He'd never been to the motel in broad daylight before, and in the rear-view mirror he noticed the drabness of the building and the old cars in the parking lot. The whole effect, he realized, was cheap and ugly.

Where would she have met a rich cattle rancher around here, Robert wondered as he drove past small cafes, pool halls, and bait shacks? It must have been at the Monticello, the luxury resort on the scenic highway where she worked as hostess in the dining room. Except hadn't she laughed once about having to walk slowly to the tables so whichever old man was following her wouldn't get lost?

When he hit the open highway, Robert accelerated to eighty miles an hour and reveled in the smooth thrust of the heavy car. The farmlands and hunting fields along Old Pascagoula Road became a blur of greens and fading yellows. And with those rocket-ship tail fins, the car looked as fast as it was. A Cadillac was the best car money could buy. Whatever car her rancher had couldn't beat it.

Having left his cigarettes at Helene's, Robert stopped about halfway to Mobile at Uncle's Corner, a clapboard house converted to a general store for the mostly black farm community. During hunting season, Uncle's stocked shotgun shells and pints of quality whiskey in addition to its staple inventory. Robert had become acquainted with the storekeeper, a quiet, mild-mannered person who was at the counter helping an elderly man in stained overalls when Robert walked in. With a wave, Robert strode on to the soda cooler. He lifted the lid, leaned over the icy vapors, and turned his face from cheek to cheek. Despite the Caddy's superior air conditioner, he'd begun to sweat a few minutes outside of Pascagoula. A fever maybe, but from what?

When his face stung with cold, Robert pulled an RC through the slider. He drank half, paused for air, and felt a rushing inside him. Not the usual kick-start feeling of enthusiasm for taking on the day, but an uncomfortable rushing as though he had to do something, anything, that instant. Helene had unnerved him. She should have told him before he spent the night that she had a damn fish on her line. He finished the RC quickly. His hand trembled so badly he couldn't get the empty bottle into a slot of the crate, so he laid it on its side. Eager to buy cigarettes and aspirin and hit the road, he glared at the owner and the old man still at the counter.

"As I said, Jethro, it's not my fault. When Bull Durham charges me more, I gotta charge more. Why not buy the Old Kentucky? It's twenty-five cents less."

"But I ain't never chewed it. Never heard of it till now. I don't see why you can't give me just one chew of it to see if I like—"

"For God's sake," Robert said, stepping up to the counter. He grabbed a twenty, the smallest bill in his wallet, and thrust it at the storekeeper. "I'm in a hurry, Frank. Give him the Durham, and I need aspirin and a pack of Luckies."

"I thank you kindly sir," the old man said as he scooped the Bull Durham into his overall pocket and grinned at Robert, his few front teeth dark as mud.

Robert nodded curtly and feigned interest in the counter displays until the man shuffled toward the door. A colorful display on a shelf behind the cash register caught his eye—Mickey Mouse and Minnie Mouse watches, one of each fastened to a board with drawings of the beaming cartoon characters below them. Robert liked to hear Ellen read Mickey Mouse comics to Wendy. She was good at faking the voices.

"Sorry, Mr. Townsend, but you got anything smaller? I'm out

of fives until my change boy comes, and I'd be giving up all my one spots."

"Nothing smaller, so how about a carton of Luckies and two Minnie Mouse watches?"

"With the aspirin, that's about on the nose," the storekeeper said, and took two watches from a drawer. "They're two-fifty apiece. I should have thought to show them to you. If I remember right, you've got two girls, don't you?"

"Damn right I do, and I'm not giving them up for anyone." How the hell could Helene think otherwise?

The storekeeper looked up at Robert with a start. "No, I'm sure you wouldn't, Mr. Townsend." He put everything in a paper bag, wrote out a receipt, and timidly counted out the change. "There's a thirty-day warranty on the watches. I put the form and the dated receipt in the bag so you can prove the—"

"Thanks, but a five-dollar warranty's not worth my time."

On his way out the door, Robert grabbed a copy of *Most On the Coast*, a free weekly of events happening along the Mississippi coastline. Not that it mattered. Helene was as good as forgotten.

Something—the thrusting sensation of the car at eighty, the aspirin, the cigarette—eased the uncomfortable rushing inside him, and Robert began to review his agenda for the day. First was the plea bargain session at 10:00 for his client, a twenty-year-old dull-normal who'd not understood that his friends intended to rob the liquor store, much less known about the gun. He'd done an especially good job in getting that plea. "Two minutes of that kid on the stand, Carl, and the jury's going to believe that he wasn't capable of intending anything, much less a crime." Carl interviewed the kid himself, and agreed. After the hearing, Robert would have lunch with the exporter he'd met at the Whitmans' party, finish that contract Gulfstream needed tomorrow, then review again those damn abstruse medical reports for his first insurance defense case. It would be a good day, in fact a damn good one, for he was through with Helene and could look Ellen in the eye when he went home tonight.

Robert saw a farm truck lumbering toward the highway on

a side road a quarter mile or so ahead. He honked a couple of times, as was customary thereabouts so farmers would wait at the intersection for faster traffic to pass, but goddamn it, that listing old truck turned north onto the highway. Robert braked hard and in seconds was inhaling black exhaust fumes despite the Caddy's sophisticated ventilation system. He banged his fist on the wheel. Unlike the first stretch of the highway, which was straight as a rifle barrel, the road had now begun a long bend in the direction of Mobile.

Robert laid on the horn, an insistent, violent sound. A boy rose to his knees amid bushels of greens and gawked at him over the makeshift wood tailgate. About Ellen's age, Robert thought. He motioned for the truck to pull onto the shoulder. The boy turned to speak through the cab window to the couple inside, then turned back, shook his head, and pointed downward over the shoulder side of the truck. Robert craned his neck to see what the boy was pointing to. Damn. An irrigation ditch. Well, all right, but at least the son of a bitch, who should have waited at the intersection, could move over enough to give him a view of the oncoming lane. Robert motioned again for the truck to pull over, this time gesturing to show just a small distance. Frowning, the boy shrugged, then lowered himself to disappear among the greens. He didn't understand, Robert thought. These farm people could be dense. Damn.

Robert felt a rushing sensation again, worse than before. Now it was a painful pressure pushing hard inside him, demanding that he move. The muscles of his right foot ached with the restraint of not accelerating. He was trapped and probably would be for the fifteen or so more miles to south Mobile, where the main farmers' market was located. He banged his fist on the wheel again. Then he got an idea. He dropped back three or so car lengths, laid on his horn, and surged forward, braking less than two feet from the bed. The truck didn't move over an inch. Well, he would keep doing it, by God, until the damn farmer pulled over enough to give him a view. Then he saw the boy flailed back against the cab with a terrified, expression as though he'd thought the Cadillac was going to keep coming. Robert was stricken with guilt. He hadn't thought about the boy.

If the other lane was clear for even fifty yards, Robert could get around the truck. Hell, it wouldn't take more than ten seconds in this baby. He crossed the center line by a couple of feet and through the smoke-hazed windshield saw a motorcycle maybe sixty yards away in the oncoming lane. He pulled out, turning to scowl at the farmer as he passed, and when he faced front again, the cyclist was about twenty feet from his windshield.

Robert slammed on the brakes, and the car fishtailed. When it came to a lurching stop astride the center line, he saw the cyclist standing upright in the field by the road. His heart beating wildly, Robert pulled off just ahead and started to get out of the car, but the cyclist, a man about the size of Jack Fry, was shaking his fist at him and shouting,"You fucking asshole!" Robert locked the car doors and watched as the cyclist walked his bike through the nettles to the road, mounted it, and roared off. The son of a bitch had done it on purpose, Robert was sure. When he saw the Caddy pull out, he sped up to make it look like the Caddy ran him off the road. Any day now, he'd be getting a call from some shyster lawyer claiming amorphous, debilitating injuries.

After a few minutes of zipping along at eighty, Robert was behind the truck again and gritting his teeth. Finally arriving at his office, drenched with perspiration, he put on one of the fresh shirts he kept for impromptu dinners with clients. With a shaky hand, he poured a glass of water from the pitcher on his desk, spilling some of it on his notes about the plea bargain. He gulped the water at first, then swilled it in his mouth to soothe the prickly dryness that the champagne had made worse than usual.

He glanced at his watch. Damn. He'd be late. As he reached across the stack of morning mail to grab the file, he saw the gold-embossed seal of the Judicial Council on the top envelope. It hadn't been opened, Ruth maybe thinking it private. His hand trembled as he tore into the envelope and his eyes raced across the text. Simmons had reported him to the council for potential unethical conduct in the Fry case, and he was to attend a meeting in Judge Keefer's chambers with regard to whether a formal hearing was warranted.

That son of a bitch. A fresh sluice of sweat broke out on Robert's forehead. Goddamn it. Simmons would be wetting his pants with excitement at the prospect of seeing him squirm, but Simmons would be the one showing his ass. Keefer, whose fair mindedness was the reason he'd been appointed council chief, would take a dim view of Simmons for making a speculative claim that could cost an attorney his license. Especially since the attorney was him. He and Keefer were friends in the indiscreet way judges were allowed to be friends with lawyers. They both fished for the big ones—marlin, tarpon, sailfish—and exchanged fishing stories at every opportunity.

He balled up the letter and threw it in the trash so his secretary wouldn't see it. He buzzed her on the intercom and told her to calendar a meeting in Judge Keefer's chambers on July 16th at four o'clock. He sighed, sat down at his desk, and tried not to think about the notice. He felt strange—weak yet jittery, like when he was behind that truck. He glanced at his watch. Too early for his noon pills, but Simmons sometimes handled the plea sessions, and he wanted to look like a man who couldn't be rattled. It took a minute for him to unscrew the bottle cap with his trembling hand.

Robert was breathing hard and sweating heavily when he entered the courtroom. Simmons, with his nose in the air as though his didn't stink, was on the bench looking down at three men—Carl and an attorney with his client whose plea was being put on the record. Inexplicably, Robert felt relieved that Carl, in addition to one of his associates, was handling this session. He took a seat in back, although he could have sat anywhere. There were less than thirty or so people in the room—attorneys sitting with their bailed clients, and attorneys whose clients hadn't gotten bail and sat in the jury box, their orange jail uniforms a rowdy burst of color in the solemn courtroom. Some young guy in the jury box waved in Robert's direction. Robert nodded, although he didn't recognize the kid.

He hoped his case hadn't already been called. He leaned over the shoulder of a lawyer in the row ahead of him, someone he'd never seen before. "Did they —" The man gestured for him to whisper. "Did they call," he whispered, and stopped. He'd forgotten his client's name. He read the tab on the file in his briefcase and leaned to the man's ear again. "Puckett," he whispered. The man's head whipped around. "Fuck it yourself, bud," he hissed, and turned back toward the front.

What the hell? A smartass with a fly-by-night practice in Pritchard or Chickasaw. Robert poked the man's neck with his pointer finger and whispered "Fuck you."

He moved up to the second row. He knew he didn't feel as clearheaded as he should, and he didn't want to miss it when his case was called. His briefcase bumped noisily as he slid in, and others nearby turned to look. Still sweating profusely, his handkerchief soaked, Robert wiped his face with the cuff of his sleeve, then skimmed through the file to refresh his memory—the police report, the charge sheet, the official transcript from the DA, and so on. It was the best plea he'd ever gotten—accessory to armed robbery reduced to …to what? To a one-year jail sentence, he was sure of that, but what was the charge they'd agreed to?

He grabbed his yellow tablet and skimmed through the notes he'd written in advance of meeting with Carl—simpleminded, no mens rea, no priors, not armed, no knowledge of gun, and so on —and then to the notes he'd made in Carl's office of the agreed upon plea, but they were illegible smears of blue ink from the water he'd spilled. Damn it. The only clear mark was a star he'd scribbled to flag a note he now couldn't read. It was probably the agreed- upon plea.

He raised the tablet to his eyes and in one of the smears made out the letters "O f f e…" What did that mean? He thought hard, nothing coming to mind. Ah, "offense," that was the word. What was wrong with him that he hadn't known that? A few smears over was maybe a "p," and a few smears further down the page a "t," but nothing thereafter. He stared mindlessly at the letters as though they might move around and form words.

The clerk calling another case broke Robert's spell. He looked up from the tablet to see yellow spots dancing in circles. He closed his eyes for a few seconds, but it made him dizzy. When he opened them, the spots were still there. Noises assaulted him from all directions—papers rustling, feet shuffling, coughing, the clacking of the court reporter's machine, which had never been more than a faint tapping even when he was as close as the defendant's table. He put his hands over his ears, but it didn't help. He shifted his tongue, which was so dry it felt like reptile scales across the roof of his mouth. If he could only assuage the dryness, the plea would come to mind. He rose. There was a water fountain in the hall. He couldn't remember where exactly, but he could find it.

"State versus James Puckett," the clerk called.

That was him. Yellow tablet in one hand, briefcase forgotten, Robert walked through the short gate toward the bench. Still dizzy, he had to concentrate so as not to wobble. A sheriff's deputy led the young man who had waved at Robert to his side. Robert recognized him then—a skinny twenty-year-old with a pimply face and big ears. Robert shook his client's hand. His own was sweaty and trembling, and the young man looked at him with concern. "Just a little fever," Robert whispered, and winked at him.

"Have counsel and the DA's office reached an agreement in this case?" Judge Simmons asked.

"We have, your honor," answered Carl.

"How does your client plead, Mr. Townsend?"

The nasal voice, the sour face, the squinty eyes looking at him over glasses pulled downward on his nose to suggest intelligence. What a fake. Simmons was a bureaucrat without the guts to be a lawyer. All judges did was listen and make rulings while lawyers faced challenges, took risks, achieved goals. Rooster was jealous of him. Funny he hadn't thought of that before. Jealousy explained why Simmons gave him a harder time than he did the other lawyers, and why he filed that report with the council. The man was one jealous son of a bitch. Robert wanted to tell him that, needed to tell him in the same desperate way he needed water. But at his side was the scared child-boy Puckett, son of one of the janitors at the Van Antwerp, which was the only reason he'd taken the case.

"Mr. Townsend," Judge Simmons said. "We're waiting for the plea."

"Not armed," Robert said, his tongue feeling swollen and the tip of it painfully tender. In the periphery he saw Carl looking at him with alarm.

"I didn't hear you, counsel," Simmons said, "and neither did the court reporter. Repeat it please."

Robert shook his head. He couldn't remember what he'd said, but he knew it was wrong. He looked to Carl for help, but Carl was biting his lower lip like he did when he was worried. Robert faced front again and blinked. The perspiration that had pooled at the base of his neck began to trickle down his chest, making him itch. He slapped at his collar to blot the moisture.

"Mr. Townsend," Judge Simmons said again.

"Our agreement, your honor," Carl said quickly, "is that the DA's office drops the charge of accessory to armed robbery in exchange for a guilty plea of—"

"Mr. Taylor, don't you think it's a little unusual for the DA's office to state the defendant's plea?"

"Yes, your honor."

Laughter rippled across the spectator section of the courtroom. Robert turned toward it and saw a span of familiar faces he couldn't name. He felt like he was outside of himself watching himself. Two of him in the courtroom, one watching his middle finger scratch the fatty part of his thumb and other doing the scratching. Both of them were desperate for water. Both of them were scared.

"Mr. Townsend?" Judge Simmons said. "Will you please do us the honor of putting your client's plea on the record? A couple of your colleagues, who, like you, didn't make it to first call, would like to take their turns, the court reporter would like to finish this session, the sheriff's deputies would like to get the prisoners back to their cells, and I'd like to go to lunch."

The sarcasm, the mocking in the nasal voice, felt like a rasp across raw skin. The son of a bitch had to give him time to think.

He would tell him to hold his goddamn horses.

"Horses," Robert said, violently pushing the word over his turgid tongue. He took a weaving step toward the bench. "Hold your—" He stopped when he felt Carl's arm around him painfully squeezing his shoulders.

"Your honor," Carl said. "Mr. Townsend is not well. I request this case be continued until next week's plea session, and five minutes to help Mr. Townsend to the washroom."

"The bailiff can help Mr....Never mind. Go ahead."

Carl loosened his grip when they reached the hall. "Damn it, Robert. I've seen attorneys drunk in the courtroom before, but this takes the cake."

"I'm not—" Overcome by nausea, Robert clamped his hand to his mouth.

"Go on," Carl said, nodding toward the men's room. "Vomit your guts out, then wait for me on this bench. I've got two more pleas, then my associate can take over, and I'll drive you home."

# Twelve

Robert hadn't asphyxiated in vomit like the winos as he'd feared while retching in the emergency room. And he hadn't died from the wracking pain—stomach, head, eyes, scalp, even his teeth. "Why the hell would my teeth hurt?" he asked Dr. Harris, who answered, "Withdrawal," and would give him nothing for it. "Nothing stronger than aspirin until your blood pressure's back to normal. You're damn lucky you got to the hospital in time."

"I know," Robert said, remembering how fast Carl had driven when he told him it wasn't liquor but Benzedrine.

Two days later, Robert was home, supposedly recovering his strength in the kingdom of Do Not Disturb, but actually sinking into despondency until he heard the sneaky peeking at the door the first evening.

"Is he dead?" Wendy whispered loudly. Her lamb-fur head appeared in the gap of the bedroom door, and stair-stepped above it was Ellen's somber face.

"No, stupid," Ellen hissed.

"Dead as a doornail," Robert said with as much volume as he could muster. He relished their giggles, and then he heard Elizabeth's voice telling them to let him rest.

After that came two days of sleep mixed with a wakeful listlessness in which he hadn't the spirit to see the girls. The only thing that roused him was masturbation, which he did several times, the covers tented by his knees and his eyes on the closed door. He imagined himself plunging into Helene's moist tightness as the orange neon light of the motel sign cast a bronze sheen on her nipples through the cheap motel blinds When he was spent, he ached with knowing he wouldn't see her again, but on the third day, just as he'd finished, he remembered how haughtily she had said, "He's a lot younger than you and he looks pretty good in a Stetson."

To hell with her, he thought. So what if she'd lasted four months as opposed to his couple of one-night stands and the three-week court reporter in Huntsville. Helene was nothing more than a diversion, as those women had been. So what if she was beautiful. Plenty of things were beautiful. Orchids, for example, which he'd not seen since his tour of duty in Hawaii during the war. Surely some florist in Mobile had orchids. He would buy some for Elizabeth as soon as he was up and about.

The fourth day he was home, Robert worked on files he'd asked Ruth to bring, but it was frustrating. When he tried to write—a contract, a pleading, a letter—the ideas he wanted to put down darted around in his mind like minnows in a bait can of water. And he had to read most things twice for comprehension.

That evening when Elizabeth brought his supper tray, she said Carl had called while he was in the shower. "He wanted to know if you would say yes if he gives you the office with the bay view. What's he talking about?"

Robert laughed. "He thinks I'm working too hard. He offered me a job."

"He did? When?"

"The last night I was in the hospital. He snuck in after visiting hours, if you can believe our Boy Scout would do such a thing." The visit had been a nice surprise even with Carl's lectures. One was about his finding a flashy earring too cheap to be Elizabeth's when he ferried Robert's car from downtown to home. "It's not my business, buddy, but I'd like to say I don't see why a man with a great family like yours would fool around." The other lecture was that Robert should come work with him as assistant district attorney. "Decent hours and tolerable pressure means no need for Benzedrine, Robert."

"I wish you'd consider his offer," Elizabeth said.

"Nope, for a hundred reasons. Let's drop the subject."

"Carl's a damn good friend. We were lucky he got you to the hospital so quickly. But I'm confused about why you were with him. Didn't you have an early hearing in Atmore that morning and that's why you spent the night there?"

"Mrs. Mims got the Atmore date wrong on my calendar. I realized it when I woke in the motel and rushed back for the plea session."

"Oh, so that's what you meant when you told Dr. Harris you'd gotten confused about the number of pills you'd taken because you'd been in such a hurry. But even confused, why did you take so many?"

"I didn't take so many. Four at the most, the usual two when I woke, and then I was so nonplussed about being late that I forgot I'd taken them and took two more on the way." It could have been a dozen, he thought. How could he have been so careless?

"Dr. Harris thinks it was at least six."

"And Gandhi thought poo-poo was candy."

"I'm not your daughters, so don't expect me to laugh at that, but I'm glad you're feeling up to being cute."

Talking about the Benzedrine had made Robert so edgy he couldn't sleep. A little before midnight he searched the bathroom cabinets for the prescription Ellen had brought home from the pharmacy on Wendy's birthday. It wasn't there. Elizabeth had probably gotten rid of it when he was in the hospital. Then he searched the pockets of the pants he was wearing when he went to the hospital. Not there. Elizabeth, the Gestapo. No matter. What he needed was something to help him sleep. He swallowed two of Elizabeth's Valium pills, which she used to take when facing difficult social events, and he soon fell asleep.

Robert felt rested and strong when he woke the next morning, almost like his old self. As he opened the drapes he saw Ellen scamper out in her nightie for the morning paper. What a sweetheart. He owed her. He called for eggs, ham, biscuits and grits for breakfast and in the shower afterwards decided that a few days at the island would revive him completely. He'd swim and collect shells with the girls and take them riding in the army surplus jeep he'd bought because it was like the one he'd driven during the war. The girls loved the jeep—butt-bumping over the dunes in the frayed plastic seats and shrieking as he skirted the waves.

"Hey, Muskogee! Hey, Birdsong!" he called through the open

bathroom door when he'd covered his face with shaving cream. He smiled to himself at the sound of their clamoring up the stairs and met them as they entered the room.

"Anybody wants to go to Dauphin Island better give me a smooch." It's been months since I've done this, he thought as he chased them around the room giving them lather kisses.

"What's going on here?" Elizabeth said, suddenly appearing in the doorway. She looked youthful in her light cotton nightgown with her hair held back by a wide white headband. And she looked eager to join the merriment. She'd seemed happier these last few days than he'd seen her in a long time, better-natured and softer-spoken with the girls. Which made sense. Wives enjoyed having sick husbands at home under their dominion.

"I'll show you," Robert answered, and chased her to give her a kiss. The three females taunted him from all sides, then ran from him, sometimes even across the Hollywood bed, Elizabeth's prize possession, but she didn't seem to mind—she even ran across it herself. Neither did she fuss about the shaving cream in her hair when he missed her cheek, or Fifi's continual barking. Robert came to a standstill a few minutes later out of breath and laughing. His wife and daughters had more shaving cream on their faces than he did.

"How about the island, Pocahontas? We can lie around and play gin rummy while the girls cook supper."

"Oh, Daddy," Ellen said. "I can't cook anything except grilled cheese sandwiches."

"Tell you what. We'll eat ready-grilled ribs from the Quick Stop. You can pick them up in the jeep," Robert said.

Ellen gasped. "Does that mean you're going to teach me to drive?"

"Does a goat stink?"

Soon after Robert had been put on retainer by Gulfstream, he bought a cottage on Dauphin Island, a fourteen mile long and two mile wide stretch of white sand dunes, gulf pines, and the ruins of a Civil War fort, only forty or so miles from Mobile. It was a barrier island and previously undeveloped for fear of tropical storms. His cottage was in one of the first residential developments.

Whitecaps sparkled in the sun and sea birds circled overhead as they drove across the long bridge from the mainland. Robert knew the girls expected him to break out in song on the bridge as he usually did, but he had a headache.

Wendy held a piece of bread out the back window to a pelican flying a few feet behind. "Slow down, Daddy," she squealed. "I'm feeding that seagull."

"It's not a seagull," Ellen said. "See the pouch under the beak? It's a pelican."

"No, it's a seagull, isn't it, Daddy?"

"Might be a stork," Robert said. "With a baby. Taking it to some lucky couple."

"That's silly, Daddy," Ellen blurted. "Babies don't come from storks."

"Well, maybe they come from pelicans. So check that one out," he said, and winked at her in the rear-view mirror. She blushed and turned away. He felt a pang of guilt. She would know about sex by now and had probably thought of it in terms of him and Helene.

Robert told Ellen the driving lesson would be after lunch, but when they'd eaten, Elizabeth insisted he rest first, and he was grateful. It was hot inside the little clapboard cottage and he sat on the porch with Elizabeth. He watched with envy as a fishing boat came from the breakwater and reached the gulf stream, a purplish band of fish-attracting warm water. Spanish mackerel, King mackerel, and Barracuda would be plentiful now. He hadn't had time to fish in months. As soon as he was up to it, he would arrange a charter for him and Ellen. Maybe next weekend. Further out from the fishing boat, a freighter steamed from the bay toward the dark water of the international channel. He pointed the freighter out to the girls, who were digging in the sand closer to the water.

"Where's it going?" Ellen said.

"Can't tell. Could be anywhere—Europe, Africa, China."

"Fifi's going to China," Wendy said. "That's why we're digging this hole big enough to put her in. But what if I change my mind and don't want Fifi to go to China. Tell Ellen she can't make Fifi go, Daddy."

"You can't make Fifi go to China, Ellen," Robert said.

"But Daddy, that's not fair," Ellen said with a mock whine. "Wendy made a deal that if we dug the hole she would send Fifi down it. And you've always told us a deal is a deal, no backing out."

"Noooo. I don't want Fifi—"

"Hush. Let your father rest."

This is the whole package, Robert thought—father, mother, children, beach cottage. It would make a good postcard with the caption "The purpose of a man's life." And it was true. Any man on that freighter, no matter where it was going, would prefer to stay in port so he could go home to his family at night. He'd noticed in the Van Antwerp how the men without families were for the most part a sorry sight at quitting time. In the hall, the elevator, the parking lot, their postures and voices had a tentative quality, as though they didn't know what to do next, like a dog circling around looking for a place to lie down.

He glanced at Elizabeth, who'd gone back to her magazine. He'd made a good choice. Had been lucky to reach her first on that platform in Atlanta, for there were maybe twenty soldiers on that train for every woman, and Elizabeth, with her long legs and lush auburn hair, had stood out like a flamingo in a chicken yard. And she'd been witty with that little tease about having a husband.

As it turned out, Elizabeth was a paradox. Fun-loving, uninhibited and bold, yet afraid of many things, like water—no swimming, no boating or even wading above her knees—walking across sidewalk grates, and thunderstorms. She'd been afraid of their new high society when they joined the club because she didn't know upper-class ways. But she'd adapted quickly and done well in making important friends.

"How about ice tea?" Elizabeth said.

"No, thanks." She was beginning to age—something of a stomach, veins showing on her legs and hands, but with that tan she was still the most attractive wife in their age group at the club. He was satisfied. It would be stupid—apples to oranges—to compare her to the twenty-two-year old Helene.

"Are you sure? You know Dr. Harris said eight ounces of liquids an hour."

"You're right. So how about eight ounces of Wild Turkey?" They laughed and he sat up. "I don't feel like resting. I might as well take Ellen in the jeep."

"Not this minute. Please. It's nice, isn't it? Our sitting here talking."

She sounded tired. This pill business had been an ordeal for her too, he realized. At his side the whole time in the hospital, even while he was throwing up. Then waiting on him hand and foot at home.

"All right," he said, and sat down again. "I hear the price of rice is going up."

"Don't be silly. I mean tell me stories about your clients like you used to, remember?"

He remembered. When he was with the DA's office in Montgomery, he would do theatrical narrations about the criminals he was prosecuting, making their larcenous hearts and foiled plots amusing, while she was the house he brought down. In the aftermath of his affair in Huntsville, those sessions had done more than anything to restore the bond between them.

"Let me think," he said. Although he wasn't in the mood, he tried to remember something entertaining, but nothing came to mind. Gulfstream was three quarters of his practice, and his loan shark cases were dull. "Sorry, but I'm a blank. Nothing's funny."

"Doesn't have to be. Matter-of-fact will do. I like hearing your voice. You've been so busy, I've missed it."

He felt a pang of guilt. Surely he could think of something to make her laugh. From the beginning he'd loved the gut-happy sound of her laughter—"uncultured" his mother said, but indicative, he knew, of her passionate nature.

"All right, a Wild Bill story," he said after a pause, having suddenly remembered the latest rumor about William Rush, a lawyer known for unusual courtroom shenanigans.

"My God. What now?"

"He was defending an itinerant who'd reached in through an open window and stolen some jewelry that was so valuable the charge was a felony. Bill had no defense because the man had the jewelry on him when the cops stopped him. So he tried to get the judge's sympathy by having the man, who was old and had a befuddled demeanor, tell the judge that his hand did it, that he didn't want to take the jewelry but had no control over his hand. The story is that the judge nodded for a few seconds, then said, 'My ruling, Mr. Rush, is that your client's hand is going to jail, and he can go with it or not.'"

Robert got the laugh he wanted. "Poor Wild Bill," Elizabeth said. "That was a loser, but I admire his creativity, the way he approaches things in unconventional ways like you often do, except you're more clever."

Robert felt a rush of warmth for her. She knew him better than anyone and admired his legal skills. He'd been itching to tell someone how clever he'd been in the Fry case. Why not her?

"As a matter of fact, I did do something clever lately, something Wild Bill would envy." He told her about the Fry case, including the words he'd whispered to his client and how Simmons had called Fry violent in front of the jury, which would assure him a mistrial. "Simmons insinuated that I'd caused Fry's outburst, which I denied. He reported his suspicion to the Judicial Council, and I have to attend a meeting Tuesday in Judge Keefer's chambers so Keefer can decide whether to proceed with a formal hearing."

As he spoke, Elizabeth's smile changed to open-mouthed dismay. "Oh, Robert. What if Judge Keefer decides to proceed?"

"He won't. He likes me, and Judge Simmons has no evidence, only self-serving conjecture. As I said, it was his yelling at Fry in front of the jury that guaranteed a mistrial. I'll point that out to Keefer to show that Simmons could be trying to shift the blame for the mistrial from himself to me. There's nothing to worry about." Damn. He'd expected her applause.

"You told me months ago you thought Fry was there that night and was responsible for the old man falling. Why did you risk your license?"

"My license is not in jeopardy, Elizabeth. And consider this: three quarters of our income comes from Gulfstream, and I would have been fired if I'd lost that case, which was about to happen."

"Well, good riddance. Look at what that company's done to you, working night and day even before this trial, having to take those damn pills to keep up. Please, take that job with Carl. I beg you."

Robert laughed. "And live on a DA's salary? You're crazy. Think about it, Elizabeth. The mortgages, car payments, Dessie's salary, the private schools, the club."

"We don't need all that."

"Yes, we do. We're accustomed to it. Scaling back sours people. Don't worry, I'm planning my escape from Gulfstream. I've got irons in the fire."

"But that will take months, and besides, new clients will overwork you too. The problem is private practice."

"There is no problem. I know what I'm doing, and I'd appreciate your confidence."

Elizabeth pressed her lips together and looked out at the water. It occurred to him that maybe she'd already interfered. "Did you ask Carl to make me that job offer?"

"Of course not."

"Good thing. You know how I feel about wives interfering in their husbands' business." He rose. "Guess it's time to get our thirteen year old behind the wheel."

"I wish you'd wait until morning when it's cool."

Her voice was low and tentative, as though she was almost afraid to suggest it. He'd been too harsh, perhaps, but she'd pushed him.

"You're probably right, but I told her I'd do it this afternoon, and...here she comes. She must have seen me get up."

# *Thirteen*

Sand on the floor, the couch, the sheets, the towels, sand in Fifi's hair, and Robert taken hostage by the girls to swim and drive the dunes in a fume-filled inferno. Elizabeth wasn't as keen as Robert about the cottage getaways, except that she loved their bedroom. Its shin-bumping size and wide louvered windows were reminiscent of the bedroom in their first apartment when Robert returned from the Pacific. "Makes me feel like a sex-starved veteran all over again," he said the first night they spent there. They always had to muffle the giggles that came from trying to muffle their moans because the girls slept a thin wall away. Robert had seemed so strong this morning that Elizabeth had packed the ankle-length chiffon negligee he liked. She felt foolish in it now since Ellen's jeep lesson in the hot sun had done him in until tomorrow morning at least, but she hadn't brought anything else to sleep in.

She bent over to lay her hand on the sleeping Robert's sunburned forehead. Still as hot as when they'd cuddled twenty minutes before. She pulled the summer quilt over his bare chest so he wouldn't catch a chill, but in a few seconds he rolled onto his side as though to shift it off. Which was worse, chill or fever? Bed rest and plenty of liquids fell far short of adequate instructions from Dr. Harris. Damn him anyway for prescribing the Benzedrine. She'd been terrified in the emergency room that day—Robert retching so violently she was sure he was losing vital parts of himself.

The Vaseline she'd applied before he fell asleep had been quickly absorbed, leaving his lips scaly and raw-looking again. Not wanting to wake him, Elizabeth set the jar on her nightstand for quick access in case he woke during the night. As she watched the labored rise and fall of his chest and heard his raspy breathing, the idea she'd had that afternoon became resolve. She would go to work so he could take Carl up on his offer without their having to scale back too much. She wouldn't tell him until she had the job, and she'd face his anger by asking if he wanted to leave his daughters fatherless at such a young age. He knew as well as she did that he would go back to the Benzedrine to cope with the pressure of his practice.

Elizabeth slipped her beach robe on over the negligee and quietly closed the bedroom door behind her. She would get the newspaper with the classifieds from the car. People were always looking for bookkeepers, the kind of work she was doing until she got pregnant with Wendy and Robert made her stop. She didn't know a debit from a credit when she applied, but she convinced them she did and taught herself at night. The prospect of bookkeeping or of any credible job pleased her. No more spending her days tiptoeing through the polished silver minefield of Mobile society. And she would still have faithful Glo and down-to-earth Marjorie for friends.

On the parking pad, the chiffon gown blowing softly around her legs, Elizabeth began to hum the song Robert had sung in a whispery voice while they cuddled. "I'd like to get you on a slow boat to China." Weak as he was, he'd made the effort to be romantic, pulling her close when she got into bed and running his fingers along the chiffon at her cleavage. "You're safe tonight, but you won't be soon," he'd said. And then he'd added—she paused when she opened the car door to remember his exact words— that he'd not been the best husband lately, but he would be in the future, and he loved her more than ever. She felt again the goose bumps she'd felt when he said that last part.

No newspaper, but she pulled a brown bag from under the front seat: a carton of cigs, aspirin, and two Minnie Mouse watches. Surely Robert knew Ellen was too told for Minnie Mouse. She would give one to Dessie for her niece. She glanced at the piece of paper that fell from the bag, a preprinted form with "Uncle's Corner, July 7, 1960" handwritten on the first line. That couldn't be. July 7th was Wednesday when he'd driven back from Atmore, and Uncle's was near his hunting club, which was in the opposite direction from Mobile. Goddamn it. Her heart racing, she remembered their conversation when he'd packed his overnight bag. She'd asked where he would stay and he'd said "Don't know. One of those little motels on the highway. It'll be late when I get there." The son of a bitch.

As Elizabeth entered the cottage, Ellen emerged from the bedroom she and Wendy shared.

"Why are you up?" Elizabeth said.

"I heard somebody at the car and thought it was Daddy. I wanted to ask if I could drive him to the Quick Stop in the morning. He said at supper that I'd caught on to shifting so fast I—"

"The answer is no. He's sun burned and too tired from this afternoon to go in the jeep again. Y'all stayed out in the sun too long."

"But he wanted me to drive to the fort."

"Why? You've been there a dozen times." She gripped Ellen's shoulder. "You met someone, didn't you, a woman, and he talked to her."

"No, we didn't meet anybody. We drank a belly wash at that concession place and then he let me drive over some dunes. Is Daddy sick again?"

"He might be. Go back to bed."

With the bedroom door closed behind her, Elizabeth shook Robert. "Open your eyes, damn you. I found the watches you bought Wednesday at Uncle's while you were supposedly rushing home from Atmore."

His eyes opened. "I'll…I'll," he muttered.

"You were with a woman, weren't you?"

His head rose slightly from the pillow, then fell back again as his eyes closed.

Elizabeth stood with clenched fists and looked at him, his white eyelids a stark contrast to the rest of his flaming face. She shook his shoulder. "You can't be asleep." But he could, she realized. That goddamn sleeping pill she'd brought along at his request. He'd probably be out for the rest of the night.

The beach was dark except for the sickle moon that cast a thin ribbon of light along the sand. Taut with anger, Elizabeth lit a cigarette at the water's edge. The other cottages were east of the Townsends' and wanting to avoid people, she followed the ribbon toward the island's deserted western end, a mile or so away. She walked quickly, consuming cigarette after cigarette with furious puffs.

Was it the same woman as on the night he was supposedly with Red, or a different one? Had there been others? She thought of all the times he had begged off from sex. No wonder. The son of a bitch had been satiated. For a few seconds she felt like she couldn't breathe. Why had he gone elsewhere for sex when she'd never refused him? That's what hurt the most.

In a minute or so she began to walk again, her thoughts and emotions like a tightly woven shroud between herself and the visible world. After a while she came abreast of a couple walking in her direction that she'd not noticed.

"Lookee here, Mama. Look who's a-sleepwalking."

"Oh!" Elizabeth said, and clutched the front of her robe as though it might be open. It was Merilee and Dale, the childless couple in the cottage next door. They were disappointing as neighbors because of their commonness, as epitomized by the way they looked at this moment: Dale in his-jockey style bathing suit, stomach flab rippling above the waistband and the vulgar bulge of his privates below, and the butterball Merilee like a walking tent in her homemade beach dress. They were about the same age as she and Robert, yet they were holding hands and swinging them back and forth like children. Totally crass.

"Sorry, Elizabeth. Didn't mean to scare you," Merilee said.

"You probably thought we wasn't coming this weekend 'cause we got here late. We got tied up in the sack, and I don't mean a croaker sack, if you catch my drift," said Dale.

"Hush, Dale. Shame on you." Merilee grinned at Elizabeth.

"We men gotta stick together. Does Robert know his wife's on the prowl?"

"He would have come, but he needed to finish some work, and I couldn't sleep."

"Probably didn't see what you was wearing, cause that's quite a getup," Dale said. "What is it, a bathrobe over—"

"I didn't expect to see anyone. Please excuse my appearance." She didn't give a damn what they thought, yet was embarrassed by the vague sense that her slipshod appearance indicated marital problems.

"Looks okey-doke to me," Dale said, "but what is it? Looks like an evening gown underneath a robe and—uh-oh, you're toting lumber, Elizabeth."

Elizabeth looked down. A small driftwood branch was caught in the hem of the gown.

"And look at that," Dale continued, pointing to a trail in the sand behind her. "You been dragging it a while. Good thing it ain't a live crab." He let out the irritating hee-haw laugh that often floated over to the Townsends' cottage.

The chiffon was caught in the splintery driftwood in three places, but Elizabeth thought she could tease it out. As she began to pick up the wood, Dale said he'd get it and reached it first. He jerked the chiffon free and held it aloft, where it waved in the breeze like an embattled flag.

"Uh-oh. Got some holes. Merilee can fix it so you can't tell."

Elizabeth held back tears. This was the gown that Robert found most seductive.

"Never mind. It doesn't matter. Goodnight." She turned to walk away. They were like the hicks she'd grown up with and moved away from at the first chance because she didn't want to be like them. Her marriage to Robert had assured her that she never would be.

She felt Dale's hand on her shoulder.

"Wait, Elizabeth. I've got some advice. If you want a jim dandy good night's sleep, tell Robert you want to skinny-dip. I guarandamntee you, he'll put that lawyer work down before you can say Jack Frost. That's what me and Merilee just done. Oohh-hh-wee. Messing around in that warm water butt-naked. You and Robert ever skinny-dip?"

They hadn't, although Robert wanted her to, had promised he'd hold her hand and they would go no deeper than her chest.

"But what if a wave comes and knocks me over, a rogue wave, you called it when you warned Ellen." He replied that they were rare and he would see it coming, but she'd still been too afraid.

"Elizabeth, I asked do you and Robert ever skinny-dip."

"None of your goddamn business," she said, and walked past him.

"No harm meant," Dale called out. "Thought we could make it a foursome sometime. Beats the hell out of cards." He let out the hee-haw.

The boar and his piglet, Elizabeth thought. At least she'd been spared from seeing them emerge naked, Dale's genitals probably as repulsive as a two-headed chicken.

She moved close enough to the water to get her feet wet and peered out beyond the breaking waves. A dark nothingness, except for the reflection of the green and white running lights of a ship in the international channel. She bent over and swished her hand in the water. Soft and warm. Yes, it would feel nice on a naked body. Maybe if she'd gone in with Robert …but that was ridiculous. A man didn't cheat on his wife because she wouldn't skinny-dip. Thanks to her uncle's cruelty, she would have been too terrified to breathe. Maybe she should have told Robert why she was afraid. Well, it didn't matter now. She was going to leave the son of a bitch. She had to or she'd be like that pathetic woman in Atlanta Emily told them about.

She stood and began to run. The chiffon caught between her legs, but she kept going, never mind the gown or the crushed shells and squishy kelp beneath her feet.

Ten or so minutes later, Elizabeth reached the island's western end: gulf pines to the north, white-capped water to the south, and a shored-up bank to the west. Heaps of kelp and seaweed were scattered about at the high-tide line, their rank smell filling the air. Elizabeth walked around trying to catch her breath and wiping strings of watery mucus from her mouth. The spot had obviously been occupied. Log-like pieces of driftwood were arranged around a shallow pit of ashes with a car grill laid across it. Empty food cans and beer bottles were gathered in a pile, and a shabby blanket hung from a low branch of a nearby pine. Someone had made this their home. Where would her home be, hers and the girls? There would be too much gossip to stay in Mobile. She stared into the darkness, unaware of the rustling of the incoming tide as the seaweed built up around her.

## Fourteen

The morning after they returned from the island, Elizabeth watched Robert pace the den with the phone cord dragging behind him like a tether. Carl phoning so early was unusual. She wished she could hear, but he'd closed the French doors. Although he'd done nothing but rest at the island the day before, he was obviously still too fatigued from the hospital ordeal to go to work. He'd had to hold on to the banister when he came down the stairs. And he looked sickly thin. Her heart ached at the way his suit pants bunched into gathers at his tightly drawn belt—the same way she'd felt when she'd returned to the cottage night before last.

He was slumped across the porch steps. Thinking he'd fallen, she raced to him the instant she saw him. He'd been coming to look for her, he said, but hadn't the strength to go further. She showed him the dated receipt from Uncle's, and he explained what happened, his voice so weak she had to lean into him to hear. When the Atmore hearing was canceled, he'd decided to go to an all-night birthday bash at the hunting lodge, liquor flowing and striptease dancers. He'd passed out and when he woke the next morning one of the strippers was still there. She told him he owed her. He didn't remember doing anything with any of the strippers, wouldn't have been able to, but he paid her anyway. His confusion about the pills came from guilt. He begged Elizabeth to forgive him and promised it wouldn't happen again. She believed him. Why would he mention the stripper if he was lying?

"That stupid son of a bitch," Robert said now, returning to the dining room table, where they'd been having coffee and reading the paper.

"Carl?" Elizabeth said in alarm.

"Of course not. Jack Fry. He told the guy in his cell what I'd whispered to him about Tanner and his wife. He was probably thinking it would make his outburst look valiant. I should be grateful. It would be a legal conflict now for me to represent him in the retrial, so Gulfstream will have to use someone else."

"Oh, Robert. This is bad, isn't it? Will Fry be there this afternoon? What if you're disbarred?"

"You'd never make a lawyer, Elizabeth, with your penchant for compound questions."

"How can you joke about this?"

"Easy. It's much ado about nothing. No, Fry won't be there. I'll tell them he misheard me. Any judge would believe a member of the bar over an ex-boxer doing collections for a loan shark company. Plus, Keefer likes me." He rose and let her help him on with his jacket. "Take that frown off your face, Pocahontas. I'm not going to get disbarred. I've got this under control. Trust me."

Elizabeth watched from the porch as he walked slowly to his car, shoulders slumped and head dropped. All bravado gone. He *was* worried about that meeting. Maybe there was something he hadn't told her. From overhead came the clamor of the girls getting up—the running around, the arguing, Fifi barking. Elizabeth went into the den, closed the door, and picked up the phone.

"I shouldn't be talking to you about this, Elizabeth," Carl said when she asked what he knew about the situation. "It's Robert's business, and besides, it sounds like he's already told you everything."

"Only what Fry told the guard. I'm scared, Carl. Will you at least tell me why Judge Simmons thinks Robert prompted Fry to attack the witness?"

"As far as I could tell, it was the timing. Robert whispered to Fry, and Fry went wild. Simmons is quick to think the worst about attorneys who don't cower."

"At least Judge Keefer likes him, according to Robert. He thinks Keefer will take his side and dismiss the matter. What do you think?"

"Yeah, Keefer does like him, but given what Fry said, he might think a hearing is necessary so people can testify."

"What people?"

"Judge Simmons, Robert, Fry of course, the deputy guarding

Fry who might have heard, and possibly me since I was at the prosecution table, theoretically within hearing distance."

The deputy, Elizabeth thought, her heart skipping a beat. "Do you think the deputy heard?"

"I don't know. But at the prosecution table I was almost as close to Robert as the deputy, and I didn't hear anything."

"But you could have, couldn't you, since you were theoretically close enough? Robert says that Fry misheard him, and he's going to tell them what he actually said. Can't you go to that meeting and say you heard some of it?" She held her breath in the silence that followed. This was their "George Washington chopped down the cherry tree" Carl.

"I'll pretend I didn't hear that, Elizabeth. You forget that I'm an officer of the court. We're not kids here deciding what to say about a broken window. "

"Please, Carl. Robert would do it for you."

"Yes, I'm afraid he would, but that's Robert. I have to go. I'm due in court and will be there the rest of the day. I'll call Robert this evening to see how things went. Try not to worry. Call me a Boy Scout if you want, but I think the truth usually wins."

Damn, Elizabeth thought as she hung up. If the matter went to a hearing and the deputy had heard any part of what Fry claimed, Robert would be disbarred. The disgrace would be too much to bear and he would fall apart. Would go back on the Benzedrine. She'd seen the spurts of euphoria the pills sometimes gave him. She looked out the window. Low grey clouds all over. The humidity would be especially hard on Robert this afternoon in his weakened condition. How could he stand up against Simmons? She thought for a few minutes, then flipped through the club phone roster.

"Of course I'd love to see you this morning, dear," Marjorie Simmons said. "Come around ten. We'll have coffee and sweets."

Oakleigh Place was one of Mobile's oldest and most revered neighborhoods. The houses were either grand—antebellum mansions, Victorians, colonial revivals, and the like—or quaint cottages with steep roofs, windows and doors of unusual shapes, and other charming features. Stately oak trees, two and three hundred years old, stood on the vast lawns like totems of the neighborhood's historical stature. The properties rarely went on the market. Most of the residents were descendants of the original owners and intended to pass their houses on to their descendants. Elizabeth remembered with a pang, as she turned onto the Simmons' street, Robert telling her they would live in Oakleigh Place someday. A dream of theirs that could be destroyed at the hearing that afternoon along with dozens of others.

When Elizabeth went to an annual Bar Association party at the Simmons' house the year before, the two-story white brick colonial hadn't looked imposing, but it did as she approached it now. The wide double doors and tall columns rising from the porch gave the house a formal look, as though only the well-bred were welcome. She dried her clammy hands with the hem of her skirt and rang the doorbell.

"I'll get it, Hattie," Marjorie said over the sustained chiming of the bell. Her tone had a hint of pompousness, a side of her Elizabeth hadn't considered when she called. She knew Marjorie liked her, had even told her to visit when she needed mothering, but she might find Elizabeth's request too presumptuous, even unscrupulous, and end their friendship in some genteel manner.

Wearing grass-stained pants and a baggy shirt, Marjorie opened the door with a happy expression, as though Elizabeth was the gift she'd always wanted. She held out a shallow wicker basket full of all kinds and colors of annuals. "For you to take home, my dear. And please excuse my appearance. I wanted to cut the flowers before the heat got to them, and I ran out of time to change. Don't tell anyone, but I practically live in these clothes. When I'm not golfing, I garden. It's the best excuse a sixty-two-year-old can have for playing in the dirt, don't you think?"

Elizabeth laughed. "Well I'm glad you do. The flowers are beautiful."

They gave them to Hattie to put in water, then headed for the side-porch, which Marjorie said was the best place to have their coffee. "The air is soft on overcast mornings like this. 'Lenient' is how I'd describe the mood it creates if I was a poet."

As they passed through the living room on the way to the porch, Elizabeth, having learned that a lady never lets a silence fall, complimented items that seemed noteworthy—the Civil War sword over the mantel, the flouncy-turn-of the-century dress in a glass box on the wall, the colorful crewelwork upholstery of a wing chair. Marjorie told her the background of each, and seeing how much she enjoyed talking about them, Elizabeth asked for more details which she got, plus a few amusing family stories. A good sign. Marjorie was treating her more like a niece than a friend.

As they approached the baby grand, Marjorie handed Elizabeth one of the gold-framed photographs atop it of a young man in an army uniform. His facial structure and broad smile resembled Marjorie. "Our son, Philip. He was killed at Normandy."

"I'm so sorry. He's very handsome. You must be proud of his bravery."

"We are. What a tragedy, that war. So many brave young men killed or maimed for life. We owe them." She handed the other gold-framed photo to Elizabeth. "And this is our daughter's wedding picture. It's about all I have of Gwendolyn since she had the audacity to marry a Yankee and move to New York."

Elizabeth studied it. The young woman was short and puny with a long nose, like her father's. The dress must have cost a fortune—a waste on such a runt. If her husband could give her twenty pounds, they'd both be passable.

"She's lovely," Elizabeth said.

"You're built more like me than she is."

"I noticed. Does she play golf?"

Marjorie laughed. "Heavens, no. She doesn't have an athletic bone in her body."

They'd reached the side porch, a large screened-in area of wicker settees and chairs with bright floral cushions and tall ferns in brass containers. The scent of the large flowerbed of annuals nearby wafted through the screen.

Marjorie motioned for Elizabeth to sit on the settee and sat beside her. Another familial gesture, Elizabeth thought. A good sign. "I'm glad you've come, dear. We'll get to know each other better. I understand you and Robert moved here three years ago from Montgomery. It must have taken courage to uproot the family like that, but then, you are a daring person—gin and poker, oh my."

"I was concerned about Robert's leaving the DA's office for an unknown future of private practice, so I wasn't keen on it. On the other hand, we lived only two blocks from his parents, who thought I was the only mistake he'd ever made. In that way, the move was a great relief." Elizabeth surprised herself by revealing such a private matter, but something about Marjorie seemed to invite openness.

"I know what you mean. Markham's mother would ask him right in front of me if he had a healthy diet. I ignored such insinuations and let her know every chance I got that he was lucky to have married me. That's the way to handle the better-than-thou's. That's what I told Gwendolyn, who had a similar problem with her in-laws at first."

"Your daughter is lucky to have you for advice. I didn't know how to react to Robert's parents."

"Didn't you ask your …Oh, I forgot. You said at your party that your mother died when you were young. What about the aunt who—"

"No," Elizabeth interrupted. "My aunt wasn't the motherly type, plus my uncle discouraged it." An understated way of saying he blew up at her aunt's attempts to be motherly.

Marjorie laid her hand on Elizabeth's. "I didn't have a chance to commiserate at your party, but I want you to know I'm very sorry. Growing up without a mother must have been hard."

Elizabeth felt a familiar bristle. She'd heard such sentiments often when she was young and grew to resent them. They'd always been expressed with an air of superiority, for anyone would rather bestow sympathy than receive it. But the concern on Marjorie's face, the kind blue eyes looking steadily at her, dissolved her ire.

"It was a long time ago," she said, and was relieved by the interruption of Hattie bringing in the coffee and muffins. Elizabeth thought she would wait until they'd talked a little more to make her request, but her hand shook as she lifted the cup to her lips. She quickly returned it to the saucer.

"What's wrong? Too hot? I'll ask Hattie to—"

"No, it's fine. I'm a little shaky because I have a favor to ask. It's about Robert's meeting this afternoon with Judge Keefer and your husband. Maybe you're aware of the situation about the man Robert was defending who tried to attack the witness during the trial. I'm afraid your husband got a mistaken impression of Robert. He would never have instigated something like that."

Yes, she was aware, Marjorie said. Markham had briefly mentioned it when she told him how much she'd enjoyed Elizabeth's party. And Elizabeth was not to worry that he'd gotten a mistaken impression of Robert, because the purpose of council meetings was to determine the facts.

"I can't help but worry. Robert just got out of the hospital from having a bad reaction to Benzedrine, a drug he was taking for fatigue, and he's too sick and weak to adequately represent himself in that meeting. If the matter is not dropped today and goes on to a formal hearing, his reputation will be hurt by the mere fact that such a hearing was called. Would you please call your husband and ask him to give Robert the benefit of the doubt, given his weak condition? "

No, Marjorie couldn't. She was sorry. She really liked Elizabeth, but she couldn't interfere, even if her husband would listen to her, which she doubted. He was a fair man who would hear Robert out and give him the benefit of the doubt if he saw that he could be mistaken.

Elizabeth sank inside. She pictured the potential formal hearing, the deputy on the stand recalling the words he'd overheard Robert whisper to Fry. It was all she could do to not get down on her knees and beg. Then the photo on the piano came to mind.

"There's something else you should know, Marjorie. Robert

fought in the war in the Pacific. The Marianas."

"I didn't know Robert was a veteran. Good for him. Those islands were the turning point, you know."

"Yes. He contracted an unidentifiable disease in Saipan, which led to serious breathing problems that still come over him occasionally, and there's no cure. I guess in a way he's one of those who came home from that war maimed for life."

Marjorie, who'd begun to sip her coffee, set her cup down, a concerned expression on her face. "There's nothing that can be done?"

"No. They don't know what the malady is. It comes on when he's run down from work or too worried or nervous. It's hell for a week or two—barely eating or sleeping, constant headaches while struggling to keep up with his practice. The breathing problem eases for a while, but keeps coming back. Each bout of it leaves him weaker."

Marjorie rested her hand on Elizabeth's forearm. "Oh, my goodness. What a horrible thing to have hanging over him."

"Yes. Horrible. That's why I've come. His worry about his reputation if he's not cleared today is likely to cause another bout. A bad one. And he might not withstand it this time because he's so weak. If you could have seen him walk to the car this morning, hunched over like an old—" The image of Robert's slumped shoulders and drooping head came to Elizabeth and she began to cry. She tried to hold back—crying in front of others was despicable—but she couldn't stop. The sounds of "Oh, my dear, my dear," and the warmth of the arm around her quivering shoulders made her cry even harder.

"I guess I could call Markham during his lunch break and tell him about Robert being a veteran and that horrid breathing problem. Markham would want to know; he watches out for veterans. That's all I can say to him, you understand. Anything more wouldn't be proper."

Elizabeth managed to restrain her exultation until she got in the car. She placed the flowers wrapped in newspaper on the passenger seat and turned to wave. Marjorie waved back, the kind of full arm wave that says the person really wants you to visit again. But she couldn't. How could she face such a kind woman, much less be friends, after having played on her grief with a lie. It was too bad. There was a warmth and genuineness about Marjorie that felt like a doorway she wanted to go through.

The scent of the flowers filled the car—roses, gladiolas, snapdragons, tiger lilies, and others she couldn't identify. Elizabeth realized she wanted a flower garden. She could start it this afternoon. The girls would enjoy helping her. When she left Jackson at eighteen, she vowed never to touch a hoe again, but this would be nothing like having to dig sweet potatoes early in the morning and get on the school bus with dirty fingernails.

# *Fifteen*

The council meeting in Judge Keefer's chambers that afternoon weighed on Robert's mind as he trudged into the Van Antwerp, and it was Elizabeth's fault. "What if you're disbarred?" she'd said, her face contorted by hysteria as though disbarment was a certainty. Her lack of confidence in him was irritating.

"Good morning, Mr. T," said Hi-Jinx, looking up from his customer's shoes. "You been on vacation, I reckon. Welcome back."

"Thanks," Robert said. He leaned against the wall as he waited for the elevator. The coolness of the marble felt good through his light summer jacket. Whap-whap-whap came the snapping of Hi-Jinx's buffing cloth. Robert wished he had even half of such energy.

Mrs. Mims had not yet arrived, and Robert's office, which had been closed while he was out sick, stank with the cloying sweetness of carpet shampoo. The eggs he'd eaten for breakfast rose in his throat, and he hurried around opening the casement windows to let in the bay breeze. He rifled through his phone messages. Nothing from Helene. His rule had been no calls, but she would have called anyway if she'd changed her mind. Just as well. He would walk the straight and narrow from now on. He was lucky Elizabeth had believed his story about the lodge.

Sorting through correspondence that had piled up in his absence, he found a letter from Dr. Greenberg, the orthodontist Elizabeth had mentioned. It was a request for a hundred-dollar retainer before starting work on Ellen. Maybe he should have been a dentist. How civilized it would be to mail a request for money in advance instead of insisting on a retainer face to face from some desperate chump in a jail cell before taking his case.

Mrs. Mims came at nine, effusively sympathetic about his hospital ordeal, telling him in detail about a cousin who'd almost died from a reaction to some medicine. "You still look a little peaked, if you don't mind my saying so, Mr. Townsend. I can call the court clerk and cancel the Southway settlement conference at two if you're not up to it."

"No thanks, Ruth. We've already postponed it once. I'm all right. Bring the file, please." He didn't feel up to the saber-rattling of a settlement conference, something he usually enjoyed, but Southway Insurance was a new client, and a second cancellation would look bad.

Robert groaned inwardly when he set the thick medical reports for Southway on his desk—one from the plaintiff's doctor, and one from Southway's. The onus was on him to get the matter settled. A jury was more likely to find a vehicle at fault in a collision than an injured bicyclist, especially when the bicyclist was first string at the University of Alabama.

Since he had no experience with personal injury damages, the tough question was how much to offer for a few broken ribs, already healed, and a surface lung puncture. The key was whether and when the plaintiff would be able to play football again. The answers would be in the reports, which he'd tried to read, but the text was so verbose and jargon-filled that he'd not found anything definitive. He'd intended, before the overdose fiasco, to read the reports again with a medical dictionary at hand. And now he had less than four hours to make the most of them and come up with Southway's position.

He opened the thickest report, which was from the plaintiff's doctor, and began to read, his shoulders creeping upward toward his neck with tension. With two bennies, the salient facts would jump off the page. He opened his bottom desk drawer. There were a few bennies left from a prescription he'd gotten to supplement Harris'. Then he heard Dr. Harris' voice: "Stay off them, Robert. You'll get addicted again, and that drug's hard on your heart." He closed the drawer. He would flush the pills out of temptation when he got back from the courthouse.

The plaintiff's attorney, Brad Tilson, was a short, wiry man with an irritating high-pitched voice. "Five thousand's a joke, Robert," he said. "A jury of that old woman's best friends would give us at least twenty. One more year with the Tide and this kid would have been playing for the Green Bay Packers or the Chicago Bears. Southway's damn lucky he'll settle for twenty."

The small, windowless conference room felt like a steam bath. Robert desperately longed to remove his jacket, lay his head on the table, and sleep. "Sounds like you got hit on the head on your way to the courthouse, Tilson."

"Let's keep it civil, boys," said the settlement judge from his swivel chair at the head of the table.

"Sorry," Robert said. Like most settlement judges, the man was retired and probably looking forward to some action despite his comment. "What I meant was that anything over five thousand is outlandish. Both reports say the ribs are healed, and there's no conclusion that that little pinprick on his lung means a damn."

"Apparently you missed something," Tilson said. "Dr. Whalen's report states lung punctures need four to five years to heal before strenuous activity. By that time, Andy will have missed his chance for the pros."

The settlement judge sat forward in his seat and looked sternly at Robert as though to say, "So what are you going to do about that?"

Robert didn't remember reading any quantified recovery time, but God knows he could have missed it in all that jargon. Tilson could be bluffing, but if he asked him to quote chapter and verse of the report, and Tilson was right, Robert's negotiating position would be damn weak.

"Chance for the pros, as you say, Tilson, is exactly the problem with the amount you want. Your boy is not a pro player now, and there's no certainty he'll ever be. You can't base damages on the loss of a job he doesn't have. That's like asking for alimony before the wedding."

The settlement judge laughed, and Robert felt better.

"You're forgetting about that invitation to play in the college all-star game this fall. I sent you a copy of it."

Robert laughed as he blotted the perspiration rolling down his neck with his handkerchief. "A first-year law student could tell you that invitation is not a job offer, but simply an invitation to compete for one. Be reasonable. Your boy is just a college player and the figure should be based on that. His becoming a pro is sheer speculation."

"Every damage award is based on speculation depending on how the jury feels about the incident. Think how a jury's going to feel about a first-string Alabama football player invited to the college all-stars getting shot out of the saddle because an old woman rammed her Chrysler into his bike."

Robert shook his head dismissively, although he knew Tilson was right. Southway would be better off if Mrs. Baker had hit a doctor or a lawyer. The trial, which would be a long one, would be sheer torture—coaching the easily befuddled Mrs. Baker so she could testify, finding a doctor to be their expert witness, burning the midnight oil over medical texts to find weaknesses in Whalen's report, all with Southway's general counsel looking over his shoulder. Where the hell would he get the energy for even half of that?

"Ten thousand," Robert said. He felt the sting as soon as he spoke. Southway had authorized ten, but the general counsel expected him to bring it in for less.

"It's a deal. I'll have the settlement agreement delivered to your office first thing in the morning."

As he shook Tilson's hand, Robert felt as though he was seventeen, and the engine of the used car he'd just bought began to knock as he drove off the lot.

After the judge and Tilson left, Robert skimmed the Whalen report until he found Tilson's reference about strenuous activity. A footnote quoted the medical journal Dr. Whalen had relied on: "Recovery time for lung punctures depends on the age of the patient and the severity of the puncture. Generally, a puncture of moderate severity in a person under twenty-five takes four to five years to heal, during which time strenuous activity should be avoided." Goddamn it. This wasn't a puncture of moderate severity. Both reports described it as a surface puncture. Tilson had deliberately misconstrued the report, the son of a bitch. But it had been *his* job to catch it. "Fatigue makes cowards of us all." It was a quote he had read once but couldn't remember who said it. He knew the truth of it now.

He crammed a nickel into the Coke machine on the first floor and took the bottle outside hoping for a breeze. Ten thousand for two rib fractures already healed and a hairline scratch on a twenty-year-old lung. He'd torn his britches with Southway. And when word of the settlement amount got around—Tilson would make sure it did—he'd be the laughingstock of the Bar.

With no breeze and dark clouds pressing the moist heat downward, it was as miserable outside as in the conference room. Tilting his head back to finish the Coke, Robert noticed the triptych on the courthouse façade, which he must have seen a thousand times but never really looked at. Each panel bore a medieval sword of shiny steel, the blades crosshatched with short metal strips a foot or so apart from the handle to the tip. The swords were identical except for symbols on the handles: one for truth, one for justice, one for equity. The cross-hatching was a nice touch, Robert thought. Make your living here, it says, and you'll be gutted as well as pierced, truth, justice, and equity notwithstanding.

It was almost time for Robert's meeting in Keefer's chambers. If Keefer decided to call for a formal hearing, Red would find out and he'd be fired. "Loan Company Counsel Accused of Ethical breach in Homicide Case' would be the headline. Then, he would be dead in the water when it came to getting new clients, regardless of the outcome of the hearing. Where there's smoke, there's fire, most people thought.

In the men's room, Robert splashed cold water on his face and combed his hair. He usually climbed the three flights to Keefer's chambers, but now he surrendered to fatigue and waited for the elevator. On the way up, he gave himself a pep talk. Keefer liked him and would believe Fry misheard him, and Simmons had no evidence otherwise. It was as simple as that. He would go to the Admiral Semmes, afterwards, where Tuesday was oysters on the half shell. He couldn't stomach oysters yet, but he'd have a drink and chew the fat with his colleagues.

As he got off on the third floor, he steeled himself to be polite to Judge Simmons, magnanimously so, as only a man confident of being found innocent could be to his accuser.

Keefer's bailiff unlocked the courtroom door when he saw Robert coming and walked ahead of him toward the chamber door at the back.

"I know the way, Frank," Robert said, the bailiff's formality making him nervous.

"I know, Mr. Townsend, but I'm supposed to announce you."

Robert fixed his face in a broad smile as he entered. It was a large room filled with shelves of case books, the judge's oversized "partner's desk" meant for two, and a conference table stacked with files.

"Good afternoon, your honor," Robert said to the tall, thin, elderly man who sat behind the desk. Robert had always felt at ease in Keefer's chambers. The thirty-pound tarpon mounted behind the desk reminded him of his running joke with Keefer that he would someday catch one bigger.

Robert took a seat in one of the two chairs facing the desk and said good afternoon to Judge Simmons in the other chair. Simmons nodded at him with a brief smile. Fake, Robert thought, and heat rose in him. Being polite to this bastard wasn't going to be easy.

"As you know, counsel," Judge Keefer began, "we're here because Judge Simmons thinks you incited one of your clients, Jack Fry, to attack a witness. My role is to listen to your explanation of the events and decide whether a formal hearing should commence. If there is a hearing and it's determined that you provoked the defendant, you could be disbarred. As you can see, this is a serious matter."

"Every time I've been in your chambers it's been a serious matter, your honor. With all due respect, this is the first time it's been horse- pucky." Goddamn it. The words were out of his mouth before he could stop them.

Judge Keefer's lips pursed. "You're out of line, counsel."

"I'm sorry, your honor. I've been out of the office sick for over a week, I've got a backlog of deadlines to meet, and I can't help but resent the time this meeting is taking when the issue is a simple misunderstanding."

"That remains to be seen, so simmer down. Markham, will you explain what prompted you to start this inquiry?"

Judge Simmons turned to face Robert. "Mr. Townsend, I want to say first that I have nothing against you personally. You're a diligent, clever attorney, but I'm concerned about your ethics in that trial. You asked that witness some provocative questions implying he had carnal interest in the defendant's wife, and then you whispered something to the defendant, who immediately lunged toward the witness. Of course, the guards handcuffed him, and then you asked for a mistrial based on jury prejudice. It looked like the trial was going badly for your client at that point, and I got the impression you might have incited him in the hope of grounds for a mistrial. It was my duty to request this inquiry."

"I'm assuming you want to respond, counsel," Judge Keefer said to Robert.

"Certainly, your honor." Robert paused for a second. Simmons's tone had been almost apologetic. Why? Maybe so Keefer wouldn't suspect that Simmons was trying to get back at him for getting the mistrial. Well, he would fix that.

"It's all a misunderstanding, but I think a fuller picture of what happened should be drawn." He turned to Judge Simmons. "Aren't you forgetting, your honor, that you called the defendant a violent man in front of the jury. That's judicial misconduct, another reason I moved for a mistrial. Maybe you're angry with yourself and trying to blame me."

"That's ludicrous."

"Why? Shifting blame is human nature. I recently heard that my client is trying to do the same—some lie about something I said to him."

"Evidently you know what I was about to bring up, counsel," Judge Keefer said. "This morning one of the guards reported that Fry told him you had whispered, and I quote, 'My guess is, he's diddling your wife.'"

"Diddling?" Robert forced a hearty laugh. "I'm a northern Alabama boy, your honor. That word's a new one on me, although I can guess what it means. What I whispered was, 'Anything else between him and your wife?' My client simply misheard me, not surprising for an ex-boxer whose ear canals have been scrambled. Seriously, your honor, what decent attorney would instigate violence in the courtroom?" He looked at Judge Keefer with aplomb.

"An attorney on a drug that affects his thinking," Judge Simmons said.

"What are you talking about?"

"The odd way you behaved in that plea bargaining session last Tuesday. I thought you were drunk, then came to find out you were taking a drug called Benzedrine."

Goddamn Carl. A reaction to some medicine was all he'd needed to tell Simmons to dispel any notion of drunkenness. What the hell was Carl thinking?

"You say 'Benzedrine,' Judge Simmons, like there's something dishonorable about it, but there's not. During the war our military gave it to pilots, paratroopers, and night patrols for stamina. The Krauts did too, but I guess we had a bigger inventory." He looked at Keefer, expecting him to smile, but he didn't. "People take it because it's useful, not because it's fun."

"It didn't seem useful last Tuesday. You couldn't even state your client's plea."

"I accidentally took too much, and it made me sick. You can't blame an attorney for getting sick." Both judges looked at Robert with dismay, and he realized that he'd pounded the leather arm of his chair.

"Calm down, Robert," Judge Keefer said. "Your being sick is the point I'm about to make. You look sick now, and that's what Markham and I are most concerned about."

"I'm not sick now. I was in the hospital for a couple of days, but that's over and—"

Judge Keefer raised his hand for silence. "As you know, the defendant's case won't be affected by what happens today—he's obviously going to get a mistrial—so I'm at liberty to consider the best course of action based on what's come to light. Do you understand?"

"Yes, your honor." What was he getting at? Was this some trick? Judge Keefer cleared this throat and continued. "Judge Simmons and I discussed the situation before you arrived. We care about the future of a bright young attorney like you. I'm inclined to drop this matter if you agree to slow down your practice. Go fishing," he said, and smiled. Robert smiled back. No formal hearing. No bad publicity. Gulfstream wouldn't fire him.

"That's what we decided, isn't it, Markham?"

"Something like that," Simmons turned to Robert. "Of course I care, counsel, especially about a veteran who's given his all. It seems to me that your workload and that drug have played a part in this matter, and as Judge Keefer says, you need to take time off. But the fact that you would come back to work so soon after leaving the hospital makes me think you won't take it easy voluntarily. Therefore you need to agree to two conditions: no more Benzedrine or anything like it and no court appearances for a month. Rearrange your caseload, postpone hearings, get continuances and the like. If you need court approval on any of that, send the motions to me and I'll make sure your requests are approved."

Judge Simmons's expression when he finished was as close as someone could come to a smirk without being obvious. You bastard, Robert thought. You don't give a shit about my health. You just want to put me in the position of having to kiss your ass.

"That makes sense to me," Judge Keefer said. "What do you say, Robert?"

Robert glanced up at the tarpon—the majestic arch, the silvery fin that would have glistened with sunlit water as the fish leapt strong and free. In his mind's eye, he stood and declared "We started with horse- pucky, and we've come full circle. My workload and my medicine is nobody's goddamn business." Weak and shaky, Robert rose from the chair, the wet imprint of his fingers staining the leather arms. "I guess that's all right, your honor."

# Sixteen


Robert made his way to his office with the image of Simmons's smirk before him. For the rest of his career in Mobile, he would face that smirk in some form or other—subtle gloating in Simmons's manner when they passed in the hall or meeting at a social function, condescension in his voice in the courtroom, and the like. All thanks to Carl. It was hard to believe Carl could have been so stupid. Keefer would have dismissed the matter if Benzedrine hadn't come into the picture. The relief on Keefer's face when Robert gave his version of what he'd told Fry had made that clear.

By the time Robert reached the Van Antwerp, the sky was blanketed with dark gray clouds, which matched his mood. He thought of the sympathy on Keefer's face when Simmons brought up the Benzedrine. Damn it. No longer would Keefer regard him as a stalwart, successful attorney, but as a weak one with a tenuous hold on his practice. Their fish talks would probably continue—Keefer admired his storytelling skills—but now the man's admiration would be circumscribed in the way one admires a good-looking car that he knows has a cracked engine.

"Get Mr. Taylor on the phone, please, Ruth," Robert said, although she was gathering her things to leave when he walked in.

"It's five thirty. The DA's office will be closed, Mr. Townsend."

"Try anyway. Not all bureaucrats quit at five."

"Yes, sir. And to let you know, Mr. Wylie from Southway just called about the settlement conference. I put the message on your desk."

"All right."

When he'd hung his jacket in the closet, Robert drank a shot of the bourbon he kept in his credenza for the occasional toast with a client. The liquor was too warm, but the familiar taste and tingling sensation that came with it, which he'd not experienced since that last night with Helene, loosened him a little. When Ruth buzzed to say Mr. Taylor hadn't answered his phone, he asked her to call Mr. Wylie. The taste of the second shot, all that was left in the bottle, was still on his lips when she buzzed again. Robert picked up the receiver and with a sophistry that turned his stomach, explained why the ten thousand had been a sound decision.

"I agree, Gordon, that the medical reports are ambiguous, but that's exactly our problem if we face a jury. They'll be at liberty to come up with whatever figure they feel like, and we know how a jury would feel about a Crimson Tide star hit by an old woman who probably shouldn't be driving. They started with twenty-five thousand, and the settlement judge looked at me as though I should agree. Having that kid on the stand lamenting his ruined football career would be like playing against the dealer in Vegas."

Robert licked his lips as he waited for a response, but the taste of bourbon had gone. Wylie, who would have a good idea of what that puncture was worth, had no doubt seen right through his baloney and was sorry he'd hired a trial-shy lawyer. Wylie's only response was for Robert to send him the settlement agreement and he would send it back signed with the check. Robert sighed heavily when he hung up. Clearly Southway wasn't going to be one of his replacements for Gulfstream.

Robert gazed tiredly out the window. Whitman Shipyards was his only real prospect. He'd start hustling for others tomorrow morning—reschedule that exporter for lunch, contact the two other businessmen he'd met at the Whitmans' party, and attend the club's midweek cocktail party to make more contacts. But he was so tired that he dreaded having to rise and close the window before the coming rain blew in. Where the hell was he going to get the energy to hustle new clients while keeping up with Gulfstream's work? He heard Simmon's voice: "No more Benzedrine, counsel, or anything like it." Up yours, he thought. He'd done his best lawyering on those pills these last six months—fast, imaginative thinking, including the way he'd saved Fry's butt and his own in that trial.

He swallowed two bennies from the bottle in his drawer. He'd keep it in his glove compartment, a secret from Elizabeth. Immediately, his spirits rose. He, and not Simmons, was in control of his life again. He'd be free of Simmons's ridiculous strictures in a month. The man would have to do something else to get the better of him, something like…like…Jesus! Simmons could subtly let it out about the Benzedrine. Other lawyers would stop referring him, and if Gulfstream's board got wind of it, he'd be fired. The thought took his breath for an instant, and then he laughed. My God. He'd turned into Elizabeth, the Hysterical, chaining himself to the ocean floor with a far-fetched hypothetical. Judges took an oath of confidentiality, and breaching it would ruin Simmons' career.

Robert rested his head on the back of his chair and closed his eyes. When he opened them, it was six-thirty. Elizabeth would be chewing on doorknobs. He would simply tell her Keefer dropped the matter. She'd be ecstatic. At bedtime, she would prance around in something sheer like that gown at the cottage. He needed a drink or two before facing all that. He picked up the phone.

"The Townsend residence," Ellen said in the new voice that she thought sounded mature and he found charming.

"This is the Alabama Highway Patrol. We're looking for a thirteen-year-old who was driving a jeep on Dauphin Island last weekend. Whoever she is better get herself a good lawyer." Her giggles sang in his ear.

"Oh, Daddy, guess what. Mama and I are digging a garden in the backyard like Mrs. Simmons's garden."

"Mrs. Simmons?"

"Yes. Mama went to her house this morning for coffee and brought back a huge bouquet. Mama says that we'll give our first blooms to her."

He felt a slight misgiving. As worried as Elizabeth had been that morning, she wouldn't have felt like going to a coffee klatch. "Was this some kind of ladies' group or just her and Mrs. Simmons?"

"Probably just them. Mama said they'd had a nice long talk. We're going to dig more first thing in the morning unless it's still raining."

"Tell your mother that I'm going to have a drink with some people and will be late."

"You want to tell her? She's in the bathroom, but I'll get her."

"No, you tell her."

"Well, what time will you be home?"

"Half past a monkey's ass, a quarter to his tail"

"Oh, Daddy. Tell me. Mom will want to know."

"Eight or so."

Robert reached Carl at home. "Of course not," Carl said. "Simmons didn't ask what the medicine was, and if he had, I wouldn't have told him. You're insulting my intelligence, buddy."

Robert remembered Elizabeth's panic that morning. *You could get disbarred.*

"Robert, did you hear? I said you're insulting my intelligence."

"I heard. I was thinking that that's how I make a good living. See you in court."

"Wait. How'd it go today with Judge Keefer? I was going to call you later."

"I'm off the hook."

"Thank goodness. I know Elizabeth's relieved."

"How did you know she was worried?"

"She called me this morning. You know how women are."

Elizabeth had told Marjorie! Impossible to believe, yet how else would Simmons know he had been in the hospital. He could imagine her begging Marjorie to ask her god of a husband to…to what, be lenient with Robert because he'd gotten sick on Benzedrine, poor man. Yes, he knew how women were; they gossiped. Granted, judges' wives seemed more circumspect than other women, but every woman had at least one confidante, and that confidant had hers, and so on down the line. The news could be all over the Bar and Gulfstream's board of directors within a week. Badly needing a drink, he put on his jacket, and left.

Having forgotten his umbrella, Robert was slightly wet when he reached the Esquire Club. He brushed the water off his suit in the foyer, hurried to the bar, and took his drink to one of the many small tables scattered around the large room, all of which had a good view of the twenty-five-foot-long stage. The Wild West saloon décor of six months ago, his last time here, had been changed to that of a bordello as depicted in movies and maybe in reality—wall-to-wall carpet, velveteen drapes, and satin skirt around the stage, all in the purplish pink color of an excited penis. A John Wayne fan, he preferred the saloon, but it didn't really matter. He wasn't here for décor, but for escape. When he finished the drink, he flagged down one of the cocktail waitresses and ordered two more, which should get him through the first show. Then he'd order a few more for the second show. He'd never hit a woman before, but only a physical impossibility would prevent it tonight.

At five minutes to show time, the thirty stools pulled up to the stage—fifteen on each side—were occupied by men laughing and teasingly vying for elbow room. Those who arrived too late to get a stool sat at tables like Robert's. All of them wore suits or sports coats, most of which were cheap, having been purchased mainly to comply with the club's dress code. Amid raised, excited voices, cocktail waitresses scurried around with drinks and stacks of dollar bills to be given in exchange for larger bills before the show began.

At eight o'clock, recorded music with a Latin beat came over the sound system. Amid catcalls and cheers, eight dancers pranced up the steps of the stage. They cha-cha'd across it single file until they were positioned so every man on a stool was within-board-inghouse reach of one of them. Their costumes—bikinis jazzed up with tassels, rhinestones, and feathers—differed in color, which made it easy for even a drunk man to spot his favorite during the break and buy her a drink. Robert was most attracted to the brunette in the red, the color of Helene's dress their last night together.

When the music changed to hard-core bump and grind, the whistles and catcalls gave way to what the men had really come for. "Over here, honey," or "Got a hot one for you, baby," or 'Come to papa, blondie. The dancer nearest to the caller would shimmy over to him smiling, squat so he could tuck dollar bills into her costume, then turn to dance for the men on the other side of the stage. When more than one man summoned the same dancer at the same time, a spirited feigned competition ensued. They knew they would get as many turns as they had bills and made a show of teasing as they did their tucking.

Life in all its fullness, Robert thought. A lot of people would find the scene disgusting. Cattle at the trough, they would call it. But he was a realist, not a judge, and knew what men wanted and deserved. He'd bet that most of these men had families and worked hard kissing somebody's ass, or getting theirs kicked as he had that day, in order to bring home the bacon. And their reward when moonlight fell across the bed was tepid sex. What was the point of life if once in a while a man couldn't press a dollar bill into a tender young thigh or firm young breast? Age twenty-five was the club's advertised maximum.

None of the dancers could hold a candle to Helene, Robert thought as he finished the last of his fourth drink. Helene was sexier as she walked across a restaurant to the ladies' room than any of these women, and they were trying their hardest. He remembered how aroused he'd been when he and Helene returned to her place after the Beau Rivage that night. He'd handled their ending badly. Too abrupt. One or two more dates wouldn't have hurt anything.

He skirted the room and went to the phone booth in the dark, smoky hall behind the stage. He closed the door and dialed Helene's number, his tenseness increasing with each ring. No answer. She'd probably already left town with her rancher, already had a horse, a closet full of cowgirl jackets, and hand-tooled boots. He lit a cigarette, thought a few seconds, then dialed the number of the fancy restaurant where she worked.

"She's on a break, Robert," her friend Suzie said.

Robert's insides relaxed. Her rich rancher must be out of the picture or she wouldn't still be working.

"Call her to the phone, will you, good-looking? I'm not at a place where she can call me back."

"It'll take a minute. She went out back for a smoke."

"I'll hold." She would come. She would have been too proud

to phone him, but she'd be glad he was calling.

As he waited in a cloud of cigarette smoke, he began to cough—a deep cough that hurt his chest and throat, still tender from the hospital ordeal. He opened the door to the booth to let out the smoke, but his coughing continued. Coffin nails, he thought. Everyone joked about it. Harris had said it was no joke and nagged him and Elizabeth to quit. He remembered seeing a girl about Ellen's age smoking in the Teen Room on July 4th, and it occurred to him that Ellen might be smoking too. Or about to start. He'd lecture her about it tomorrow and she would obey him. A good girl...Ellen, whom he'd promised...He hung up and returned to his table. Two more drinks, he thought, and he'd be drunk enough to go home.

# *Seventeen*

It was an evening of quickening sounds—the clatter of her mother's mules pacing the house, the splats of rain blown against the kitchen window, Fifi's sudden barks for no apparent reason. The sounds unnerved Ellen, who stood at the stove teaching Wendy how rain was made. She was keeping an ear out for her father's car and her mother's whereabouts. Her mother had burst in twice within the hour to ask Ellen essentially the same questions: Was she positive her father said eight? Positive he didn't say who he was going to have a drink with or where? Positive he didn't mention a meeting with some judges? Ellen said yes, she was positive, but Elizabeth snarled that she probably hadn't listened to him carefully.

Her father frequently came home late after work, so Ellen couldn't understand why her mother was so upset, especially since she'd been happy all afternoon as they dug up the ground to prepare for their garden.

Splat. Another gust against the window. Ellen, startled, dropped the ice cube she'd been about to put in a pitcher. Fifi chased it across the floor. Wendy hopped off Dessie's stool and yanked the cube from the dog's mouth. "No, Fifi. Bad for your teeth." She was repeating her mother's admonition to her.

"Ssh. Not so loud. You'll bother Mama."

Back on the stool, Wendy dropped the cube in a pitcher next to the stove. "I want to count."

"Go ahead." Wendy's curls glistened in the light from the stove hood as she bent over the pitcher counting the cubes. Ellen wondered if Madame Curie had had a younger sister whom she taught science stuff like this. She certainly wouldn't have had a mother who paced around in a huff when her husband was late from work.

A few minutes later, bubbles began rolling over each

other in little fighting spits. Ellen said it was time and held the pitcher slightly above the pot. The pitcher was soon enveloped by a gray haze.

"It's smoking," Wendy said.

"Not exactly. That's steam from the water." Ellen raised the pitcher a few inches. "See how the steam bunches all together. That's what a cloud is. Watch carefully now, any minute you'll see—"

"What the hell are you doing?" Their mother clomped across the floor to the stove, her red silk lounging pants billowing around her legs, and turned off the burner. "You're going to burn the house down."

"We was making rain," Wendy said. "You messed it up."

"You told me to keep her busy, so I was showing how rain is made."

"You know better than to use the stove unsupervised. Take her upstairs and keep her busy until bedtime. But first, have you remembered anything else your father said?"

"No. I told you everything."

Her mother exhaled in frustration. "Then tell me at least how he sounded?"

"Well…like Daddy."

"Damn it, Ellen. You know what I mean—happy, sad, tired?"

"None of that, really. Just ordinary." A sort of lie. He had sounded tired until she told him about her mother and Mrs. Simmons that morning. Then he fired off questions about it. But if she mentioned it, her mother would hound her further.

"Well, it's two hours later than what he told you." Her mother glared at Ellen as though his lateness was her fault.

"Maybe he had a flat tire and nobody stopped to help him in the rain," Ellen said.

"And maybe there's a Santa Claus. You're always looking for excuses for him."

"Is Santa Claus coming tonight?" Wendy said.

"Get off that stool before you fall. You know by now, Ellen, to call me to the phone when he's on the line. See what happens when you don't?"

"Yes, ma'am. I'm sorry." She didn't dare mention that he'd told her not to.

"Take Wendy upstairs and keep her busy."

Wendy sat cross-legged on the carpet in Ellen's bedroom with Fifi lying next to her. She peered into the glass jar Ellen had given her that afternoon, containing a dozen or so roly-polys, and began to sing: "Roly-poly under a rock. Now I find you in my sock. You can curl up in a—"

"Be quiet, I'm trying to hear. And anyway I've told you I hate that stupid song." Ellen sat on her bed scribbling down the lyrics of "Lonely Boy" as it played on her record player.

"I can sing it if I want." Wendy raised the jar above her head and looked through the bottom, hoping to see dozens of tiny feet crawling around. "Wake up, wake up," she said, shaking the jar, but the little gray balls, dull as BBs, simply rolled around. "They're not crawling like you said. See?" She opened the jar and tilted it toward Ellen.

"They're probably dead. Why did you put the lid on? I told you not to until I punched holes in it. You've killed them."

"I kilt them? I didn't mean it," Wendy said with a sniffle, and began to cry.

Good grief. Ellen tossed her pad on the bed and pretended to examine the corpses.

"They're not dead. They're just scared. I guess they don't like being in a jar. I'll put them in the yard when it stops raining."

"But you said they would crawl and I could see their feet through the glass. Now I don't have anything to do. Let's play with my jewelry kit."

"It's too late. We'd just get the beads laid out and then it would be time for bed."

"Mama said you have to keep me busy. I'm going to tell."

"What? You would do that after I tried to teach you to make rain?"

Wendy nodded. "Mama said."

"Then I've got news for you about those roly—" She stopped

at the sound of the front door opening.

"Daddy's home," Wendy said and scrambled to her feet.

"No. Stay here. I'm warning you," Ellen said. She turned off her record player so she'd be able to hear them.

"Where have you been? You told Ellen eight o'clock and I've been worried sick. What happened at Judge Keefer's?"

"Just what you wanted."

"So they're not going to have a formal hearing?"

"That's right. They wouldn't have had one anyway—Keefer believed what I told him, but I still had to kiss Simmons's ass, and I'll have to keep kissing it thanks to you."

"Ooh. Daddy said a bad word. Why does he sound funny?"

"Hush."

"Why thanks to me? What are you talking about?"

"You know damn well. 'Oh, Marjorie, ask your hubby to be nice to Robert 'cause he was taking Benzedrine.' Simmons told Keefer about the Benzedrine, and both of them were so worked up about my well- being, a pretense on Simmons's part, that Keefer dropped the matter with the condition that I agreed to Simmons's dictates about my workload. If word gets out about the Benzedrine, I won't have a law practice, damn you."

Ellen's skin had crawled when he mocked her mother's voice. Even slurring badly, his tone was hateful. She didn't know he could be like that. What had her mother done?

"Get away from me, Elizabeth. I'll get my pajamas and sleep in the den."

Ellen heard his rapid footsteps up the stairs, and her mother's pleading voice fast behind him. "I was only trying to help."

"And instead you've probably ruined me. I told you this morning to trust me, goddamn it."

"Daddy's mad, isn't he?"

"Hush."

Through the gap of her door, Ellen saw him go into their bedroom, her mother following. The door slammed.

"Stay here. I'm going to listen at the grate," Ellen said, referring to the heating register halfway down the hall.

"Noooo. I'm scared."

"Dang it, Wendy." Ellen closed the door. She dug her stamp album from the closet and sat on her bed to show it to Wendy. Grandfather Townsend had helped her begin it shortly after Grandmother Townsend died, but she hadn't looked at it in a long time and couldn't remember where most of the stamps were from, though she pretended to. "This one's from Africa where lions live. This one's from Egypt where they have hootchie-coochie dancers, and this—"

"Robert, listen to me, please."

Their voices were louder than normal. Her father said something Ellen couldn't hear clearly, then her mother cried out "I did it for you. I didn't think she would mention the—" She broke off sobbing.

"Can you really be that stupid, Elizabeth? To think that telling Marjorie, or anyone, about the Benzedrine was harmless? I'm half a breath away from hitting you, so I'm leaving."

"Uh-oh. Daddy called Mama stupid and he's gonna hit her."

"Don't pay any attention to them. Daddy's had too much to drink. This stamp is from France like Fifi. That should be her picture instead of—"

"Please don't leave."

"Don't touch that suitcase!"

Wendy pulled Fifi to her lap and rocked back and forth. Ellen, who'd hurried to her record player, told her to stick her fingers in her ears until the music started.

"But I have to go to the bathroom. And I'm afraid to go alone."

Ellen groaned. They would have to pass their parents' room, which meant a possible encounter, but Wendy had a nervous bladder, and making her wait, worsened it. Ellen took her sister's hand. "Tiptoe, and don't talk."

On the toilet, Wendy looked as though she was sitting in an inner tube—fanny hanging into the bowl, knees thrust upward, and legs draped over the seat. Ellen gestured for her to be quiet and put her ear to the wall adjacent to her parents' room.

"Move before I make you. I need to get in that drawer."

"For God's sake, Robert, don't do this. You're drunk, and I can see by your pupils that you've taken those pills again. You don't know what you're doing. Go ahead, sleep in the den. I'll let you alone, but realize that I had to do it. What if the deputy had heard…your silk pajamas! Why would you want…You son of a bitch. You never intended to go to Atmore, and that business about the lodge and your feeling guilty was a lie. You're using this Simmons thing as an excuse to go to—"

"Get out of my way."

"No. You can't go. I won't let you."

There was a thud, then sounds of scuffling—grunts and groans, bumps into furniture and thuds against the wall. Their bedroom door flew open and hit the hall wall with a bang. Ellen opened the bathroom door to see her father running down the stairs with his overnight case, her mother in pursuit. She hurried to look over the balcony as Wendy hobbled toward her, trying to pull up her underpants.

Her mother reached her father in the entry hall before he could open the door. She grabbed his suitcase, and he struggled to pry her hands off. They reeled in one direction and then another with the red silk of her mother's lounging pants whipping around like flames. Finally, with a loud "umph," her father jerked the case free, which sent her mother careening into the hall table. The glass vase holding Mrs. Simmons's flowers crashed to the marble floor. As her father ran out, his dark hair shone in the porch light for an instant like the pelt of a wild animal. Ellen felt a flicker of happiness, then the pain of his leaving. She wanted to cry out, "Wait for me."

The blue shade of the lamp on Ellen's nightstand cast a blue tint on Wendy's sleeping figure and the Madame Alexander doll in her arm. In the best of times, Wendy was not an easy bedmate. She chattered to Ellen or Fifi or to herself, until she fell asleep, and once asleep, she kicked like a mule. Usually Ellen didn't let Wendy sleep with her, but she took pity on her that night. And now was glad she had. She felt the warmth of Wendy's body.

Ellen lay for a long time wondering where her father had gone and what would happen next. After a while, she tiptoed down the hall toward the bathroom, forgot the creaky board under the carpet, and stepped on it.

"Ellen, come in."

Her mother was perched on the edge of the bed in a faded blue nightgown, arms encircling her stomach as though in pain. Her eyes were red and puffy, and her thick hair was matted and jutting out in all directions.

"I guess you heard. He's gone off with some woman."

"But it sounded like you did something that made him really mad. Maybe he wanted you to think he had another woman just to punish you."

"That's right, Ellen. Blame me. But you're wrong. I made a mistake, which he knows I thought would help him, and he's using it as an excuse. He's tired of me and wants someone who is…" Her voice broke, and she covered her face with her hands.

I should feel sorry for her, Ellen thought as she watched the heaving shoulders. I should reach out and touch her arm like Dessie or Mrs. Taylor would do. She looked around at the disarray. Two drawers from her father's highboy lay overturned on the carpet, the dresser lamp lay on the floor, and an ashtray had spilled on a nightstand. "Do you want me to straighten up in here?"

Her mother shook her head and blew her nose on a crumpled tissue. "Your face is a stone, Ellen. You don't feel anything for me, do you? But think of this: his leaving me means he's leaving you too. So what do you think of your hero now?"

"Kind of what I said. That he was trying to get even with you for whatever you did. He'll come back."

Her mother sat up straight and gave a bitter two-note chortle. "Over my dead body. He's made his choice, and any judge will back me on that. Go on now."

When Ellen returned to her room, she opened the window that looked over the porte cochere, for she wanted to hear if her father came back that night. Her mother's words about his making his choice and any judge backing her up sounded like she was planning on a divorce. Her father needed to know that, so he could talk her out of it. This girl at school whose parents' got divorced could see her father only on holidays. She eased into bed and carefully released the doll from Wendy's grasp so she wouldn't roll on it. Then she turned onto her stomach, and glancing to ensure that Wendy was still asleep, stuck her pillow between her legs and rocked.

# *Eighteen*

Elizabeth shimmied the shovel blade under the roots and tossed the chunk of grass and earth aside. At five in the morning the sky was a shallow darkness except for a few weak silvery stars. She didn't need light. The ground, at least, was where it was supposed to be. Shovel and toss. The shoveling would have been harder had the ground not been damp from last night's rain. Still, her face, neck, and arms were slick with perspiration.

For hours after Robert left, Elizabeth had lain in bed drenching one Kleenex after another. Then she'd remembered how her uncle stopped her crying spells when she was a teenager. "Get off that pity pot and get to work," by which he meant physical labor on the so-called farm. The labor turned out to be an antidote to self-pity. As it was now. Each bladeful of roots tossed aside felt like she was sloughing off the soft, vulnerable layer of herself and getting to the hardness that would sustain her.

After a while, she paused and lit a cigarette. The sky had lightened to grey, and she saw for the first time the results of her three-hour effort: irregular sections dug out helter-skelter across the yard, only one of them contiguous to the garden area she and Ellen had dug the day before. Sondra Miller would be amused. "Our little farm girl gone off her rocker," she would say, or something like it. To hell with Sondra and the rest of Mobile society, except for Glo. An attractive divorced man would be on everyone's guest list, but a divorced woman had the social status of a collard patch. For a heart-pounding instant, she imagined Robert walking up the terraced steps of the club with a shapely young thing on his arm.

Elizabeth tossed the cigarette and shoved the blade into the ground again. She was over the son of a bitch. No more tears. It was her gullibility at his deception that stung her the most—the thought of her wasted efforts, emotions, and sacrifices. She would make him pay.

Dessie came at seven, and Elizabeth went in the house with her for coffee. When Dessie praised her for working on the garden so early, she explained it was because she couldn't sleep. "I don't give a damn about the garden, Dessie. Mr. Townsend left me last night for another woman. I'm sure the girls will tell you about it. I'd appreciate it if you'd keep them out of my hair for a day or two."

At nine o'clock, Elizabeth phoned Robert's office, eager to tell him she was going to divorce him. When Ruth said he hadn't come in yet, Elizabeth told her it was critical that he call her right away. She called again at ten, and Ruth said he still hadn't arrived. The son of a bitch must have had a big night. Even hung over, Robert was always at his desk by ten. She dragged herself up the stairs and lay on his side of the bed to be near the phone. She closed her eyes and fell asleep.

When Elizabeth woke around three, she called his office again.

"Still haven't heard from him, Mrs. Townsend. He could have come in and left again while I was at the dentist, although I left him a message to call you."

Probably lying, Elizabeth thought. He could be standing at her desk giving signals. "Oh God, Ruth," she said, making her voice quiver. "Wendy's been in an accident and I need to reach him."

"Oh my, let me look at his calendar…Nothing listed for today. But he has a plea bargaining at nine tomorrow in Department Five. He could be at the DA's office now working on the plea."

Elizabeth hung up and called Carl.

"He's not here, Elizabeth, and I don't expect him. We've already agreed to the plea bargain on the calendar for him tomorrow, so we don't need to talk about it. It's the Puckett plea that was postponed the day he got sick. You sound upset. Is something wrong?"

"No. I was hoping he'd…yes, there is something wrong. We had a fight last night and he left to go to some woman. I need to find him. Do you know anything about his having a mistress or something like that?"

The long pause told her he did. "I thought he might."

"Damn, Carl. You should have told me. For how long? Who is she?"

"I don't know. He never mentioned it. Little things gave me that impression, that's all. I'm sorry."

"A lot of good that does me. Did you tell Glo?"

"It bothered me, so yes I told her. You know how close we are."

"How sweet," Elizabeth said, and hung up. She imagined Carl and Glo talking about it: "Poor Elizabeth. Do you think she suspects?" "I wonder where he met her?" "How long do you think he's been seeing her?" A titillating topic for marrieds. Good for foreplay. The brass silent butler that the Taylors gave them for Christmas clanged as it hit the bottom of the metal wastebasket. How could Glo, her best friend, who'd taught her and encouraged her and laughed with her about Mobile society, have kept it from her? She heard her uncle's voice: "To see the only person you can trust, look in the mirror." Sometimes the son of a bitch had been right.

That night Elizabeth bathed in water close to scalding, for the pain was a welcome distraction. As she dried off, she scrutinized her figure in the mirror. Her tan was striking, but the areas her bathing suit covered were sickly white and appalling—blaring stretch marks on her breasts, jiggling cellulite on her buttocks, and worst, a stomach that in profile looked like a fourth or fifth-month pregnancy. She'd known she was gaining weight this last year, but Dr. Harris said it was middle-age spread and she shouldn't worry. Fine advice for a woman married to a faithful husband, but not for a middle-aged divorcee. Who would want her now? When she got into bed she was too exhausted to cry or rage.

Elizabeth arrived at the courthouse the next morning at eight o'clock in case Robert came early. She wore the sophisticated beige walking suit she wore when shopping in New Orleans. She couldn't compete in the realm of young and voluptuous, but Glo said once that she looked statuesque in that suit, an effect that had its own appeal. She'd woken with renewed anger. Robert may have been too drunk to realize how much his leaving would hurt her, but he would have sobered up for this hearing, and he still hadn't contacted her. She stood on the landing at the top of the courthouse steps, which was the best vantage point to spot him. She would tell him she'd come downtown to hire a lawyer for a divorce in which she would get enormous alimony and custody of the girls and he wouldn't be allowed to visit them.

By eight-thirty there was a steady flow of people trickling in. Elizabeth took note of the camaraderie of the lawyers, their briefcases making them easy to identify. They hailed each other, shook hands, and chatted and laughed as they gathered in pairs or clusters as jovially as if going to a ballgame. She'd always imagined lawyers, including Robert, to be tense and preoccupied with their cases before court, but that wasn't so. The outgoing Robert would be in the thick of them, thoroughly enjoying himself. His enthusiasm for life would stay the same after their divorce, except for his missing the girls. But hers wouldn't. She would wake up miserable every morning with nothing to look forward to.

The merry chatter of the lawyers felt like pinpricks to her now. The girls and his money were not enough to get even with him. But she knew what would be. She would tell Judge Keefer what he'd done in the Fry trial. That would be perfect.

Although it wasn't like Robert to be late for court, Elizabeth waited on the steps until quarter after nine. Maybe she'd missed him. Inside, she asked directions to Department Five. Through the glass panel in the courtroom door she saw a judge she didn't recognize on the bench, with three men standing before him, two in suits and one in a jail uniform. From behind, none of the men she saw were Robert—not enough hair, shoulders too broad, neck too short. But that was only one side of the courtroom. She tiptoed in and took a seat in the back row on the other side of the room. In a minute or so she spotted his wavy dark hair, narrow shoulders, and the tan suit he'd worn the night he left. She eagerly anticipated his reaction to her plan for revenge. He would see that he couldn't take her for a fool.

The men in front of the judge left, and the clerk called, "State of Alabama versus James Puckett."

Puckett. That was Robert's case—the boy whose plea session had to be postponed. She waited for Robert to rise as a deputy led a frail- looking young man in a jail uniform from the jury box to stand before the judge.

"Is defendant's counsel present?" the judge said as he looked out at the courtroom. "Mr. Townsend, are you here?" When no one responded, the judge said the case was continued until the plea session next week. Elizabeth watched with alarm as the deputy returned the boy to the box. Something bad must have happened to Robert, or he would be here. He'd said he'd felt so guilty about letting that boy down before that he wasn't going to charge him a dime.

Elizabeth hurried from the courtroom to the phone in the lobby. Still not heard from at home or office. Her hand trembled as she lit a cigarette on the courthouse steps. Not a car accident or the police would have called. He must be drunk or doped up on Benzedrine despite Harris' warnings. She had to find him before he collapsed again or something worse. Whoever he was with might be too stupid or inebriated to call an ambulance.

The hallway of the Bail Bond building was rank with the odor of perspiration, and so dimly lit that Elizabeth had to squint to read the nameplates on the doors. The first was the investigator Robert sometimes used, so she knocked on the door of the other: Morris White. She cringed as she sat in the chair opposite his desk in the smoky cubbyhole of a room. Some of his teeth overlapped, and he wore a transparent nylon shirt under which his chest hair looked like moss. He was a stereotype right out of *True Detective*.

To avoid looking like a stereotype herself, Elizabeth sat in her most ladylike posture and spoke with composure as she told him the circumstances: Robert leaving Tuesday night drunk and angry at her and having taken the pills that had hospitalized him the week before.

"He gave me the impression that he was leaving to go to some woman, but I don't think he knew what he was doing. I'm afraid he's still taking those pills and they could kill him. I need to find him as soon as possible."

"I see," said Mr. White. "I need to ask you some questions."

Aside from the basics—description of Robert, model of his car, favorite bars, and the like—the man's questions annoyed her: the names and dates of Robert's previous liaisons, the names of attractive women in their social circle, and other women she'd had suspicions about. She told him about Huntsville, although she didn't see how it mattered so many years later.

"Look, Mr. White, I don't think you understand. I'm not your typical jealous wife. Robert is not a philanderer, or I wouldn't be married to him. One instance in fifteen years is not philandering."

"One instance that you're sure of. A wife can usually triple that number. And he may well have gone to some woman night before last. You need to realize that even if he was drunk and on pills, he knew what he was doing. It's not liquor or pills that cause a man to stray. It's his particular nature. Some men are—."

Elizabeth stood. "Never mind, Mr. White. I'll find him myself."

Ruth was walking out the door, handbag on her arm, as Elizabeth arrived. She still hadn't heard from Mr. Townsend and was miffed when Elizabeth said she'd gone to the plea session. "His calendar is confidential, Mrs. Townsend. I only mentioned the hearing because you said it was a family emergency and I thought you might find him at the DA's office."

"This *is* a family emergency. He's off with some woman, and the danger is that he's still taking the pills that put him in the hospital, so I need to find him as soon as possible. Do you know anything that might help?"

"No. And besides, my professional loyalties are with him."

Elizabeth stepped forward to block her. "For God's sake, Ruth, what could be more loyal than saving his life? Those pills could kill him. You weren't surprised when I mentioned another woman, so you know something. Please, tell me."

"Well…a young woman came maybe two or three weeks ago at lunchtime, no appointment or anything. He took her into his office before I could get her name. She was dressed more for a party than business. She said hello when she walked in, and I thought I recognized the voice from a couple of phone calls. It might not be anything, Mrs. Townsend."

"All right. Thanks. Go ahead to lunch. I need to use the phone. I'll lock the door behind me when I leave."

Anger swelled in Elizabeth as she looked around the reception area. She had carefully decorated it to be "masculine and dramatic" as Robert requested: maroon leather sofa, glass-topped mahogany coffee table, a huge oil painting of a three-masted schooner on a storm-tossed sea. She'd decorated his inner office too—the credenza, the bookcase, the artful framing of his license, diplomas and awards, and family photo. The office was like an extension of their home, yet in the middle of the day when he wouldn't have been influenced by liquor or pills, he had let that woman come here. He was probably with her now. The concern she'd felt for his welfare disappeared. She was going to track him down and make him sorry.

The door to Robert's private office was locked. Not having the key, Elizabeth smashed the glass panel with the heel of her shoe. She thrust her arm through the opening to grab the knob and instantly felt pain. A shard lodged in the frame had scratched the underside of her forearm, making a shallow trench that quickly filled with blood. Inside his office, she yanked off her half-slip and managed to wrap it around the cut. She rifled through the papers on his desk looking for clues—a phone number on a scrap of napkin, a matchbook cover, a florist bill, a love note. Next were the desk drawers and the pockets of the jackets in the closet. In his suede jacket, she found a woman's scarf, a cheap one judging from the flimsy fabric and gaudy colors. She stuffed the scarf back in the pocket and hurried to the elevator with the jacket draped over her wound.

"Nice to see you, Mrs. Townsend," Hi-Jinx said, looking up from his customer's shoes as Elizabeth rushed past.

Dr. Harris' voice seemed to come from far away. Only the smelling salts his nurse held under her nose kept Elizabeth from fainting.

"Why the hell didn't you call a locksmith, Elizabeth?" he said when he finished stitching. "I would think you'd have better sense."

"There was no time. Like I told you, my friend's dog was suffocating in that hot car."

"You're going to wish you'd let it when this local wears off. Do you want to call Robert or someone to come take you home?"

"No. I can drive."

"Well, here's a sample of pain pills so you don't have to stop at the drugstore. Get home before you take them. They'll knock you out."

Elizabeth's suit and the suede jacket were smeared with blood. She hurried up the stairs to her bedroom as soon as she came in the house so the girls wouldn't see her, then called down for Dessie to come up. "I tripped and fell on some glass," she told Dessie who helped her change into an old nightgown, then she told her to throw the suit and jacket away.

"This looks like a nice jacket, Miz Elizabeth. Too small for Lester, but I reckon my nephew could use it."

"Suit yourself." It struck her then that Dessie, like Ruth, hadn't seemed surprised when she told her that Robert had left her for another woman. "Dessie, have you suspected Mr. Townsend might have a woman?"

"Can't say that exactly, but I saw some hairs on his undershirt a time or two that weren't none of yours."

"Damn it, Dessie, you should have told me."

"I can't go interfering where it ain't my business, Miz Elizabeth. But I'm sorry. I surely am."

"Don't be sorry for me. I'll get even. I'll be asleep in a minute—some pain pills Dr. Harris gave me—and probably won't hear the phone. Wake me if Mr. Townsend calls."

Carl, Glo, Ruth, and Dessie, Elizabeth thought. Four people who knew or suspected, and no telling how many others. Maybe it was already a topic of conversation at the club. Elizabeth reached for the scarf which she'd laid on the bedspread and angrily balled it up in her fist. Robert wouldn't have worn his suede jacket since early February when they had their last cold spell. So he had known the woman as far back as that, and maybe before then. She tried to remember the last time they had had sex, but she felt like a thousand horses were dragging her from consciousness and closed her eyes.

# *Nineteen*

Wendy was more high-strung than usual the two days after Robert left. It was as though she couldn't stop talking, which was mostly to Ellen.

"What happened to Mama's arm?"

"You heard Dessie say she fell on some glass."

"Why did Mama dig the garden bigger while we was sleeping?"

"You asked me that yesterday."

"What did you tell me?"

"Because she couldn't sleep and wanted something to do."

"Why did she make it look all messy?"

"Because she was tired."

"If she was tired, why couldn't she sleep?"

"That's enough, dang it. Stop pestering me."

"Well, when is Daddy coming back?"

"I've told you three times I don't know. You think I know everything but I don't, so stop asking."

When her father left night before last, Ellen felt sure he'd gone to a hotel to cool off and would come back the next morning at the latest. And last night, she was sure he would know they were worried and would come home today. But it was almost suppertime. She had to admit to herself that maybe he had gone to Sleeping Beauty's to get back at her mother, and was probably still with her because he was too drunk to leave. Ruthie's father, who drank a lot before he died, would sometimes disappear for days because he wasn't sober enough to get home. "Off on a toot," Mrs. Kelly would say.

The girls sat on boxes at Ellen's worktable looking into a five-gallon glass jar in front of them. Suspended in the mouth of the jar was a metal funnel full of rich deep earth, with Ellen's gooseneck lamp positioned so the light warmed it. Insects rarely seen because they preferred cool soil would burrow deeper for it and fall through the spout. Ellen had set the apparatus up to keep Wendy from waking her mother. So far, only a couple of small everyday spiders had fallen through.

"I haven't seen any scary spiders like you said, and I'm bored. You could show me how to tell time."

"Not now. I'm thinking about something, so be quiet."

Wendy hopped off the box, sat on the concrete floor, and whispered to Fifi that they had to be quiet.

Ellen's thoughts went back to her parents. She felt more and more sure that her mother was going to get a divorce and keep her and Wendy from seeing their father. Maybe that's what she was up to today after she left the house early, all dressed up. Even though her mother would probably yell at her, she would ask her when she woke. Ellen looked at her watch. Six thirty. Possibly she was awake now.

"I bet Dessie's got supper ready, Wendy. Let's go in."

Ellen saw her mother on the phone in the den through the French doors. Her heart quickened. Must be her father. Who else would her mother bother to talk to when she was in pain which Dessie had cautioned them about when they came in? (So y'all be quiet as you can.)

Ellen tiptoed through the living room to the French doors on the other side of the den, where her mother wouldn't see her, and pressed her ear to the glass.

"I'm not accustomed to hiring investigators, Mr. White, so I don't have that much cash lying around. I'll bring it to your office when the bank opens at nine, along with a picture of him, as you mentioned."

Ellen's heart sank. A private investigator. "Bottom feeders," her father called them because they lived on other people's dirt and would do anything to find it, he said.

"It's not custody I'm worried about—mothers always get it. I want to make sure he's not even allowed to visit the girls. So get pictures. You know the kind."

Ellen took a deep breath and opened the door. "Mama, no."

Her mother turned to her with a scowl. "Quite the sneak, aren't you," she said when she'd hung up. "I've done some sneaking too. I found out he's had another woman since February at least and no telling how long before. I told you he wanted someone younger. He doesn't love me anymore."

"Yes, he does," Ellen said. "He told me he loves you, not her. He said he was going to drop her like a hot potato."

"What the hell are you talking about?"

Ellen told her how she and her father met the woman after a Mardi Gras parade, and how she'd seen them together in his office when she went to get him for lunch that day, and how she told him July 4th that she'd seen them together. "That's when he said the part about loving you and dropping her." He hadn't said the love part, but it felt like the right thing to say.

"Damn it, Ellen. Why didn't you tell me about her when... never mind, I'll deal with you later. What's her name?"

"I don't know. He called her Sleeping Beauty because she was on a float called Sleeping Beauties of the Coast. Please don't send that man to find him. I heard you tell Daddy when he left that he was drunk and had taken some pills and didn't know what he was doing. I bet he's still that way and that's why he hasn't come home or called. I'm sure he left just to punish you and he'll come home when he's able. Please talk to him before you do anything."

"I can't talk to him if I don't know where he is."

"I know where he is if he's with that hussy," Ellen said after a pause. "Although we had just met her, she asked for a ride home, which was all the way to Pascagoula."

"Are we going to a party?" Wendy asked as their car backed down the driveway. Ellen looked over the seat at Wendy, and put her finger to her lips.

"You know we're not. Now be quiet."

"Then why did I have to wear my party dress?"

"Hush. No more talking."

Ellen knew. Her mother wanted to make her father as sorry

as possible that he was losing them, so she wore the green silk dress he liked, and had insisted Ellen wear her sailor dress, and Wendy wear her yellow organdy frock. Ellen wished she hadn't mentioned Pascagoula. Now she thought her mother was too furious for anything good to come of it, and she was afraid.

As the car turned onto Government Street, a bark came from the backseat. So that's why Wendy had run to the car and climbed in back, when she always clamored for the front.

"Damn you, Wendy. You knew better. I'm not taking her home. One more peep and I'll put her out."

"But she'll get runned over."

"You heard me."

"I'll get in back and help keep her quiet," Ellen said. This angry, her mother might really put the dog out.

"No. You can spot the place more easily from where you are."

Ellen looked longingly at each of the familiar landmarks they passed—Weinacker's, Lafayette Library, St. Catherine's, Ladd Stadium. If only she could reach out and anchor herself to any of them. When they passed the club, she felt a knot in her stomach when she thought of her father's reassuring words on July Fourth.

"So was your little talk with him before or after the fireworks?"

"Before. When he came to the Teen Room to get me for supper."

"And you still believe every word he said, don't you?"

"Yes."

"Well, you shouldn't. He was with her the night before he went to the hospital, and that was after he told you he would dump her. Plus, he left night before last to go back to her, so he still hadn't dumped her. His leaving had nothing to do with punishing me. No man would leave his wife simply because she'd made an honest mistake. Do you believe me?"

"I don't know." It was hard to believe her father had broken his word.

Her mother's cut-glass eyes glinted at Ellen for an instant. "You'd lie down in front of a train before you would say anything bad about him, wouldn't you?"

"Where's the train? I want to see the train too."

"There is no train, Wendy. Now, be quiet."

In another ten minutes, the sky, which had been cloudy all afternoon, ripped open and the rain sounded like a band of pygmies drumming on the roof. Ellen felt hopeful. Her mother hated driving in the rain after dark and might turn back, especially with her arm hurting so badly that she groaned when she had to raise it to hold the wheel. A glance at her mother said no such luck. Her eyes were fixed on the headlight beams like the road ahead was an animal she was determined to run down. The rain tapered off in another few minutes, and then the car was silent until they saw Uncle's Corner.

"That's where we were going to get a belly wash when we took that fancy woman home at Mardi Gras, remember Sissy? But it was closed. The lights are on now. Mama, can we stop? I'm thirsty. Pleeeease."

"No. Be quiet. So, Ellen, he'd been going to stop for refreshments. That sounds more like a social event than just driving her home. There's no telling what else you haven't told me. How many times did you see them together?"

"Just what I said—after that Mardi Gras parade and at his office that day."

"Don't lie to me."

"I'm not."

"You said you'd seen them kiss. Did they kiss a long time? Were his arms around her? I want to know exactly what you saw."

"It was hard to see details through that orangey glass. You know how it's wavy. It was like trying to see someone under water."

"Surely you could tell if they were embracing."

" Yes, I guess they were."

"You saw that, then lied to keep me from catching them, didn't you?"

"Yes."

Her mother's right hand came fast. Ellen touched her cheek as much in surprise as to salve the pain. Her mother had never done that before. Fifi started barking.

"Shut her up, Wendy. This is my last warning."

When the lights of Pascagoula came into view, Ellen dug her nails into her palms. It had been five months since she'd been here. What if she couldn't find the place? That investigator would find her father and take pictures of him and Sleeping Beauty as her mother asked, and then a judge would think her father was so bad that he shouldn't be allowed to see her and Wendy.

As Ellen directed, they kept on the main thoroughfare, passing gas stations, boat repair places, bait and tackle shops, and a few motels, none of which Ellen recognized. Then came the small downtown of mostly one-story buildings, followed by houses, grocery stores, and schools, then gave way to a stretch of open fields.

"No more town, Ellen. I think you saw the place but changed your mind about showing me, damn you."

"No, I didn't. None of them looked anything like...there," Ellen said, pointing toward an orange neon sign just ahead: Best Deal Motel. Daily, Monthly, Weekly. Kitchenettes.

"Looks awful. Are you sure?"

"Yes." She remembered the ugly orange neon sign and the word "kitchenette" because she'd wondered what it was.

"There's Daddy's car," Wendy said when they turned into the gravel parking lot. The Cadillac was easy to spot among the old cars and pickup trucks.

Ellen's heart skipped a beat. Funny how she'd expected his car to be here yet was shocked to see that it was.

"Daddy-waddy, Daddy-waddy, Da—"

"Hush!" They pulled up next to the Cadillac. It was in front of Unit Eight where light seeped out from around the window blinds.

"Is that it? Number Eight?"

"I don't remember. Probably, since his car is parked here." Ellen had been so glad to get rid of the woman, she'd not paid attention to much else.

"I want to see Daddy-waddy, Daddy—"

"Damn it, Wendy! Shut up!"

"Do you realize it wouldn't have come to this, Ellen, if you'd told me about the woman the day you saw them in his office?"

"Yes, ma'am," she said, although she didn't know for sure.

Her mother got out of the car and banged on the door of Unit Eight. "Your daughters are here, Robert. I'm divorcing you and getting custody, and I thought you'd want to see them one last time." She turned toward the car and gestured for the girls to come.

"Daddy, it's me," Wendy called through the door with Fifi struggling in her arms to get loose.

"For God's sake, Elizabeth. Are you crazy? Take them home," Robert said.

"Listen. He's slurring," Ellen whispered to her mother. "Still drunk like the night he left as I told you. He doesn't know what he's doing."

"He knows he's here instead of at home where he should be. That's all he needs to know." Her mother banged on the door again. "Open up goddamn it."

Ellen glanced toward the front office, which had windows all around. The desk clerk was looking in their direction. Please come and make us leave, Ellen prayed.

Wendy put her mouth to the keyhole playfully as though talking into a walkie-talkie. "Daddy-waddy, I want to see you."

The door opened the width of the chain lock, and a vertical swath of her father's suit pants and bare chest appeared.

"Here I am, Birdsong, but I'm sick and can't—"

"Oh, no!" Wendy cried. Fifi had leapt from her arms and disappeared through the narrow opening."Fi-Fiiiiii." Wendy futilely tried to wedge herself through the gap.

Her father said he would get her, and they heard him calling Fifi in the falsetto voice she usually responded to. Then the swath appeared again, and Robert said he would have to raise the sofa bed to reach her so they should go back to the car and he'd bring her out. "Please, Elizabeth. For God's sake take them home."

"Nooooo. I want Fifi." Wendy began to cry hysterically.

"The desk clerk is looking our way, Robert. Better let us in or this will be in the papers tomorrow."

"Goddamn it, Elizabeth." He opened the door and they filed in.

There, like a life-sized painting suddenly unveiled, was Sleeping Beauty. She sat erect in the sofa bed holding up the sheet to cover her breasts. She didn't look embarrassed or scared like Ellen expected. Only smug. No one spoke or moved. Like a game of statues, Ellen thought as her eyes roamed the room. The Miss Pascagoula banner with its red and gold sequins hung over the open closet door. Her father stood near the sofa bed—hair messy, face unshaven, chest and feet bare. One of his shoes lay nearby, half buried under a lacy black gown, but where was the other? He liked things orderly and always kept his shoes together. His dress shirt lay crumpled on a chair, and his blue-and yellow-tie wound a serpentine path on the dresser between dirty glasses, overflowing ashtrays, perfume bottles and scarves.

Ellen wondered how he could stand such a mess or the stink— stale cigarette smoke, sickly sweet perfume, and something like rotten seaweed. It was more than anger at her mother that had brought him here. It was what he'd said July 4th about middle-aged men and attractive women: "It's like when you can't stop gobbling ice cream on a hot day." She hadn't known then what he meant. But she had a sense of it now, and flushed with shame.

After a few seconds, her mother made a guttural sound that could have been a sob or a laugh of derision. As though it meant statues was over, Wendy dropped to her knees, stuck her head under the bed, and called the dog, her voice sounding tinny, as though it came from the bottom of a bucket. Ellen grabbed the doorknob. She would take Wendy and Fifi to the car.

"She's just a child, Robert. Less than ten years older than Ellen, I bet, and already a whore."

"Don't call me a—"

"Shut up or I'll tear your eyes out." Elizabeth took a step toward the woman.

"Daddy." Ellen looked at her father with alarm.

"Calm down, Elizabeth, and for God's sake, take them home.

Don't you care about your daughters?"

"Don't I care! How dare you? You're the one who's trading them for this piece of trash. How could you choose a whore over two lovely daughters? Get up, Wendy, so he can see how nice you look. Ellen, turn around and model your new dress, the dress you *would* have seen, Robert, had you not been with this whore in your office the day she came to show it to you."

Ellen's eyes met his for an instant. "I showed her here because—"

"Ellen!" her mother exclaimed. "Are you apologizing, for Christ's sake?"

"No. Just to explain."

"Listen, Elizabeth. I'm not trading—"

"Yes, you are. Like I said, I'm divorcing you and getting custody of them. And you're trading your license too. I'm going to tell Judge Keefer what you did in that trial."

Her father started. "But I'll be disbarred." His lips trembled as though he might cry.

Ellen shuddered. She didn't know what her mother was going to tell that judge, but she knew what disbarred meant. It would be horrible.

"Yes, disbarred," her mother said. "You deserve it. You had a right to be angry with me, but not to do what you did. Don't you care how much it hurt me, haven't you thought about—" She stopped. Anger crumbled from her face. She put her hands on his shoulders.

"You're not in your right mind, Robert. Look at you—half naked, glassy eyes, slurring and weaving. And you've been in this hellhole for two days, for God's sake. Please, come to your senses. "This," she said, sweeping her arm around to include the whole room, isn't something you could possibly want. Not this place, and not someone who, in addition to being immoral and willing to destroy a family, didn't have the decency to put on some clothes before your daughters came in. Your being here is the liquor and the pills talking. It breaks my heart. I implore you, come home. I need you. The girls need you."

Ellen was shocked—her mother begging him, no longer angry. "Ellen, tell him you need him. Beg him to come."

Ellen looked down as though she'd spotted something on the carpet. Yes, she needed him, but what was he doing here in the first place? He said he would dump the woman. Had her mother really done something bad enough to deserve his coming here? She looked up at him and said simply "You should come home." She wasn't going to beg.

Her father cleared his throat. "All right, I'll come. Y'all go ahead. I'll be about ten minutes behind you."

"You're in no shape to drive. Come with us and we'll get your car in the morning."

"But Robbie," Sleeping Beauty whined. "What about the divorce?"

"Whore!" Her mother jumped on the bed, straddling the girl with her long legs and slapping her with the hand of her good arm. The girl fought back as she struggled to get away, and the sheet slipped down until it was completely off.

"Look. That woman's nekkid!" cried Wendy, emerging from under the bed.

"Daddy, do something," Ellen said.

"Elizabeth! Helene! Stop!" her father yelled, yet they kept on fighting and screaming. He tried to elbow his way between them, but their flailing arms and legs knocked him off balance. He clutched her mother's sleeve, which ripped when she jerked her arm away to grab Helene's hair.

Somebody could get killed. Ellen stepped forward to help her father stop the fight, but Wendy tugged on her dress.

"Sissy, get Fifi? I can't reach her."

"Not now, and you shouldn't be watching this. Go to the car and I'll bring her in a minute."

"Nooo. Not without—"

"You heard me. Now go or I won't get her ever."

"Okay, okay," Wendy mumbled.

Ellen watched Wendy wrestle with the doorknob a few seconds, and finally leave, closing the door behind her. When she turned back to the fight, her father had plunged in between the women and was trying to separate them and block their blows. Ellen stood still, transfixed by the howling tangle of green silk, long dark hair, bare flesh, and tan trousers tumbling on the bouncing mattress, its springs squeaking loudly. A faint whimper reminded her that Wendy was waiting, and she knelt to look under the bed.

"Here, Fifi." Raisin eyes in a ball of cotton gleamed at her from the far corner of the bed. When the dog didn't budge, Ellen lay on her stomach, her face scraping the carpet, and shimmied forward as far as she could. Her outstretched arms fell a foot or so short. She wiggled her fingers, pretending to have food in her hand, and coaxingly called the dog, but Fifi didn't move. Scared by the squeaking springs and bouncing mattress, Ellen figured. She was too. The frame could collapse any minute.

Someone banged on the door and a voice boomed out, "Open up. It's the sheriff." The door burst open and male voices yelled "Stop, break it up!" Ellen twisted her head toward the black boots and in that instant felt a soft brush of hair across her outstretched forearm. "Fifi!" she shouted as a blur of white flashed across the doorway.

Ellen crawled backwards as fast as she could until her pony tail caught in the coil of a spring. By the time she freed herself and reached the doorway, Fifi was heading toward the road, Wendy was running close behind, and her barefoot father was hop-skip-ping across the gravel yelling for Wendy to stop.

Ellen heard the deep blast of a truck horn and the screeching skid of rubber. Her back pressed against the outside wall of the Best Deal Motel, she saw yellow organdy rise in the air like a butterfly, anomalous in the night sky.

# *Twenty*

The parking lot of the Best Deal Motel filled quickly in the hot, humid night—people from other units and from a nearby cafe, motorists attracted by the gathering crowd. The incredulous tones of their voices rose in the orange-tinted darkness.

"I heard it's a child." "Is the driver drunk?" "Those must be the parents."

In a corner of the lot near the road, a man in overalls beat his fist on the hood of a delivery truck. One of the deputies standing by him laid a hand on his shoulder as though to calm him. A heavyset woman holding a blanket came out of one of the units calling, "I have one," and waddled quickly toward where Wendy lay in the light of the neon sign.

Ellen stood immobile, back still pressed against the building as though impaled on the prickly stucco. She could tell by the manner of her parents and the deputies hovering over Wendy that she wasn't dead, but she wasn't awake either. Wanting both to join her parents and to run the other way, Ellen could do neither.

Sleeping Beauty's scent was strong as she came to the open doorway from the room. She was dressed—shorts and a halter top—and her hair looked freshly brushed, but she was not so pretty now, Ellen saw with satisfaction. The skin around one eye was badly puffed, and her face had scratches too deep for makeup to hide. She coiled a strand of hair around her finger as she looked out. "Must be pretty bad, huh."

"You whore," Ellen said, her mother's word coming to her lips. She pushed Helene against the door jamb and ran to join her parents. She crouched between her kneeling father and her mother, who sat on the gravel with Wendy's head on her outspread-skirt. Wendy's face was turned mostly away from Ellen, but she saw blood running from her nostrils onto her mother's dress. Her father, who'd been saying, "Birdsong, can you hear me?" over and over, glanced at Ellen and muttered "Skogee." Her wild-faced mother was railing at the deputies about where the hell was the ambulance.

Suddenly the shriek of an ambulance split the air, and in seconds a monstrous-looking vehicle—the lower part with sleek lines and rocket fins like her father's car, and the upper part a high hump like the roof of a bus—pulled up within a few yards from them. The huge front grill looked like the teeth of some man-eating ogre and the six headlights, three on each side, like eyes no one could elude. Wendy would be terrified if she woke and saw it. Two young men in dark blue uniforms grabbed some equipment, an oxygen tank and mask the only things Ellen recognized.

A deputy made everyone, even the Townsends, move back so as to not crowd the medics. Ellen craned her head, but couldn't see anything beyond the steady, urgent movements of the medics' backs and arms. They soon rose with Wendy lying on a long board and carried her to the back of the ambulance. Ellen and her parents hurried forward to watch as they laid the board on a gurney. One medic hurried around to the driver's seat and started talking on the radio, while the other one, bending beneath the low ceiling, began to fasten straps to hold Wendy in place. Ducking her head, her mother climbed in. The medic told her there was no room and she was to sit up front, but she plopped down on the metal floor, her back pressed to the back of the passenger's seat, and pulled her knees to her chest. "I'll stay like this, out of your way."

"But the rules—" he said, and stopped. He tossed her a blanket to sit on and told her to hold on to the metal rail that ran along the interior wall the whole time they were in transit. When he closed the back door, Ellen followed her father to the front.

The medic in the driver's seat reached over to open the passenger door. "We're going to Providence Hospital in Mobile, Mr. Townsend. It's the closest for getting a neurosurgeon. Hop in. The sheriff will bring your daughter. "

Her father glanced at his bare feet. "Let me grab—"

"No sir. We can't wait. You can come with the sheriff too."

"I'll go with you." Ellen climbed in.

"Sorry, miss. No one under sixteen can ride as a passenger."

"She is sixteen," her father said, and stepped forward to close the door.

He'd done that at least, Ellen thought, and as they pulled away she turned to see him hop-skipping over the gravel toward the room. If he'd had his shoes on, he might have caught Wendy in time.

"But my husband," came her mother's panicked voice across the seat back.

"The sheriff will bring him, ma'am," the driver said. "Sometimes they get there before we do."

As they wove in and out of town traffic, Ellen leaned forward as though it would help them go faster. When they reached the open road, the driver told her to relax, that it was a fast shot from there.

Ellen looked over the seat toward Wendy but could see only the blanket pulled up to her neck and the oxygen mask the medic held over her face. A few minutes later, when he moved the mask to his left hand to adjust something with his right, Ellen saw that Wendy's head was wrapped in gauze like a mummy's and cradled in a contraption that looked like bookends. To keep her head from moving, Ellen figured. Her head must be broken. Warnings from childhood roared through her mind: "Keep that up and you're going to break your noggin," or "crack your head," or "bust that noodle wide open." She remembered the illustration of Humpty Dumpty having fallen from the wall in their Childcraft book of nursery rhymes—a frowning face on a badly cracked egg-shaped figure lying on the sidewalk.

"Mom, is she going to be all right?" Ellen turned her head as far as she could, trying to see her mother, who glared up at her for an instant, then drew back out of sight. Blames me for not watching Wendy, Ellen thought.

"Your sister's holding, miss," said the medic attending Wendy, "but it's too early to know anything more. We'll be at the hospital soon."

Holding, Ellen thought. Holding on to life is probably what he means. And it was her fault for sending Wendy outside. If Wendy had been in the room when Fifi ran out, she or one of the deputies or even her barefooted father could have caught her. But she'd sent her outside to protect her from seeing the fight, hadn't she? Ellen slumped back in her seat and stared at her reflection in the window. No. There was more to it. She had been thinking to help her father stop the fight when Wendy asked her to get Fifi, so she didn't want to do it right then. But she should have gotten her and gone out with Wendy.

The wind was blowing hard, and the pine trees, which turned red and white in alternation in the sweep of the ambulance lights, seemed to wave ghostly goodbyes as they sped past. Red pines, white pines, red, white. Ellen's head began to swim, and her chin dropped toward her chest.

The driver touched her shoulder. "Bend over, miss, head between your legs. The lights make people dizzy sometimes."

"I'm all right." She wasn't, but she didn't want to be a problem.

"Do what he said."

"Yes ma'am." Relieved that her mother was concerned about her, Ellen gladly bent over.

At the hospital, Ellen hurried to keep up as she and her mother followed the medics pushing the gurney toward the emergency room. Inside, two young men in green uniforms took over, and a hefty middle-aged nurse with arms as big around as Lester's came forward from behind a desk. She had a mustache. Ellen couldn't help but stare. Pale brown hairs and sparse, but still a mustache.

"Mrs. Townsend, I presume," the nurse said in a gravelly voice.

"Of course." Her mother continued toward the gurney, which the men were hurriedly rolling toward some double doors.

The nurse stepped forward to block her. "They're taking her up to the pre-op room. Dr. Franklin, the neurosurgeon, is waiting for her. But I need you to sign the admission form and answer some questions before he can treat her. Come to my desk."

Her mother wanted to sign right away, but the nurse insisted on getting information first, starting with the name of the family doctor so he could be notified. Her mother said John Harris, then the nurse asked for his phone number. Her mother started cussing at her, but stopped at the sound of the ER doors sliding open. Robert, unshaven and in his wrinkled suit, rushed toward them with two deputies close behind.

"Where is she?" he said.

"I assume you're Mr. Townsend. Your daughter is in pre-op. Fluid will have to be released from her brain immediately. The neurosurgeon, Dr. Franklin, will explain, but you have to sign this form to get her admitted."

He grabbed the form. "Why the hell did you bring them there, Elizabeth? No decent mother would have."

"Why the hell were you there?"

"You should have waited at home."

"Waited for what? The divorce, *Robbie?*"

"Keep your voices down," said one of the deputies. "You're disturbing other people."

Ellen looked toward the waiting area. Two dozen people at least, and all looking their way, even a toddler in a woman's lap. Ellen wanted to melt into the linoleum.

"Disgusting," the nurse said. She held a pen out to Ellen's father. "Sign at the bottom, and I still need some questions answered."

Her father's hand shook as it raced across the line, the last two letters spilling onto the metal desk, but the nurse didn't notice. "Our daughter will answer your questions and then join us. Now where's Wendy?"

"Room 314. Through those double doors to the end of the hall, elevator to the third floor, take a right, then a left. She'll have to stay here. Minors aren't allowed on the third floor."

"But I'm sixteen and I'll be quiet as—"

"You don't look sixteen, and anyway, you're a minor until you're eighteen."

Her father gave Ellen a quick hug, then hurriedly followed her mother, who had started across the room.

"We'll make sure you don't get lost," said one of the deputies.

Ellen watched them go through the swinging doors, one deputy next to her mother, and the other next to her father. They probably wanted to make sure her parents wouldn't keep arguing.

"Have a seat. Let's see what you can answer."

There were a lot of questions, and some were hard. Ellen tried to ignore the nurse's sigh of irritation when she didn't know the answer.

"Could I please join my parents now?" she said when they were done. " I swear I won't make a sound."

"No minors, I told you. Have you no respect for rules? Wait for your parents over there. But first tell me how it happened."

"She ran in the road and got hit by a truck."

"Dispatch told me that. I mean, wasn't someone watching her? Where were your parents?"

Ellen felt her cheeks reddening. That certainly wasn't a question on the form. The woman was nosy.

The ER doors slid open, and a colored woman in a flour-sack dress came in with a boy around seven or eight who was holding one of his arms up with the other and bawling. With a snort of disgust, the nurse went to them and led them through a doorway.

Ellen darted across the room and through the same double doors as her parents. The elevator took a long time to get to the third floor and she was afraid every minute that the nurse would find her first.

One of the deputies was waiting when the door opened. "Howdy, miss. Sorry, but sweetie pie downstairs called to say she's lonesome without you. If it was up to me, I'd let you stay, but it ain't."

"Only for a minute. Oh please, I just want to see my parents."

"They're with the doctor and can't be interrupted. I'll let you peek at them, then down you go."

On her tiptoes Ellen could see through the small glass panel of the consulting room. Her parents sat next to each other at a table listening to a man dressed in gray scrubs who was pointing out areas on a piece of paper clipped to a light box. If only she could hear him.

"Come on. I'll go down with you," the deputy said after a couple of minutes.

Ellen flushed. "I'll go by myself. You can trust me."

"Not saying I can't. I was going down for some fresh air and a nail in my coffin, and I thought we could both use the company."

The nurse smirked as they came through the double doors. "Thanks for bringing her back. Wildness must run in the family."

"I don't know what you're talking about lady. I happened to be coming down and figured to enjoy the young lady's conversation."

"I'll wait over there for my parents," Ellen said in her most grown-up voice as the deputy walked away. His treating her as mature made her swell with a sense of pride and optimism. Wendy was in good hands now, with people who knew what to do. And her parents, who'd been sitting there together calmly listening to the doctor, would see that it got done.

"You'll wait, but not for your parents. They'll be here all night because your sister's getting surgery. Your father just called down and said to tell you a Dessie Moore is coming to pick you up. Now, where were we before you rudely ran off? Oh, yes, how did your mother's dress get torn?"

"It's none of your beeswax." Shoulders back and head up, Ellen walked to the waiting area and sat in a chair that faced the glass doors. After a while, she recognized the headlights of Dessie's old Rambler, which were small and narrowly set like the eyes of a cat.

# Twenty-One

Grievously late, Robert hurried toward the hospital entrance the morning after the accident. He'd gone home after the operation to change clothes and catch fifty winks, intending to go back to relieve Elizabeth, but he'd inadvertently slept for three hours. Despite the fresh suit, he looked like a man undone with his bloodshot eyes, shaving nicks, and hair hastily combed with his fingers. His right hand held the handle of the overnight case Dessie had packed for Elizabeth, and he leaned toward it as he walked as though in deference. His hand shook as he opened the glass entry door. Withdrawal from the pills he'd taken at Helene's. Well, he was through with Benzedrine, had flushed the rest of his pills down the toilet during the surgery as part of a deal he'd made with God.

"Mr. Townsend, I assume," said the nurse sitting by the bed as he tiptoed into the room in Critical Care where Wendy had been moved after the surgery. "My name is Sarah. No need to be quiet; she's still unconscious. Your wife just went out for a smoke."

Robert leaned over the bed rail to peer through the oxygen tent that covered Wendy's head and shoulders. Hell was not red, but white—the goblin-shaped gauze around her head, the ghostly white of her olive complexion, and the sheet under which tubes fed into each arm as though clutching her like the pinchers of some monstrous crab. He felt an urge to snatch her up and run. Her hands were folded on her chest, and he cupped them with his.

"She's freezing."

"Cooler than normal, yes. Her temperature's been lowered to reduce the fluid to her brain."

"But she doesn't like being cold. For God's sake, put some blankets on her."

"That would defeat the purpose, wouldn't it? Don't worry, Mr. Townsend. She doesn't feel anything."

"She will when she wakes, and can you take this plastic tent off her then? It will scare her."

"Depends on how well she's breathing. It's lucky the part of her brain that controls breathing is still working. Otherwise she would have tubes in her nose or mouth."

"I guess that's something anyway."

Robert turned back to look at Wendy. He wasn't responsible for this. He shouldn't have been with Helene, but this had not been foreseeable. Any law student knew the principle: If a man starts a fire in a wind and it carries over to his neighbor's property, he's liable for the damage. But he's not if the wind sprang up after he started the fire. And that's what happened, wasn't it? He couldn't have foreseen Elizabeth's bringing the girls to the motel. This was her fault.

"Robert." Elizabeth's voice came from behind.

Another part of his deal with God was to do whatever it took to save them as a family. Accordingly, he feigned an expression of sympathy as he turned toward her. Then he actually felt sympathetic—her baggy-eyed gaunt face and the bloodstained dress. He put his arm around her shoulders, but she shrugged it off.

"Any change, Sarah?"

"No, Mrs. Townsend. Her vitals are still up and down, which often happens after major surgery, as I explained before."

"Where's Dr. Franklin?" Robert said.

"He's in surgery today at another hospital, but he'll come about six to check her. Remember his telling us last night that the brain is a mystery to medical science and all we can do while she's unconscious is wait?"

"Maybe more of a mystery to him than others. He should have been able to give us some inkling of what to expect. And he should be here now, not seven damn hours from now. We need another opinion. A specialist from a big city." Yes, that's exactly what we need, he thought, and he would see to it.

Elizabeth looked up at him eagerly. "Who?"

"I don't know, but Dr. Harris will. I'll go to the office and make some calls," His hand at her waist, he steered her toward the window. "Listen, Pocahontas," he said in a hushed voice, "that woman never meant anything to me. I only went there because I was angry with you. You heard me say I was coming home. Let's put this behind us."

"Behind us? How? You'll always blame me. What decent mother, you said last night and—"

"Excuse me," Sarah said. "There's a lounge at the end of the hall if you want to talk in private."

Elizabeth shook her head and turned toward the window.

"Well, I'll go make those calls, check in on Ellen, and come back." He gestured toward the case he'd left by the door. "Dessie's idea if you decide you want to stay here. Toothbrush, change of clothes, and what- all. I put your car key in it. The deputies found it in the ignition last night when I asked them to bring your car here as well as mine. Wendy will be all right, you'll see. And we'll be a family again. Call me if there's any change, all right."

Her back still to him, Elizabeth nodded. He hurried to his car, and then all but recklessly veered through traffic on the way to his office. The sooner he talked to Dr. Harris, the better.

"I've got Dr. Harris on the line, Mr. Townsend," Mrs. Mims called through the open doorway of his office, the glass panel Elizabeth had broken not yet replaced.

"Has there's been a change?" asked Dr. Harris, who had come to the hospital to give them both a sedative during the surgery.

"Still unconscious. We need another neurosurgeon right away." Robert explained the situation, and Dr. Harris gave him the names of three well-known neurosurgeons, and in case they weren't available, the name of a large hospital in Chicago known for its neurosurgery department. "Hospital policy requires patients to go there for treatment, but I've known their doctors to travel in exceptional cases, if you get my drift."

"How much?"

"I'd start at five hundred. How is Elizabeth holding up?"

"Not well, but not hysterical like last night."

"And you?"

Robert looked with dismay at the nearly unintelligible scrawl of his shaking hand as he'd taken down the doctors' names. A couple of bennies would stop the shaking and get him through this, but he'd made a deal. "I'm all right."

Four hours later Robert was a tightly coiled spring. He'd had to wait for call-backs from the three doctors Harris recommended, and when none of them were available, he'd called the referrals they'd given him and waited for them to call back, in one case the referral of a referral. He called the Critical Care unit only to be told that there had been no change in Wendy's condition and they couldn't let him talk to Elizabeth on the unit's phone. A little after three, the administrator of the Chicago hospital returned his call. This was his last resort.

"Yes, Mr. Townsend. Your doctor was right to recommend us. Our chief neurosurgeon, Dr. Cohen, is world renowned for severe brain trauma, but hospital policy requires patients to be brought here."

"Impossible. She can't be moved. I know you make exceptions. I'll pay a thousand, plus expenses."

"I can't respond to that except to say that our benefactors are some of the nation's wealthiest people. I'll transfer you to Dr. Cohen's office. He'll give you some top-notch referrals."

Damn bureaucrat, Robert thought as he waited. Why didn't he give me a figure? He would tell Cohen two thousand and keep increasing it if necessary, but Cohen had just left for the day, his secretary said. Robert explained the situation and asked for the doctor's home number. Her broad Midwestern accent full of sympathy, the secretary said that he'd been in surgery for fourteen hours, had gone home to sleep, and she would have him call Robert first thing in the morning.

"That's too late. I told you how bad off my daughter is, and the doctor here doesn't know what he's doing."

"I'm sorry, but Dr. Cohen needs his rest. He has obligations to his patients here too."

"But are they five years old and... Please, I beg you. Call him now. Wendy could—" He burst into sobs.

Robert felt Ruth's hand on his shoulder. She took the phone, and he listened as she gave the doctor's secretary phone numbers where he could be reached the next day. When she hung up, he looked away from her and busied himself wiping his face with his handkerchief.

Robert paced his office, thinking about how to get Cohen to come. Three thousand ought to do it, but he'd have to hustle to get that much. His thousand, five hundred from his father, though he wouldn't tell him what happened until they knew more, and five hundred on a signature loan from the bank. Selling the cottage should give him the rest, but that would take time and Cohen might want the money up front. Gulfstream! Of course. As the corporation's attorney, he was uniquely positioned for at least a thousand-dollar loan on his signature.

"I'm going to Red's office, Ruth. If Elizabeth or the hospital calls, give them Red's number."

When the elevator door opened at the lobby, Carl was waiting to get on, his somber expression telling Robert that he knew. He stepped back and put an arm around Robert's shoulders. "Dessie said you'd be here. I'm so sorry. How's Wendy?"

"Unconscious since it happened. How did you find out?"

"The early evening edition," Carl said, and handed him the front page of the newspaper. The headline was "Mobile Girl Hit by Truck in Pascagoula." The terrifying reality of the accident pained Robert anew as he saw it in print: "The five-year-old daughter of prominent Mobile attorney Robert Townsend and his wife, Elizabeth, was hit by a truck around nine o'clock Thursday night in front of the Best Deal Motel in Pascagoula. The Townsend family was visiting someone staying at the motel, when, according to the desk clerk, an altercation broke out—"

"Fleabag motel, altercation. Even the dim bulbs in Mobile will get the picture. Damn newspapers. Gulfstream will fire me. The board of directors won't use a lawyer with a tarnished image."

Carl took the newspaper from Robert and threw it in a trash can.

"Don't let it get to you, buddy. Granted, there's enough for speculation, but nobody knows for sure. It'll soon be forgotten. I've got a meeting in ten minutes. Walk with me and we can talk."

It was hot and muggy under the blanket of low-lying clouds, but Carl slung his arm over Robert's shoulder as they walked. Robert told him about Dr. Franklin being a dud, about his intent to bribe this specialist in Chicago to come treat Wendy, and about his plan to borrow the money from Gulfstream. "I'll be like any other borrower to them now, and they'll want collateral, which will take a while to get in place."

"Glo and I can loan you a thousand. Let me know when you need it, and I'll pull it from the savings account."

Afraid he might cry if he spoke, Robert nodded.

"Of course, there's thirty-percent interest over ten years and a whopping prepayment penalty."

Robert laughed, and for an instant the tightness in him loosened. He had one hell of a friend. "Guess I'll support that usury bill after all."

"Here's my turn," Carl said when they reached Government Street. "I don't know how this all came about, Robert, and I don't need to, but however it happened, my heart goes out to both of you. I bet Elizabeth is strung out."

"Yes, but it's her fault." He explained the chain of events: Elizabeth's telling Mrs. Simmons about the Benzedrine, Simmons lording it over him, his anger at Elizabeth and going to the motel, and her bringing the girls there. "I don't know whether she brought them to punish me or to help convince me to come home, but either way she had no business doing it."

"No, she didn't," Carl said. "But then you had no business being there."

Robert stiffened. "It's not the same, Carl. No decent mother would subject her children to such a scene, while plenty of married men fool around, the ones who have anything on the ball."

He was immediately sorry. He didn't need to see Carl's face to know how badly he'd hurt him.

"Guess I don't have anything on the ball then, quite the opposite in fact, being short, fat, and gutless enough to settle for government work. Is that how you see me, Robert?"

"Jesus, Carl. Not at all. I didn't mean—"

Carl raised his hand. "Never mind. You're overwrought. Good luck with this doc in Chicago, and let me know about the money. Meanwhile, let Glo and me know if you need anything. Ellen's welcome to stay with us through all this if it will make things easier."

Robert watched Carl disappear into the complex of government offices. Jesus, how could he have said that about married men. As for having something on the ball, look where it got him. And as for all his teasing Carl about substandard government salaries, look at who was about to borrow from whom.

Robert crossed Water Street, intending to go down to the docks for a minute or two of respite, but stopped halfway. The docks would make him feel worse. This wouldn't have happened if he'd stayed in Montgomery. He'd had a couple of one-night stands there, but wouldn't have dared an ongoing tryst like Helene. Given the strict mores of Montgomery society, he would have been ostracized professionally and socially if he'd been caught. Whereas here, his weekly evenings with her had seemed on a par with activities Mobile society readily accepted: a striptease joint in the center of town, all-night bars, wives of prominent men doing risqué can-cans, the indiscretions of his hunting club members.

"Mobile compared to Montgomery is the difference between the Saturday night South and the Sunday school North," someone at the club told him." And Mardi Gras season, Robert supposed, was the epitome of that Saturday night South—a month of parties, costumed drunk revelers in the streets, and parades with floats of provocative beauty queens. If only he'd stayed home with Elizabeth, who had a cold that night.

Robert called the hospital when he got back to his office. Wendy was still unconscious, and Dr. Franklin had been delayed until six thirty. Damn. Six o'clock had been bad enough. The extra half hour could be critical. He asked for the supervisor of the unit and railed at her because another doctor hadn't been called in to check Wendy since Franklin wasn't available. She said no other doctor would have done it because Wendy was Franklin's patient, and that meanwhile they were doing all they could. "It's not enough," he said, and hung up. He would go see the administrator and threaten to sue.

Robert started the car, then waited a few minutes in idle. Threatening to sue was not going to get him anywhere. The nurse was right that no doctor would have taken over Wendy without consulting Franklin. He could go on to the hospital anyway and wait with Elizabeth, but he'd go crazy watching Wendy for three hours, unable to do anything to help her. Was there really nothing he could do? When Wendy had that nervous bladder problem last year and Harris said a non-allergy-inducing pet, like a poodle, might calm her nerves, he'd driven to a breeder in Houston and back in eighteen hours with Fifi. Fifi! Maybe she hadn't been hit and he could find her, and when Wendy regained consciousness, he'd sneak her into the hospital. Surely someone around the motel knew what happened to her. It was a few minutes after four. If he stepped on it, he could be there by four thirty.

When the Best Deal Motel came into view, Robert started shaking. He should turn around and go home, he thought, but knew he couldn't. He sensed that Wendy's survival was tied to his finding Fifi.

He parked in front of the office. The middle-aged woman who often sat in the breezeway a few doors from Helene's was the only person there and she was behind the counter. He'd thought the woman was mentally off because she stared at him every time he came until Helene answered the door. She simply glanced at him now, but otherwise looked the same—a faded house dress and frizzled gray hair pinned haphazardly with bobby pins.

"You was here last night, warn't you? You're the father of that little girl who got kilt. What a shame." She spoke in an eager voice.

Hair rose on the back of Robert's neck. He'd interviewed enough witnesses to recognize the perverse glee that tragedy brought out in some people. He clenched his fists and pictured the woman's head, which appeared to sit directly on her shoulders because of her fleshly chins, fall to the floor.

"My daughter's not dead. She's in the hospital, and I'm looking for her white poodle. Have you seen it or heard anything?"

"Surely have not. I knew a dog was part of all that. I heard a cop tell the man what was driving that truck that the girl was chasing a dog. That man was crying like a baby, and the cop was telling him over and over that it warn't his fault." Her eyes narrowed to a squint as she looked at Robert, a look that said she knew whose fault it was.

"It was an accident. Nobody's fault." He handed her a business card and a five-dollar bill. "Here's where you can reach me if you find out anything. I'll give you another five if you do. And there's a fifty- dollar reward for whoever gives me the dog."

After ten minutes of looking through bramble weeds on each side of the road in front of the motel, Robert spotted a dark stain that ran from the edge of the road across the dirt shoulder and ended in a patch of flattened weeds. He knelt and smelled the stain—oil and something else indiscernible. Then he saw bits of what could have been an animal bone or dog hair pressed into the asphalt.

He glanced at Helene's window as he walked toward his car. The blinds were closed. This was her night to go to work at six, so she was probably napping. She might know about Fifi. Anyone around when it happened could tell that her room was connected to the accident and might have told her about the dog.

"Who is it?" came Helene's sleepy voice a few seconds after he knocked.

"Robert." He winced at the familiar reverberation of the sound of his name in the breezeway.

"Just a minute."

Unwittingly, he anticipated how she would look—large dark eyes hazy with sleep, lush hair falling over her shoulders, and blush-colored cleavage in the opening of her silvery pink robe.

The chain lock rattled and the door opened.

Not much more than a teenager, as Elizabeth had said. She wore a cotton summer nightgown that could have been Ellen's, and her hair was in a ponytail. He noticed then her dark nipples under the nightgown. Erect.

"Oh, Robert." She grabbed his arm and pulled him in.

He looked around the room—the unmade bed, clothes strewn everywhere, dirty glasses, his tie partly buried in the overflow of an ashtray. To think that his daughters, especially Ellen, had seen him here half-dressed and half-drunk with a naked woman. He shuddered.

"How is your daughter?"

Robert cleared his throat. "It's too early to know. I came to find out what happened to her poodle. Have you heard anything?"

"No, sorry. I'm sorry about it all. You look really beat, Robert. A shot of bourbon will help."

Helene poured him a couple of inches from the bottle he'd brought the month before, handed him the glass, then sat on the edge of the bed and patted the place next to her. "Lie down. A five-minute rest."

Robert hesitated. Nothing relieved stress like sex. Without a sip, he set the glass on the dresser. "Please call my office if you get news of the dog. My secretary will know where to find me. There's a fifty-dollar reward for whoever gives her to me."

Whether it was the bright sunlight, or lack of sleep, or the strain of coming back here, the world seemed to swirl under Robert's feet as he shuffled to the car. He rested his head on the steering wheel, closed his eyes, and the world started swirling again. What was happening to him? If he lost consciousness, somebody would notice and call an ambulance, and good lord, his coming here would be in tomorrow's newspaper. Please, God. Just let me get back to Mobile. He jerked his head up at a tapping on his window.

"Whatsa matter? You sick?" said the woman from the office.

"I'm all right. I'm leaving"

"I got news about the dog. The man in Unit Twelve says he saw a deputy shoveling a dog off the other side of the road into a burlap bag after the ambulance left."

Robert sighed. "Well, thanks for letting me know." He started the car, expecting the woman to step back, but she stood still and stared at him as she'd done all those times in the breezeway. Her eyes had been mousy brown then, but now the pupils were dark gold and he couldn't look away. "You're right," Robert blurted. "I know what you're thinking and you're right. It was my fault; I'm the one who started it."

"I don't know what you mean, mister," she said. "I'm waiting for the five."

A mile or so up Old Pascagoula Road, Robert pulled onto the shoulder and rifled through the glove compartment, hoping he'd overlooked a bottle with a few bennies left when he'd thrown the others away. No luck. He remembered the disdain on Ellen's face last night when Elizabeth begged him to come home. How could he face her without some help? At least he would have Elizabeth's Valium. He'd told Dessie five o'clock. He'd better step on it.

# Twenty-Two

Elizabeth listened to Robert's retreating footsteps down the hall as she looked out the fourth-floor window. The sky was a jaundiced gray, the tincture of a feeble sun behind massed clouds. She watched him hurry across the parking lot to the car. It had been good to see him, although she'd seen in his eyes that he blamed her, despite what he said. She turned back to the room. Shadows cast by the half-open blinds looked like prison bars as they fell across the bed. Let her be all right, Elizabeth silently pleaded. Not in prayer, for she didn't believe in God, but as a cry of desperation.

"Sorry we were loud, Sarah," she said as she approached the bed.

"No need to apologize. I've been in critical care units almost twenty-five years, and I know how hard it is on families. My heart goes out to you."

"I guess you've seen a lot of head injuries."

"All kinds."

"What do you think of her chances?"

"Oh, Mrs. Townsend. I wish I knew."

"What about our getting another doctor like my husband said?"

"I don't suppose there's any harm, but Dr. Franklin has an excellent reputation. No doctor could have a prognosis so soon or maybe ever. Head trauma cases this severe are unpredictable. Patients can lie comatose for months, then die, or open their eyes one day and say good morning, although that doesn't happen often. It's usually something in between."

"In between?"

"Partial functioning."

"You mean like she can't walk or feed herself or—"

"Better to wait for Dr. Franklin to explain. It sounds from what your husband said that you have another child."

"Yes. Ellen." Elizabeth felt a pang. She hadn't thought of Ellen since Robert called Dessie the night before to come get her. "She's thirteen and quiet. Keeps her own counsel. This one is the pistol ball. Bright, talkative, and a great manipulator in getting her way. Artistic too. We were thinking about private art—" She stopped to keep from crying.

"This must be so hard for you. There's coffee down the hall."

"No thanks. I was gone long enough."

Elizabeth sat in the chair pulled up to the bed, the post she'd kept all morning to watch Wendy closely. Dr. Franklin had said when he popped in that morning that any movement – the wiggle of a finger, the tilting of her head—could be significant, and Elizabeth thought that Sarah, occupied with monitoring the oxygen, checking Wendy's vital signs, and so on, might miss something. She rested her chin on her hands on top of the bed rail and looked at Wendy. She felt again, as she had each time she left the bed and returned, the jolt of Wendy's chalk white complexion and the lifelessness of her normally animated features. The long eyelashes, tiny nose, and heart-shaped lips might have been no more than brush strokes on china.

The day passed slowly. The door was left open, and hospital smells hung thick as smoke in the small room—rubbing alcohol, disinfectant, the oily odor of floor wax, and at mealtimes the indistinct aroma of various foods merged with the smell of their sanitized plastic covers. The room was quiet except for the low hum of a machine next to Wendy's bed. Occasionally, hushed voices in the hall or the sound of footsteps caused Elizabeth to look toward the door hoping to see Dr. Franklin, or Robert with some big-city specialist in tow. Reason told her he couldn't have found one that quickly. But it bolstered her to know that he would find one.

The most dramatic times were Sarah's periodic checking of Wendy's vital signs. Elizabeth all but held her breath then. She breathed easily again only when Sarah announced that there'd been no change. It seemed like a good sign that Wendy's condition wasn't worsening. These continuing good signs and Sarah's calm competence held in check the swarming of bees inside her that had begun that morning when Dr. Harris' sedative wore off.

Having slept little the night before, Elizabeth had to struggle to stay awake while watching Wendy. Periodically, she dozed off, and when startled awake by a noise, she chided herself and focused on Wendy again. Around three o'clock, her dedication paid off.

"I saw that, Wendy." She leapt to her feet. "Open your eyes. I know you can hear me."

"Saw what?" Sarah rushed to the bed.

"She moved. You didn't see it?"

"No. Where?"

"Her eyelids. They twitched like they do when she's pretending to be asleep." Wendy, the great possum player at nap time. "Wake up, Wendy, sweetie. It's Mama." She turned to Sarah. "It's a good sign, isn't it? Dr. Franklin said any movement."

"I'm sorry, Mrs. Townsend, but he didn't mean involuntary reflexes. Comatose people can twitch without it meaning anything."

"How can that be? Even if it is a reflex, doesn't it mean her body is capable of movement, and isn't that a significant sign?"

"Not necessarily."

Sarah could be wrong, Elizabeth thought. Even with twenty-five years' experience, Sarah was still just a nurse. She would ask Dr. Franklin.

A little before four, another nurse came to tell them Dr. Franklin had been delayed and would arrive around seven.

"Oh no," Elizabeth said. "I can't stand it." Three more hours of not knowing seemed intolerable. "I can't believe this happened. I've always been so careful with the girls, much more so than other mothers, strict about what they could do, hovering over them at the playground, taking temperatures around the clock when they're sick."

"I can see that from your vigilance now, Mrs. Townsend. Try not to blame yourself, though mothers often do. I was told that Wendy ran into the road after her dog. I wish I had a nickel for every time my son chased a ball into the street faster than I could stop him. This is nothing like cases I've seen where the parents were so negligent I could hardly be civil to them."

"Negligent how?" Elizabeth was eager to know; it might let her believe for an instant that she wasn't as reprehensible as Robert thought.

"In all sorts of ways. For example, one mother left her three-year-old in the kitchen with a pot of boiling gumbo on the stove while she was in the bathroom dying her hair. He climbed up on a chair and turned the pot over on himself. Another left the wringer washer going when she went outside to hang clothes, and her four-year-old stuck her fingers in the roller. These mothers put their children in harm's way by their carelessness. You see the difference, don't you?"

Elizabeth nodded. She'd not put Wendy in harm's way by taking her to the motel. She'd taken her only because she thought seeing the girls would make Robert come home and thus the girls as well as she would benefit. And it worked. He had agreed to come home. They could have left right then, but... She put her hands over her face.

"Oh, dear. It looks like my stories upset you. I should have mentioned that both children recovered."

"That's not it. My stamina's giving out is all."

"No wonder. All this strain and no breakfast or lunch. We have a cafeteria on the second floor. It's not Morrison's, but the food is tasty enough. Why not wash up a little, put on fresh clothes, and get something to eat. It will make you feel better."

"No. I'll be all right. I want to stay here and watch her."

"I know, but with no food and the strain you're under, you might be too lightheaded to understand what Dr. Franklin tells you. I'll have you paged if something changes."

In the adjoining bathroom, Elizabeth took off her bloody dress and slip and washed away the blood that had seeped through to her body. Next she tackled her face, scrubbing at her smeared mascara so hard that the skin around her eyes crinkled like dried apple peel. She thought again of that whore, her youthful, flawless skin, and the shameless way she'd sat in bed watching them with a smug expression, all the while sure that Robert was going to marry her. *Robbie, what about the divorce?* Elizabeth gripped the porcelain basin with both hands until her fingers were as white as the bowl and her wounded arm shrieked with pain. She wished she'd killed the bitch.

"Do you need something?" Sarah called through the door.

"No thanks. I'll be out in a minute."

"Oh, that's much better," Sarah said when Elizabeth came from the bathroom wearing a tan sheath. "It's lovely. I wish I could put a fresh dressing on your arm, but since you're not a patient, I'm not allowed when I'm on duty. I'll do it when my shift is over."

Elizabeth looked at her dressing, bloodstained gauze jutting out from twisted tape. She tried to tuck it back under the tape, but it was too painful.

"Go eat something hearty. I'll watch her with your eagle eyes and page you if there's any change, Mrs. Townsend."

"Thank you, and please, call me Elizabeth."

At the entry to the cafeteria, the talking, laughing, scraping of chairs, and clatter of dishes seemed disrespectful of the silent room upstairs, but the aroma of red beans and rice made Elizabeth's mouth water. A basket of cookies next to the register caught her eye. The cashier told her they were applesauce except for that one last peanut butter cookie, which Elizabeth chose because Wendy would like it best.

When she had almost finished eating, a tired-looking young woman sat down a few chairs away and hefted a girl who looked just a little younger than Wendy into the chair beside her. The girl had a fresh cast on her wrist, the plaster aroma wafting over. There was something wrong with the girl. Her eyes were set too deep in her head, and her lower jaw hung slack.

"Off," the girl whined as her fingers raked at the cast.

"No, Christy. Don't pull at it, precious." The mother glanced at Elizabeth as though in apology.

"Hot. Christy hot," the girl said, trying to wedge her tongue between the cast and her skin.

"Don't do that, honey. The plaster will make you sick. Here, precious, Mama will cool it." She blew at the edge of the cast, now and then stopping to kiss the hand jutting out from it. "Isn't that better?"

Ridiculous, such coddling, Elizabeth thought. Seldom had she kissed away tears, blown on stings, consoled with endearments. She glanced toward the woman, and their eyes met.

"She fell off the slide and broke her wrist," the woman said as if Elizabeth had asked. "I told her it was too high for her, but she climbed up when I wasn't watching. Kids are like that. Do you have children?"

"Yes," Elizabeth said curtly, stacking her dishes on the tray.

"Then I guess you know what I mean."

"Hot," the girl said, and licked the cast again.

"No, Christy, darn it. I said no." The mother whipped a handkerchief from her purse and wiped saliva from the cast and her daughter's lips. "Don't do that again."

Christy began to cry. Her mother sighed. "Oh, my sweetheart." She lifted the girl onto her lap. "My good girl, my sweetheart, my precious, it will be all right." She kissed the girl's tears away one by one, and wiped away her drool. "Mama loves you."

Christy's crying subsided to sniffles, and her good arm crept upward to her mother's neck. "Mama wuv," she said wetly.

"Yes, sweetheart, I love you."

Elizabeth felt a pang. She remembered times like that with Wendy. When she was three or four they would sit together on the porch of their old house waiting for Robert to come home from work. She couldn't turn the clock back, but she would become a mother who coddled, and was patient and loving to both her girls. She remembered with shame how she'd wanted to say to Ellen in the ambulance, "Why weren't you watching her." Thank goodness she hadn't.

As Elizabeth rose quietly to leave, the girl reached her arm out toward Elizabeth's milk carton. "Christy want."

"We'll get you some milk in a minute, Christy. That's the lady's."

"It's empty," Elizabeth said, and held it open for the child to see. Christy reached toward the cookie, which sat on a napkin by Elizabeth's purse. "Christy want."

"No. It's for my daughter."

The girl lunged forward and grabbed it.

"No!" Elizabeth cried. She wrenched the cookie from the little fingers, most of it crumbling to the floor. "Look what you've done!" she shrieked as the girl threw her arms around her mother's neck and bawled.

"Lady, what's wrong with you?" the mother said, rocking the girl. "I would have bought you another one."

"There aren't any more. I told her no."

"Maybe she didn't understand you. What kind of monster are you to snatch a cookie from a retarded child?"

Elizabeth grabbed her purse and rushed from the cafeteria. She fumed as she strode down the hall toward Wendy's room. She wasn't a monster. She'd distinctly said no. Not her fault if the child wasn't disciplined. Suddenly she saw the scene as from a distance—the child's small hand barely grasping the cookie, and her own hand angrily tearing it away. Yes, she had been monstrous. That familiar swell of anger she could rarely quell when she was a child, or even now that she was a grown woman, had overwhelmed her, as it had when she dumped the creole on Wendy's head, and, oh my god, as it had last night with that whore. She had to push that out of her mind for now, or she would go crazy.

Elizabeth slowed to compose herself as she approached the nurses' station, their white caps like tiny sails. One of them was reading from a newspaper. "According to the desk clerk, the family was visiting a young woman who was staying there and an altercation broke out."

"That explains how her dress got torn."

"Probably explains that ratty bandage too."

Damn, Elizabeth thought. The evening paper. She wondered if Robert had seen it. She would call him. She needed to let him know Franklin wasn't coming until seven anyway.

Sarah looked up from the chart when Elizabeth came in. "There's been no change, Mrs. Townsend, and it's the end of my shift. Emily, the nurse for the next shift, will be here any minute."

No first name, no warmth, no offer to change her bandage. Sarah had read the paper.

"Please, Sarah, listen. He'd been drinking and popping pills and I took the girls there because... Well, anyway, we needed him to come home. He'd only gone to the motel because—"

"It's none of my business, Mrs. Townsend," Sarah interrupted. "My business is nursing."

"But can't you understand that—"

"I said it's not my business. We have a hospital chaplain. Would you like to talk to him?"

"Hell no. It's not religion I need. It's the milk of human kindness where a person who says their heart goes out to you means it unconditionally. I guess you'll be adding me to your stories of negligent—"

"Oh, here's Emily," Sarah said as the new nurse walked in.

While Sarah and Emily conferred over the chart, Elizabeth went to Wendy's bed, pressed her chest to the bed rail, and whispered, "You're going to love it, Wendy. It's the biggest peanut butter cookie you ever saw, big as a flying saucer."

## Twenty-Three

Ellen had pretended to be asleep until her father left for the hospital the morning after the accident. When he called around one, she gestured to Dessie that she didn't want to talk. "She's taking a nap, Mr. T. I'll tell her when she wakes."

"Wendy's still unconscious," Dessie said when she hung up. "He's gonna pick you up around five and take you to the hospital. Ain't you shamed, making me lie to your daddy? You gonna have to talk to him sooner or later. Try not to be mad at him."

"I'm not."

"Well, you is *something* at him. I ain't never seen you not wanting to talk to him."

Ellen shrugged. Yes, she was *something* at him, but she didn't know what. She dreaded his coming at five, but she'd be glad to see Wendy, even if she was still unconscious.

"I finished cleaning the bathrooms. What's next?" she asked Dessie. Grandfather Townsend was coming on the train the next morning, and her mother always wanted the house to be perfect when he visited so he wouldn't have anything to criticize.

"How 'bout bringing in the laundry?"

"Okay, and then what?" Ellen wanted to stay busy.

When the housework was finally done, she and Dessie sat in the kitchen booth drinking Cokes. It was after five, but Ellen didn't mind that her father was late. Her stomach was in a knot from having to see him at all. When they heard the plop of the evening paper hitting the porch, Ellen went to get it. She came back and slammed it on the table.

"Look at that. It tells everything about Wendy and last night, which is nobody's business but ours. Darn newspapers just want to give people something to gossip about so they'll keep buying papers. Mama's gonna be furious."

"What's this mean?" Dessie's pointer finger, which she moved along as she read, had stopped under a word.

"Altercation?" They say it a lot on *Perry Mason*. It's a fancy word for fight. Mama and that girl fighting like I told you last night."

"I been thinking about that. Who started it?"

"That hussy. When Daddy said he'd follow us home, she whined something about a divorce, and boy, was she sorry. Mama pounced on her and slapped her silly and pulled her hair. That hussy fought back, but Mama was winning. I wish you could have seen it." Ellen paused for breath. "Why are you frowning?"

"Because your mother's probably hating herself for jumping on the woman after your daddy said he would follow y'all home."

"You're right." Ellen hadn't thought of that. Her mother had made a big mistake too, and that lightened her guilt for an instant.

Dessie shook her head. "With all those deputies in the room like you said, I don't see why somebody didn't stop Wendy from running out."

"I don't know. I was scared, and there was a lot of confusion." She would never tell anyone, especially Dessie, that she'd been so irresponsible as to send Wendy outside alone.

"I don't mean you. Nobody would expect a thirteen-year-old to know what to do in all that craziness."

A car door slammed in the porte cochère, and Ellen ran to the bathroom. Holding her ear to the door, she heard her father the second he entered the hall.

"You're a star, Dessie. Anytime you want to double your salary, just threaten to quit."

"Oh, Mr. T, I ain't gonna quit. What you got there?"

"Mrs. Phillips brownies. Here, take them. She ambushed me as I was getting out of the car."

The sound of her father's voice had always enlivened Ellen, his enthusiasm making ordinary life seem like more fun than it was, like how the word "ambushed" brought an image of old Mrs. Phillips crouching behind the box hedge with her brownies. But now neither the idea nor the image amused her.

"Has Elizabeth called?"

"Yessir, 'bout four. No change in Wendy, and she said to tell you the doctor can't come until seven-thirty."

"That quack. Good thing I'm getting a different doctor tomorrow, a specialist from Chicago. I know you must be tired, Dessie. Go on home. I'll take Ellen out for supper, and then we'll go to the hospital."

"Y'all can eat here. There's chicken, potato salad and corn in the refrigerator."

"Thanks, but my nerves are getting to me. I need to be moving. Where's Ellen?"

Ellen opened the bathroom door. "Here I am."

"Skogee," he said, opening his arms to her, and Ellen went to him to avoid embarrassment.

"Ouch, your whiskers." She was glad for an excuse to step back.

"How about the Dog River Grill," her father said as they backed out of the driveway? The accident's in the evening paper and I don't want to run into anyone we know. Fifteen miles ought to be far enough, and you like their hamburgers."

"Okay," Ellen said, although it wasn't. The family often ate there coming home from the island and it would feel lousy without Wendy. To lessen the possibility of conversation, she tuned the radio to her favorite station and turned up the volume.

"Goodness, gracious, great balls of fire." Ellen bobbed her head to the beat of the piano keys as the belting voice resounded in the small space. "You shake my nerves and you rattle my brain. You got a love drives a man insane. Goodness gracious..." The next song was soft, so she turned the dial until she found another loud one. A minute later, her father said he had a headache and asked her to turn the radio off for a while. The silence that followed felt awkward, for they usually chattered incessantly when it was just the two of them. Ellen lowered her window for road noise and pretended to scrutinize the salvage yards and warehouses on of the outskirts of Mobile.

"Looks like we're in for it," her father said as he glanced at the sky.

"I know." She had seen a few dark clouds when she brought in the laundry, but now they almost blanketed the sky.

"That big one's a thunderhead if I ever saw one. I bet the lifeguards at the club have cleared the pool."

It does look bad, Ellen thought—cumulus clouds stacked like a tower with a dark gray underbelly. Nimbus, which meant rain, was the name for the dark cloud at the bottom. The chapter on clouds in science had been one of her favorites.

"That's a cumulonimbus cloud."

He glanced at her, and she felt embarrassed. Her tone had been haughty instead of teasing as it usually was when she dropped some tidbit of science on him.

"Listen, Skogee, I want you to know I dumped that woman like I said I would. Do you believe me?"

Ellen hesitated. She wished she could. She had never not believed him. "Well, Mama said you were with her the night you were supposed to be in Atmore." The statement was more than she felt the nerve to say, but she was glad she had.

"Yes, I was. I went to the motel to tell her it was over."

"But you spent the night there," Ellen said after a pause. She had to keep going if she wanted the true picture, which she did now because of Wendy, no matter how nervous it made her.

"It was late and I'd been drinking, so I didn't want to drive home. Listen, the only reason I went back to the motel when I stormed out that night was to punish your mother for something she'd done."

"What did Mama do?" He looked as surprised as she was at the question. It wasn't her business, but the answer was import- ant. She wanted to judge for herself whether his punishment had been fair.

"I had a business problem of sorts, which I told her to trust me to handle. Still, she interfered and made things worse. I was furious with her when I got home, but I had no intention to leave or to punish her until she wouldn't let me alone. If I had sobered up, I would have come home yesterday. You heard me say last night that I would come home, didn't you?"

"Yes."

"So do you understand?"

"I guess." Which was true if understanding meant having a picture of how one thing followed another. But he'd not said *why* he needed to see Sleeping Beauty to dump her when he could have just called. Or *why*, after he'd told Sleeping Beauty in person that he was dumping her, had he gone back to her, which was the very opposite of dumping her. She would have a lot more understanding if he told her those things. But maybe nothing he could say would make a difference. She didn't feel the way she used to about him.

"Let's leave," Ellen said as they stood behind the Wait To Be Seated sign in the foyer. The huge room of twenty or so tables, booths, and a wall-length bar was practically deserted. The dark wood and dim lighting, normally a relief from the sun-glared beach of Dauphin Island, was now a bane, for the drizzling sky outside the picture window gave the place a gloomy aspect.

"It's like a dungeon. Can't we go?"

"Well… maybe this wasn't a good idea, but since we're here, we might as well eat. It won't take long."

A young woman carrying menus hurried to them from behind the bar and led them to a booth by the window.

"Wasn't easy, but I got you the best seat in the house."

Ellen felt uncomfortable. The woman was pretty, with long blond hair and a curvy figure made obvious by her tight black skirt and white low-cut blouse.

"My name is Darlene. We have a skeleton crew on rainy weeknights, so I'm your hostess, bartender, cocktail and food waitress. Sort of a jack of all trades."

"You're as far from a Jack as a person could be, Darlene."

Ellen started. Could he possibly be flirting with her? "I want a Cherry Coke."

"She meant to say please. And I'd like a double bourbon and Coke as soon as you can, please."

"All right. A double on the double."

Her father laughed as though it was the wittiest thing he'd ever heard, and Darlene beamed at him. Ellen interrupted to say they should order now since they were in a hurry.

Robert watched Darlene sashay across the room with their orders, her rounded buttocks shifting in alternation with each step. "Like two little boys fighting in a croaker sack," her father said as he usually did when they saw a female with a shapely rear walking ahead of them. Instead of laughing, as she usually did, Ellen bit at the inside of her cheek.

"Come on, Skogee, don't mope. We'll eat up and be on our way. I'm gonna put that doc on the witness stand soon as I see him. We need some answers, don't we?"

Ellen nodded. She was grateful that he was smart and was getting a better doctor. "What did Wendy look like when you saw her this morning?"

"Like she was sleeping." He choked up. Ellen looked away, sorry she'd asked.

When the busboy brought water, her father took two pills from a bottle in his pocket.

"I don't think you should take those. Remember what Mama said last night about the pills talking?" She'd spoken out of place, but was worried.

"For your information, these aren't the pills she was talking about. These are Valium, which she used to take when she got in a tizzy about some social event. All they do is calm you down."

"Here we go," said the tight skirt at her father's elbow. "Cherry Coke on the rocks, and a double on the double. Better taste it. I tend to make my doubles too strong."

Robert took a swallow. "Fine as a horse hair split three ways."

The bitter aroma of bourbon wafted across the table. Maybe he was becoming like Mr. Kelly, Ruthie's dad, who got drunk every night before he died. Ellen wanted to tell him that and ask him not to drink, but he was having an animated conversation with the waitress. It angered Ellen that he would be so friendly to the waitress after all that had happened.

The jukebox, Ellen remembered. Then she wouldn't have to listen to them. She interrupted her father for change, then hurried across the room toward the orange-yellow glow of the Wurlitzer as though it might lead her to safety. None of the titles appealed to her—she wasn't in the mood to play music—but she had to play something or go back to the table where her father and the waitress were still talking. As her quarter clinked into the slot, she felt a pang. She would usually be pushing Wendy's fingers away at this point to keep her from randomly pressing buttons. *Stop. You don't know what you're doing. Yes I do, and Daddy said I could pick so—*

The sound of laughter from a small private dining room nearby broke her memory. She turned toward it. A family was gathered around the table—a couple about her parents' age, a boy of eight or nine, two girls around Amanda's age who looked like twins, and an older woman she figured was the grandmother.

Not wanting the twins to think she was immature, Ellen selected the titles most popular in the Teen Room, and the first one started to play.

"Since my baby left me, I found a new place to dwell. It's down the end of Lonely Street at Heartbreak Hotel. Oh baby I..." She glanced toward the family and saw one of the twins smiling at her. She smiled back as though good music was the most important thing on her mind. As she was picking the songs for her second quarter, the family rose to leave—chairs scraping, reminders to not forget things, teasing about who had eaten the most. They walked across the room, the boy following close behind the trio of his parents and the grandmother, with the twins behind him. The talking and laughing continued while they helped each other on with their raincoats in the foyer.

As they opened the door to go out, Ellen noticed a yellow slicker on the coat rack. In her mind's eye, she slipped into it, pulled the hood forward to conceal her face, and went out the door with them. Six came in and eight went out. It sounded like a line from some fanciful children's book about counting. There would be a picture of six dwarves in yellow slickers coming in a door and then another picture of eight going out. And underneath it would be a question: How many more dwarves went out than came in? The answer would be two. Her and Wendy.

"Hey, Muskogee," her father called across the room. The food had arrived.

Ellen strode to the booth. "You promised you wouldn't call me that in front of people."

"I forgot. Your hamburger's getting cold."

Ellen froze. His slurring was worse than it had been at the motel. An empty cocktail glass and a half full one sat in front of him, and the waitress had probably removed some empties.

"Eat while it's warm."

"I'm not hungry, and besides you're not eating." His steak was intact.

"Do what I say. I'm still the father here." He downed his drink in a few swallows.

"Looks like I'm just in time," said the tight skirt. She put the empty glasses on her tray. "How about another?"

"Better not, or I'll be looking for a pillow. You ought to call your doubles triples, Darlene, but I'm not complaining."

At least he knew he'd had enough, Ellen thought.

"Want me to heat that up for you, honey?"

"No."

"Well, okay." The waitress leaned over the table for a better look out the window. Ellen's father's eyes fixed on her cleavage in the low-cut blouse.

"Just a drizzle, but it's gonna get worse. Guess I better get back to work."

Ellen shoved her plate toward the wall as the waitress sauntered away. It wasn't true, as her father had said on July 4th, that most men his age fell for attractive young women, certainly not the father in the family that had just left, or Mr. Taylor, or even Mr. Kelly, as far as she knew. And it wasn't true, as he'd also said, that it did no harm. It had harmed her and her mother and most of all Wendy.

"What happened was an assident," he slurred. When Ellen didn't speak, he continued. "Your mother shouldn't have—"

"It's your fault, not Mama's. You shouldn't have taken up with that woman to begin with. It's like you tell Wendy and me when we're fighting—the one who started it is to blame."

A frown crossed his face, and his lips turned down like they did when he teased with "Do you want to make a grown man cry?" Ellen couldn't bear it. She leapt from the booth and ran to the ladies' room. A waitress emerged from one of the stalls and began washing her hands. Darlene's voice wafted from the other stall. "He tries to be friendly and funny, but his eyes say, 'Forgive me for living.' Something terrible must have happened in that family, and that girl's not helping him any." The waitress at the sink glanced at Ellen.

"Please tell my father that I'm waiting in the car and we have to be at the hospital in thirty minutes."

# Twenty-Four

The drizzling rain looked like shattered glass as it blew at an angle across the lighted entry of the Dog River Grill. Ellen checked her watch. What was keeping him? "Forgive me for living," the waitress had said, which meant he felt guilty, but he'd made things worse tonight by drinking so much. They would never get to the hospital by seven-thirty in this rain.

Her father came out a few minutes later and gazed around as though searching for his car, although there were fewer than a dozen in the parking lot. Ellen honked, and he staggered toward her. When he fumbled with the door handle, she reached across the seat to open the door, and he plopped behind the wheel. Without looking at her, he wiped the rain from his face with his handkerchief, then tried without success to get the key into the ignition.

"You're drunk. Give me some change and I'll call Dessie or Mr. Taylor to come get us."

"No siree bob. Not drunk. I'm fine as a horse hair split three ways soon as I get this damn key in—"

"I'm not riding with you."

"Come on, Skogee."

"Nope." She opened her door and got out. "I'm going to call someone to come get us."

"How 'bout this? I snooze while you get me coffee. Extra strong, tell her. If I can't walk a straight line after I drink it, we'll call a damn taxi." He fumbled for his wallet and pulled out a dollar bill.

"Something wrong, hon?" Darlene asked from behind the bar.

"I need to use the phone. Could you give me change for a dollar, please?"

Ellen let Dessie's number ring for a long time. Then she called information for the Taylors' number but got no answer there either. She was wet from running back and forth to the car, and the phone booth was deliciously warm with the glass door closed. She stayed there for a minute, thinking of what to do.

When she got back to the car, her father was asleep, which is what she was hoping for. He lay on his side, head propped on the armrest of the passenger door, legs curled to his chest. She eased herself into the driver's seat, quietly closed the door, then lifted the keys from his upturned palm, gently as though playing Pick-up Sticks.

She adjusted her seat forward and upward as she had when he'd let her drive the Cadillac once before. With the windshield wipers and lights on, she would be ready. Her only real worry was that he would wake and insist on driving.

She turned the key, and the engine hummed to life, which both excited and frightened her. Barely touching the gas pedal, she eased the car toward the road and stopped to look for traffic. When she stepped on the gas to pull out, the Cadillac bolted like a runaway horse, and when she braked to slow down, it lurched. Her father rolled forward but not off the seat, thank goodness. She'd forgotten the controls on the car were so sensitive.

The drizzle soon turned into heavy rain, and the storm they'd expected came blowing across the highway, sweeping up branches and debris that flew everywhere. The Cadillac shimmied in the wind, and power lines sparked off and on like flash cubes. A long stream of lightning zigzagged ahead, and Ellen silently counted seconds—one thousand one, one thousand two—until thunder boomed on six. The storm was only a mile away. Dang close. Ellen liked thunderstorms when she was inside, but now she was scared. Lightning was attracted to metal, and the whole car was metal except for the upholstery and carpet. If lightning struck the car, it would burst into flames and they would burn along with it. Lightning was six times as hot as the sun.

Suddenly, rain crashed so heavily on the windshield that Ellen thought she'd driven into the Gulf. Even with wipers on high, she couldn't see the hood of the car. With a trembling hand, she flipped on her signal light and slowly pulled onto the shoulder. In a minute or so came another flash of lightning which illuminated the interior of the car, and at about the same time, a deafening thunder clap. Ellen screamed.

"Wha...what's happening?" her father said, popping upright.

"A thunder storm is on us, and lighting is going to strike us any second. Since the car is metal, should we get out and lie on the ground like you're supposed to do if you're in a field?"

Her father blinked as though trying to wake.

Ellen burst into tears and shook his shoulder. "Answer me. Should we get out of the car?"

"No," he mumbled. "Windows shut."

Ellen looked around, checking the windows. Only the front window vent on the passenger side was open, and she reached across him to shut it.

"Good girl." He leaned his head against the window and closed his eyes.

"No, Daddy, don't. Please stay awake."

He opened his eyes. "Trying to... Valium... sit tight." He blinked a few times then his eyes closed again.

The next lightning streak looked far away and the lagging thunder barely a noise. The blowing rain soon eased to where Ellen could see the road. A car ahead pulled out from the shoulder and headed north. She did the same and followed its taillights for a while.

It was still raining when they reached the outskirts of Mobile. Ellen, who'd only been to Providence Hospital the night she rode in the ambulance, didn't know how to get there. She roused her father, who was a little drowsy and couldn't see well enough in the dark and the rain to direct her.

"It's almost eight thirty, Muskogee. Let's go home, call the hospital and tell your mother we're coming. I know how to get to Providence from home."

They were surprised to see her mother's car at the house. Ellen thought it was a good sign. Her mother wouldn't have left the hospital unless Wendy was better. She was probably sleeping for the house was dark, except for faint light in the living room.

As soon as Ellen parked, she got out of the car and hurried through the rain toward the house, her father coming behind. Suddenly Ellen stopped. Somebody was moving behind the living room sheers. A burglar! She moved in closer. It was her mother. She had something in her hand and was pounding the poker table with it.

"Mama!" Ellen cried and started forward, but felt her father's hand on her shoulder.

"No. Wait on the porch until I call you," he said and rushed into the house. From the open doorway Ellen saw her mother staggering around the poker table, stabbing it with an ice pick, sobbing and babbling incoherently. Ellen could make out only two words: "blood clots." She watched in horror as her father struggled to take the ice pick, finally twisting her mother's wrist until she dropped it. "No! No decent mother," her mother screamed as her father kicked the ice pick away from them. All this could mean only one thing.

Her father then called out for Ellen to phone Dr. Harris' exchange for him to come right away. His exchange told her that the hospital had already notified him and that he should arrive any minute. When Ellen returned to the living room, her father had her mother, thrashing around to get free of him, pinned to the sofa.

"Dr. Harris will be here soon," Ellen said, and went up to her room.

# Twenty-Five

$W$hen Ellen woke the next morning, the sky was smeared with gray clouds of no particular shape. No science words to call them came to Ellen's mind. "Cigarette ashes," is what Wendy had said once about a similar sky.

Under the gray sky and inside the shadowy house everyone but Elizabeth, who chose to stay in her room, gathered in the living room crying and embracing—Grandfather Townsend, who'd arrived on the morning train, the Taylors, Dr. Harris, Dessie, and Ellen, who didn't cry, but allowed herself to be hugged. Her father and Grandfather Townsend embraced for a long time, and the sight made Ellen uneasy. She'd never thought of her father as a boy, much less one seeking comfort from his father. Dessie laid out the food people had dropped off, but no one did more than pick at it. No one talked much either—what was there to say?

In the days thereafter, Ellen got tired of people looking at her intensely—searchlight eyes, she called them—and asking how she was doing as though she knew and would tell them. She tried to escape to her room or the workshop, but often as she tiptoed up the stairs or scurried out the back door, her mother or father or Dessie would say, "Where's Ellen?" in an alarmed tone as though she might have fallen overboard into the sea. Worst of all was being alone with her mother or father, or both of them at the same time. They kept saying that they were sorry and encouraging her to cry with them if she felt like it, which she didn't. She was determined that she never would. They were to blame for Wendy's death just as she was, and none of them deserved the comfort of being together.

The funeral was held on the fifth day after Wendy died. Ellen didn't want to go. She would have dug in her heels about it except for two things: Dessie would be allowed to sit in the family section—her father had insisted on it—and Dr. Harris had told her that Wendy hadn't felt a thing the whole time.

After the service, people gave her parents their condolences. Her mother, who hung on her father's arm like a blossom about to fall from a bough, said nothing, letting him speak for both of them. Not wanting to be approached, Ellen stood off to the side close to Grandfather Townsend, but she got hugged anyway by Ruthie, Mrs. Kelly, the Taylors, and several teachers. The hugs brought her close to crying, but she didn't. Crying in front of a bunch of people would have felt like putting on a show. By the time they got home from the cemetery, she had an awful ache in her jaw from the strain of holding her tears in.

The funeral was like a milestone after which household life seemed to go back to normal: Grandfather Townsend went home, her father went to work every day, although he came home midafternoon, her mother got up and dressed to see him off in the morning instead of moping around in her nightgown, and she sometimes had Mrs. Taylor over for coffee.

But things weren't really the way they'd been before. Dessie cooked substantial suppers like she used to, but nobody ate much, especially not Ellen, who'd given up her favorite foods as a private penance. Her mother would burst into tears at random day and night wherever she happened to be in the house. Ellen often heard her father trying to console her when she passed their door on the way to the bathroom. No one was enthusiastic about anything, and no one laughed, except her father when he was trying to cheer her up. Once in a while she heard her parents arguing in their bedroom about which of them was most at fault for Wendy's death. It was disgusting and made her feel sadder than she already did.

Through Dr. Harris, Ellen's parents made arrangements for her father to go to a month long treatment program at a military hospital in Washington, D.C. It would help him stop taking the wake-up pills and drinking, her mother told her. Ellen knew from eavesdropping that Dr. Harris had given him enough pills the night Wendy died to get him through the funeral, and then, when he agreed to go to the treatment program, enough pills to hold him until the program started. When she found out she would have to go to D.C. too because Dessie couldn't stay with her a whole month, she called Ruthie and got Mrs. Kelly's permission to stay with them.

The day before her parents were leaving for Washington, her father's morning shave-and a haircut knock on her bedroom door came earlier than usual. Ellen, who was in the process of dressing, jumped into bed, pulled up the covers, and told him to come in.

"I'm going to the train station to check on the tickets and then to the office for a couple of hours. Mrs. Mims won't be there and I know you like to practice on her typewriter. Want to come?"

"No thanks. I didn't sleep much, and I'm tired."

"Well, the best sleep in the world is on a Pullman. The clack-ety-clack of the wheels is a thousand times better than counting sheep. Come on, Skogee, change your mind and go with us. You and your mother can see some museums, the Capitol, and the White House. You might even run into ole 'I Like Ike.'"

"But I'm looking forward to staying with Ruthie." A lie. Mrs. Kelly would talk about Wendy being with Jesus, and she would have to bite her tongue about Jesus not stopping that truck. Still, it was better than going with her parents, who were suffocating her with attention.

"I'll need cheering up with all those doctors poking around and sticking needles in me, and I'll be gone for a whole month. Aren't you going to miss me?"

"Do you still love me?" That was what he was really asking, Ellen knew, and had been asking indirectly since the funeral. He'd sought her out three or four times a day to see if she wanted to go for ice cream or play gin rummy or ping-pong. She'd said no thanks except for a few times when he looked so down-in-the-mouth she couldn't stand it. Whatever they did together took for-ever because he'd regale her with funny stories about his clients or things that happened during the war, like his trading a cooler of ice to Alan Ladd for an army jeep. Unlikely, Ellen thought, as she did about most of his stories now.

"But I wouldn't get to see you much since you'll be in the

hospital. I'll write you."

"Guess that'll have to do. No Dear Johns, I hope. You still love me, right? You're not going to run off with the paper boy?"

"No." She was taken aback. How could he know she had a crush on the paper boy?

"No, you don't love me," or "No, you're not going to run off with the paper boy?"

"I'm not going to run off with the paper boy."

He paused, waiting, she knew, for her to say she loved him.

"Well okay. Later, gator."

Ellen stared at the door for a long time after it closed. How could she love him? She blamed him for Wendy's death as much as she blamed herself, and except for the first few days after the funeral, he didn't seem to feel as guilty about it as he should. He made jokes, and barbecued and sometimes watched Perry Mason. She then had to make excuses as to why she couldn't watch with him. The only times he looked miserable enough to suit her was when they went to the cemetery.

When she heard his car drive off, she finished dressing, tip-toed past her parents' door in case her mother was still sleeping, and hurried downstairs. Dessie who'd been gone three days helping Mother Moore, was to return early that morning and Ellen had things saved up to tell her. Hearing the clatter of dishes in the sink as she rounded the corner from the hall, she felt a rush of exuberance and cried out "Geronimo!" as she bounded into the kitchen.

"What?"said her startled mother, who was washing dishes.

"Sorry. I thought you were Dessie."

"She called and said she had to help Mother Moore again this morning. I fixed pancakes for your father, and I have batter left over, or I can scramble some eggs."

"I'm not really hungry. I'll get cereal."

"No. Sit down, I'll get it." Her mother usually worked quickly in the kitchen so she could get on with her business—arms and hands fluttering, burners on high, cutlery and plates clattering to the table—but now she placed a bowl, a spoon, a box of Cheer-ios, and bottle of milk on the table with deliberation, as though serving Ellen's breakfast was her business. She was different in other ways too, like not being so critical or so insistent that she wouldn't listen to Ellen's point of view. And like her father, her mother sought her out several times a day to see if she wanted anything—new 45s or comics or "something for your laboratory." Ellen knew her mother too was asking a question: Will you let me love you now? No, Ellen thought to herself, because her mother's moods could change in an instant. The only people she could count on were Dessie and Grandfather Townsend.

Her mother sat down in the booth and said she had something serious to ask Ellen.

Uh-oh. Here comes "Why weren't you watching Wendy?"

"Your father thinks you won't go to Washington with us because you think I don't want you to. Is that true?"

"No," Ellen said, exhaling with relief.

"Good, because I really would love for you to go. You and I could sight-see—there's a big museum of science there, I'm told—and then we could tell your father all about it to cheer him up. The three of us need to stick together now, you know."

"I know. It's just that I'd rather stay with Ruthie." Ellen was surprised that her mother looked truly disappointed.

"It was nice of Martha to invite you to stay with them. I'm glad the Kellys are still good friends. We'll be seeing more of them in our new life."

"New life?"

"You know, one car, no country club, no private school and a smaller house. We have to be careful with money now that Gulfstream is out of the picture. When we get back from Washington, I'll find a job and your father will start building his practice back up. You look surprised. Didn't he tell you last night?"

"No."

"But he went in your room specifically to tell you. What were the two of you doing for over an hour?"

Ah, the green-eyed shrew is back, Ellen thought.

"Oh, Ellen, I'm sorry. I didn't mean that like it sounded. But it's not fair that he gets to have fun with you and leaves me to tell you the hard stuff."

"What hard stuff? I'll miss swimming at the club, but somebody in the Teen Room said the public pools are going to stay open. And I'd rather go to a public school than Wright's."

Her mother laid her hand on Ellen's shoulder. "It's that we'll have to let Dessie go."

"No." Ellen jumped up. "Not Wendy and Dessie both. I'll run away."

"Wait," Elizabeth called out, but Ellen was halfway out of the kitchen.

Ellen slammed her door, threw herself on her bed, and sobbed. Without Dessie, she had no one to confide in.

"Ellen, I'm sorry," her mother said breathlessly through the door a few seconds later.

"Does Dessie know?"

"Yes. She knew you were going to be upset. If I'd known your father wasn't going to tell you, she and I would have told you together. Please come out so we can talk."

"There's nothing to talk about." Ellen sat upright and blew her nose. She would go to the Memphis Academy like Amanda had said she should when she visited a few days before. "Why not? You said you're not happy with your parents without your sister."

Ellen flipped quickly through the brochure Amanda left for her, which was mainly pictures—pool, stables, dorm rooms and so on. It all looked fine. Anywhere would be better than here. Grandfather Townsend would pay for it; he'd said to let him know if she needed anything. She would call Amanda after her parents left in the morning, find out how to get into that school, and then write her parents about it. Her father wouldn't like it, but he would let her go if she begged. Her mother probably wouldn't mind because then she would have him to herself.

"Don't be mad at me, Ellen," Dessie said that afternoon. I thought it was your parents' place to tell you. None of us is happy 'bout it. I thought your daddy was gonna cry when he told me, so don't go making him feel worse."

"Course not. I'm not a child. But I don't want to live with them unless you're here." Dessie would fuss about boarding school, so she wouldn't tell her until she had to. She would miss Dessie like the dickens in Tennessee, but she'd be missing her here most of the time.

"You feeling that way now, but it'll pass. When school starts you'll be busy making new friends. And it ain't like I moved to Chicago. I'll pick you up and we'll go on picnics on weekends. How does that sound?"

Ellen knew better. After working hard all week, Dessie would want her weekends for her own family.

"All right."

Dessie was making blueberry muffins for her parents to take on the train. When she squeezed the handle of the old flour sifter, it made little mouse squeaks. The loneliest sounds Ellen had ever heard. She bent over to blow off the white dust that had settled on Dessie's arm.

With the muffins in the oven, Dessie sat in the booth and lit a cigarette. She said Mother Moore couldn't get out of bed so she'd been fetching things for her every minute—snuff, church fan, fly swatter, and that old one ton tabby that kept jumping off the bed but couldn't jump back on. Instead of sitting across from Dessie, as usual, Ellen slid in beside her. She folded her arms on the table and rested her head on them. Dessie blew a smoke ring that slowly expanded to become a large circle over them. If only it were a lasso that would come down and tie them together with a knot so tight that no one could undo it.

"You feeling kinda sad, huh?" Dessie said, and began to scratch Ellen's back. Dessie's fingernails were stubby, but she had a way of digging in that felt better than long nails.

Ellen nodded.

"Listen, baby. I've had lots of family pass, and I know how the sadness comes and goes. You got to keep busy. I think you should go to Washington with your parents like they been asking."

"I don't want to," Ellen said and sat up. She knew Dessie wouldn't let it go at that.

"Why not? It would be good for all y'all. Both of them is miserable as can be."

"They don't look miserable to me, and even if they are, they deserve it." She'd blurted it out without meaning to; she'd not told anyone she felt that way about her parents. But she was tired of Dessie feeling sorry for them.

"Now, that's as wrong as wrong can be."

"No, it's not. Parents are supposed to be responsible and they weren't. Mama shouldn't have taken Wendy to the motel, and Daddy shouldn't have taken up with that hussy."

"I ain't saying they did right, but what happened to Wendy was an accident. I know you hurting and missing Wendy, but they're gonna be hurting long after you a married woman with a husband and children and hardly ever thinking 'bout Wendy. You is all they got left; you ought to take pity on them."

"I can't."

"What's holding you back? Pity comes natural if you don't get in the way of yourself. Soldiers at war feels it. Lester told me that when they seen them Germans lying in—"

"Ssh," Ellen said at the sound of her mother coming down the hall.

"Custer's last stand," her father said at supper, raising his bourbon and Coke as though for a toast. Her mother didn't raise her glass, and her deadpan expression was as good as a frown. Ellen knew she didn't want him drinking.

"And," he said, looking at Ellen, "I'm going to make enough money when we return from D.C. to hire Dessie back at a salary she can't refuse."

Ellen felt ashamed. Her mother must have told him that she'd pitched a fit about Dessie.

"Daddy, I'm not worried about losing Dessie. She said we would go on picnics on weekends."

Her mother gave her a rueful look, as though she thought Ellen was counting on it and would be let down.

Around ten, Ellen helped put their suitcases by the front door.

The taxi was coming at dawn when Ellen would be sleeping, so they said their goodbyes right then. She tolerated their hugs more easily because she was getting a month long reprieve.

When she went to take a bath, she heard them talking through the wall. Her father was worried that she'd get sick while they were gone. Her mother reminded him that she could fly back in a few hours, and that Mrs. Kelly would take good care of Ellen in the meantime.

"Not as good as we would. I don't think I should go."

"Robert, please, you promised."

Ice clinked on the other side of the wall. Another Custer's last stand.

"Only because you and Harris ganged up on me. With the pressure of Gulfstream gone, I can get off the pills and the drinking by myself."

"Maybe, but getting new clients is going to be so hard that you might go back to the pills if you don't take the program. Like Harris said, the counseling makes the difference."

A long silence followed. Ellen crossed her fingers. Her mother was right. Don't back out, she urged her father in her mind, then remembered it wouldn't matter to her because she'd be in Tennessee.

"I beg you. You're getting cold feet, that's all. You know you should go."

"I don't know a damn thing, Elizabeth, except that I'm going crazy thinking about Wendy. I told you I was coming home. Why the hell did you start that fight?"

Not again, Ellen thought with disgust. She turned on the faucet trying to drown out their voices.

"Stop it Robert. No more finger-pointing, remember. We agreed to split the blame fifty-fifty and not argue about it again for Ellen's sake."

"Nothing I do seems to be for her sake anymore. No matter how enthusiastic I pretend to be about things, she doesn't want to be around me."

Pretend! So he had been feeling miserable all that time after all.

"Or around me either. I suggested we go shopping for school clothes and she said she had enough. Maybe in time she'll forgive us."

"But how much time? I can't stand this. Surely if I show her... show her...," Ellen pulled back from the wall. It sounded like he was going to cry. She should tell them that she'd sent Wendy outside. It was only fair for them to know that the blame was not in halves but in thirds, or maybe her share was more since Wendy's being outside made all the difference. Despite her mother's niceness since Wendy died, she would be furious with her. Maybe her fear of that fury was why she hadn't told them already. But she was ready for it now; it would be a relief to be yelled at. She deserved it and any other punishment her mother gave her. Not eating her favorite foods and the other little ways she punished herself every day were not enough. She turned off the faucet, put her clothes back on, and knocked on their bedroom door.

Ellen woke a little after dawn. She heard noises outside and hurried to her window. A taxi was parked in the driveway, and the driver was putting the suitcases in the trunk. Her mother, with purse, overnight case, and a paper bag that likely contained the muffins, was a little way behind him. Although her mother had gone to the beauty parlor the day before, her hair looked like a bird's nest in back, as though she'd only combed what she could see. Since Wendy died, she often looked disheveled in some way.

"I'll run up and say goodbye," came her father's voice from the porch.

"No. Let her sleep. We've already said goodbye, and she's probably still exhausted from last night."

Ellen was in fact exhausted, but she felt lighter than she'd felt since Wendy died, because she'd told them that she'd sent Wendy outside and explained why. She had cried a little at the end when she said she hadn't realized it could be dangerous.

Her father had looked startled. Her mother did too, but Ellen knew her mind was churning. Any second she would hear, "How many times have I told you to think before you act?" Instead, both of them rushed to embrace her. "Of course you couldn't think in all that craziness," her mother said. "You wanted to protect Wendy from seeing the fight" her father said, and "You couldn't have known Fifi would run out." Ellen knew she was guilty no matter what they said—her carelessness had paved the way for the accident—but their not blaming her meant something.

They'd begged her again to go to D.C. Her father said he'd bought an extra ticket just in case, and her mother said they could have her packed in twenty minutes. Turning them down had felt awkward.

Now her father appeared in the driveway with a thermos in one hand and his briefcase in the other. In khaki pants, a light blue polo shirt, and loafers, he could have been going on vacation. Ellen felt a catch in her throat. He was *her* full moon, her Mardi Gras parade—swimming, fishing, skeet-shooting, go-carting, and most everything else that was fun. But he had taken up with that hussy and look what happened. How could anyone so wonderful do anything so horrible, and which should matter to her the most? She'd thought about that question many times since Wendy died but still didn't know.

As her father climbed into the taxi, he turned to look at Ellen's window. She jerked her head back and didn't look out again until she heard them drive away. For an instant, she wished she'd gone with them, but just for an instant. She would call Amanda right after breakfast to find out about getting into the Academy and whether she could take her portable record player and 45s. She couldn't imagine doing without them.

Ellen sat on her bed and looked more carefully at the pictures in the brochure than she had the day before. The main building was three times the size of Wright's. The stables consisted of a huge barn with corrals close by. There were several pictures of smiling girls in riding outfits sitting on horses, big horses. Ellen was a little afraid of horses, but she would learn to ride. She'd driven through a tropical storm, so she was certainly brave enough to ride a darn horse. The swimming pool looked as big as the club's. The dorms had two girls to a room: two twin beds, two dressers, and two desks. She could picture her record player on one of the dressers.

She put the brochure down and felt a fluttering inside her. The very idea of going was exciting—packing up and riding the train to Memphis, and then bingo, she would be a boarding school student in Tennessee. But did she really want to go? She wasn't so angry with her parents now. After all, they hadn't held it against her for sending Wendy outside. And it was like Dessie said—they would be hurting about Wendy for the rest of their lives. Plus, Mobile was where she'd lived with Wendy, and she could bike to her grave every day.

Yet if she stayed, her parents would constantly watch her and worry about her like they'd done since Wendy died. And they would be too strict when she got older, setting an early curfew and grilling her about where she was going and who with. And what if her parents didn't get along, or if her father went back to drinking and taking pills and maybe even got another woman. So what should she do? If only she could pick the petals off a daisy—go, stay, go, stay—and do what the last petal said. A childish notion.

The morning paper thumped on the porch, and she ran to the window. The newspaper boy was on the sidewalk, adjusting the pouch on his bike. Darn, he wasn't the one, but of course not. This wasn't the evening paper.

The house was quiet. Dessie, who'd come early so Ellen wouldn't be alone in the house, wouldn't think she was awake yet. This would be a good private time to go to Wendy's room. She'd wanted to since Wendy died, but she'd been afraid. Now, though, she really wanted to be in Wendy's world, to sit on Wendy's bed and tell her things aloud instead of just in her head. And she could cry if she felt like it without worrying that someone might come in.

The door to Wendy's room was closed, as it had been since she died. Maybe because Wendy's room was so cheerful—walls, rug, bedspread, curtains all bright yellow—that even just glancing into it would make anyone feel sadder than they already did. Ellen squeezed the doorknob as she might someone's hand in a scary movie, paused for an instant, then opened the door and went in.

After Ruthie and her mother picked Ellen up that afternoon, Dessie started in on shutting up the house. She locked the windows, closed the drapes, blinds and curtains, and sprayed the kitchen baseboard for cockroaches. It took less than an hour but tired her out. She plopped down in the booth, looked out the window and remembered them laughing at Ellen's story about the farmer and his mule. Then she thought of nothing at all like folks with heavy hearts do. Now and then the evening breeze blew the branches of the crepe myrtle tree against the pane, and the tiny pink blossoms floated downward.

## About the Author

Virginia Johnson is a retired attorney and first time novelist who grew up in Alabama. Her memoir, "Rocketman", about Katrina was published in Issue 55 of the *Oxford American, The Southern Magazine of good writing.* Her play, *The Last of Everything,* received a staged reading in Santa Monica, Ca. Her fiction has received an honorable mention in a national fiction writing contest for lawyers and has been presented in Stories on Stage presentations in Sacramento and Davis, California.

## Acknowledgements

My thanks to the instructors and my fellow workshoppers at the Squaw Valley Writers Conference for their input to my work and to the faculty of the Bennington College MFA low residency program for their rigorous mentorship and high standards. Thanks also for the guidance and encouragement I received from the instructor and classmates in the Santa Monica College creative writing class through the years.

Many thanks to those in my writing groups in Santa Monica and Davis Ca, respectively, for their frank and insightful comments, with a thanks in particular to Zen Chang for his generosity in reviewing my work and his excellent critiques. And a very warm thank you to my editor, Joy Johannessen, for her meticulous work and encouragement.

A heartfelt thanks to Elizabeth Keller, Linda Hax, Carol Rogers, Jon Courtway, and my family for their support and belief in me, and a particular thanks to Aaron Wedra, whose production talent, efforts and enthusiasm made this book possible.

www.ingramcontent.com/pod-product-compliance
Lightning Source LLC
Chambersburg PA
CBHW030923120626
46554CB00001B/249